THE
UNTI
DEATHS
OF ALEX
WAYFARE

M.G. BUEHRLEN

DIVERSIONBOOKS

Also by M.G. Buehrlen

The Fifty-Seven Lives of Alex Wayfare

Diversion Books
A Division of Diversion Publishing Corp.
443 Park Avenue South, Suite 1008
New York, New York 10016
www.DiversionBooks.com

For more information, email info@diversionbooks.com

First Diversion Books edition April 2016.
Print ISBN: 978-1-68230-058-9
eBook ISBN: 978-1-68230-057-2

For Hay,
who can always find the crocuses in the snow.

ANOTHER DISCLAIMER

Some stories are about a boy. A second glance, a teasing smile, the promise of a kiss before you turn the last page. Love pursued and gained, the peaks and valleys and never-ending tension that lead two people from First Sight to Ever After.

Some stories are like that.

Not this story.

This story is about death. Two kinds. The tiny deaths, like finding out all the bright, diamond-cut things you thought you knew about your life were a lie. The light they used to shine on your path has gone dark, leaving you lost. And the big death, the one that looks like a polished, gleaming gun barrel pointed between your eyes. The one that says: *You don't have much time left.*

I don't know when the gun will fire, or when Death will take my hand. I don't know how many days I have left to make everything right again. All I know is that I have to do something good while I still have breath. Something that makes a difference. Something that makes my fifty-seventh life worthwhile.

So even though some of this story is about a boy, his glances, his smiles, his arms around me and a dance beneath stardust, it doesn't end with him. It doesn't end with a happily-ever-after kiss on his lips. No forever and always. No happy ending.

And I thought it would.

Oh, how I thought it would.

CHAPTER 1

UP IN THE AIR

I'm standing at the edge of the world.

The last time I was in Chicago, staring out across Lake Michigan, Blue had his arm around me, and I was struck by the vastness of the water. We stood on a concrete pier, the waves lapping beneath our feet, the glittering lights of the Roaring Twenties at our backs.

This time it's not as magical. This time, I'm standing at the edge of the world and there's no one beside me.

Well, no one with blue-green eyes that haunt my dreams at night.

The Signature Room is a posh restaurant on the ninety-fifth floor of the John Hancock building, the kind where a burger costs thirty bucks and comes with snobby-sounding ingredients like brioche and aioli and chipotle. But the room is gorgeous, so maybe you're paying for the atmosphere. Floor-to-ceiling plate glass windows surround the entire restaurant, overlooking the lake on one side and the city on the other. If you stand close enough to the windows, so close your breath fogs the pane, you can trick yourself into believing you're hovering over the city, and one step forward could send you tumbling down, down to the busy, snowy streets below.

I'm not looking down, though. I'm looking out, where sky meets water. Right now it's midday. The waves are ruffling lazily toward the shore. The pale blue of the sky, of the water, makes it almost impossible to look away. On the horizon, the faintest pink mingles between them. No wonder Monet spent his life trying to capture the way light glints off water. How it plays with color and shadow, so pale yet so vivid at the same time. You feel like you could walk across, clear to the horizon.

It's too bright, though, too cheery, for how I'm feeling at the moment.

It's been three days since I landed at Chicago's Midway airport with Porter waiting for me at the baggage claim. If it weren't for him I wouldn't be here now, on New Year's Eve, so close to finding Blue in Base Life. If it weren't for Porter, I wouldn't have known about the 3D bioprinting workshop offered at AIDA's Chicago branch for students interested in biomedical engineering. I definitely wouldn't have gotten selected to attend, since my application was submitted way after the deadline, and I certainly wouldn't have received a full scholarship for the travel and hotel expenses. That was all Porter's doing. I'm not exactly sure how he did it. I'm not exactly sure I want to know.

I learned seconds after meeting him that Porter makes things happen. He weaves reality to suit his needs. He plays by rules I don't completely understand. And somewhere along the line, I realized I didn't need to know the gritty details. I'm good with blindly reaping the rewards, especially this one, this trip to Chicago so we can find Blue.

For the past three days I've been up to my ears in biomedical geekery, sitting in on lectures and exploring labs, poking a finger into the fleshy, 3D-bioprinted human tissue created by some of AIDA's top engineers, surrounded by a group of awkward, nerdy kids like me who plan on making a difference in the world. I must admit, it feels good being immersed in normalcy for once. Discussing college plans like I'm any other kid headed off to school with grand, and probably foolish, ideas in my head.

Of course, none of the other kids realize I'm not going to college, not really, that I've seen too many things, know too many secrets, to ever walk down a normal college-to-career path. I'm a Descender, a protector of the past, present, and future. That's my job, now and forever. College used to be my own Monet painting, a pale yet vivid smudge of color on my horizon, back before I met Porter and he upended my world, pulling the shade down on that shining future and turning my eyes in the opposite direction. Showing me how to navigate the Black instead of the Light.

I used to spend hours lying on my bed longing for my future college days, flipping through brochures and picturing myself on those bright, happy campuses with fellow bright, happy students, hoping by the time I graduated I'd have my life figured out. I'd have my visions fixed and I could focus on real, everyday life. But that never happened. My visions, which I once believed were a burden, became my lifeblood. The reason I get up in the morning. They've given me a different purpose. And I'm OK with it. Because I get to travel back in time. Because I get to see things no one else gets to see, touch them, taste them, feel them brush against my bare skin. Because I get to see Blue. Because I'm going to bring Gesh to his knees and make him pay for all the atrocities he's committed against this unsuspecting world.

All those he's committed against me.

And even though this student workshop won't amount to anything on my nonexistent college applications, I'm learning a lot. I have renewed faith in humanity and all the ways we dedicate our lives to healing the sick. I've had an amazing time, and all I have to do is try not to screw it up for the other students. Make sure I don't create any more Variants, so their futures remain bright and golden and they can eventually touch those dreams waiting for them out there, on their own horizons.

This morning was the last lecture of the workshop. Then our hosts brought us here, to the Signature Room, for lunch. After this, they're taking us on a tour of the city and later tonight, we're all watching the New Year's Eve fireworks from Buckingham Fountain. Another one of Porter's arrangements, I'm sure. Placing me right where I need to be, at the exact right moment.

It's all too perfect.

Which means something's bound to go wrong. Isn't that the way of it?

One of the workshop hosts steps up to me beside the window.

"You OK, Alex? You haven't touched your lunch."

Her name is Dr. Micki Shah, and she seems pretty cool so far. She told us her family is from Dubai, but she was born and raised in Detroit, and she studied at Johns Hopkins, where I wanted to go, once upon a time. She's the youngest—and by far the least stuffy—of our hosts, and I like her, I think, although I haven't quite figured her out. While the other workshop hosts wear boring clothes in bland colors and sensible shoes, and don't seem to care that their hair is going gray (or receding), Micki wears heels, always heels. *Clop, clop, clop.* God, her feet must hurt. She wears her black hair in a sleek ponytail. Her eyes are smoky and dark, her lips and fingernails painted bright red. She dresses in trendy styles and leather jackets. She looks like she belongs at a swanky club, not a biomedical lab, even with a white lab coat draped over her chambray shirt and black skinny jeans. She looks so out of place that it's hard not to pay attention to her. And I can't figure out if that's her game, if she wants to be noticed, or if that's just who she is and I'm simply in awe, like I've discovered a rare species in the wild. There's nothing wrong with a girl who's passionate about the latest fashions *and* engineering. I've just never met one in real life.

I kind of admire her for it.

"Not that hungry," I say with a shrug. Which is true. How can I eat when my stomach is tangled and twisted in knots? When I can't concentrate on anything or anyone other than Blue? Anything other than our fountain, and our cold hands kept warm with entwined fingers. "I've felt kind of out of it all day."

"Sick?" She cocks her head to the side, and I can see her mind whirring as she tries to diagnose me with her dark eyes. "Want to go back to the hotel for the night?"

"No," I say, almost too quickly, too loudly. "I feel fine. I want to stay with you guys."

Dr. Shah quirks a sharply tweezed eyebrow at me. "You tell me if you think you're gonna barf, OK?"

I laugh. "You'll be the first to know. Promise."

• • •

THE FOUNTAIN

Hours later, deep into the evening, I'm standing at the edge of Grant Park, my fellow workshop mates around me, the bus we took to get here pulling away from the curb. I turn and watch it go with my hands in the pockets of my army-green parka, swallowed in a gust of exhaust. The last time I was here it was 1927, and Blue stood in the exact same spot, hands in his own pockets, watching me drive away in a yellow cab. I have no idea what happened to him after that, not until I pulled him from his home in Base Life (wherever that may be) to Cincinnati in 1961, then to Missouri in 1876, and then to AIDA Headquarters in our most recent past lives. I have no idea what he's been doing since he died in my arms outside Washington, DC, my last words begging him to meet me here.

Now.

Under a clear, frigid sky, beneath clear, frigid stars.

I square my shoulders toward the fountain and the lakeshore, biting my bottom lip, and scan the park for any sign of him. Buckingham Fountain is cold and dry, shut off for the season but covered in elegant strands of glittering holiday lights. More lights are strung up around the plaza, bathing the park in an orange glow. A crowd has gathered for the fireworks, even though they won't start for another hour.

With a deep breath, I make my way to the fountain. The rest of my group follows aimlessly, then disperses, blending in with the crowd. My winter boots crunch across pink gravel and pull me to the spot where Blue and I first kissed. Where he gave me a penny and told me to make a wish. Where he took my face in his hands and stole my breath away.

Everything looks the same.

Everything looks different.

The fountain seems larger than I remember, but it still looks like a fat wedding cake. The strands of twinkling lights are draped on each layer like icing. It doesn't feel as magical without the water shooting toward the clouds. The massive, gleaming copper seahorses stationed at the four corners have turned green from oxidization since the last time I saw them, but the wide, smooth pool stretching out at my feet remains the same. I wonder if our wishes still lie at the bottom.

Blue wished for a kiss. I wished to see him again. Both of our wishes came true.

I pull a penny from my pocket, one I brought along for this occasion. A 1927 Lincoln wheat penny I found by sifting through Pops's penny jug. It took me an hour to find the right year. I wasn't about to use any old penny. Not for this.

I close my eyes, make the same wish I made back then, and press the coin to my lips. It arcs through the air and slips beneath the icy water, sealing my fate for the evening.

I hope.

My heart warms as I run my gloved fingers along the railing Blue and I climbed over. After I make a complete turn around the fountain, the crowd in the plaza has doubled in size, full of red noses and thick with winter coats. People pose for photos in front of the fountain. The twinkle lights reflect off the glassy pool. The more crowded it gets, the more I wonder how Blue and I will find each other. Maybe meeting on New Year's Eve in a huge city wasn't the smartest of plans.

I move through the winter coats, locking eyes with each person. I bounce on the balls of my feet. I breathe warm air into cupped hands. I nestle my chin down into the warmth of Gran's scarf bundled around my neck.

Waiting.

"Coffee?" Dr. Shah stands behind me, holding two paper cups in her leather-gloved hands. The twinkle lights glitter in her dark eyes. "I spied you sipping some yesterday, so I know you're a fellow coffee-holic."

I grin and take one of the cups. "Definitely. Thank you, Dr. Shah."

"Oh, please. We're done with workshops now. Call me Micki."

"OK. Micki."

"Why are you hanging out over here all alone? Haven't you made friends with anyone in the group?"

I shrug and take a sip, let the heat warm me from the inside out. "I'm not very good at making friends."

"I'm not an expert, but talking to them usually helps."

I glance over at a few of the kids from the workshop. The boys are laughing and horsing around, running and sliding in the gravel. The girls are watching, huddled together and giggling.

It's just not my scene. "I'm good by myself."

"Riiiiight." She hunches her shoulders against the cold. "I'll be over there on that bench if you need me."

I nod, then turn back to cataloging the faces around me. The later it gets, the more anxious I become. I sip my coffee with trembling hands, too nervous to gulp, even though gulping would help warm my bones. My stomach turns and turns, and every guy who walks by resembling Blue's familiar shape has it turning yet again. I look for his gait. The slope of his shoulders beneath a wool coat.

And I wait.

What will he look like this time? If he even shows at all? Tall, handsome, and fit like in 1927? Will he wear his dark hair short, with no hat to ward off the cold? Or will he be tan and lean, with hair down to his jaw like in 1876? With a hat casting a shadow over his eyes?

Will I still find him attractive?

Would that even matter?

Will he recognize me in this body? My long, straight, dusky blond hair parted in the middle and spilling over my shoulders? My gray eyes behind the fake black-rimmed glasses Porter gave me? My button nose? My freckles? Blue's never seen me like this. Will he like what he sees? Will he still want to kiss me?

As the clock ticks closer to midnight with no sign of him, doubts roll in my chest. They tumble against my ribcage—*thump, thump. He doesn't remember you. Why would he remember you? No one remembers you.*

It's the usual reel of self-fueled vitriol I have running on repeat in the back of my mind, but a text from Dad helps silence it for a moment. He asks if I'm having fun and sends me a photo of the corned beef and cabbage Pops makes every New Year's, a tradition from his childhood in Ireland. Then Dad sends a photo of the whole family gathered around the table. Gran's arm is around Mom and they're both laughing so hard that their eyes are closed. Pops is piling a mound of mashed potatoes on my youngest sister Claire's plate, and Afton, our tiny black cat, is curled on her lap. My other sister, Audrey, isn't in the shot, which means she must not be feeling strong enough to join in with the festivities. A pretty common occurrence, unfortunately. I reply by shooting Dad a picture of the fountain and its glittering lights. We wish each other a happy new year. I tell him I'm having fun and really liked the workshop this morning.

All truth, which is a rarity. My replies to him usually contain plenty of lies sprinkled throughout. My whole life is made up of lies now. I wear them like scarves and hats and little flowers in my hair.

But then again, doesn't everyone?

I shoot a text to Audrey with the same photo. She usually responds right away, but this time she doesn't. Not even the quick NPILT (Not Participating in Life Today) she uses when she's too sick to chat but wants me to know she's OK. For a split second I imagine my worst fear coming true, that she's at the hospital, that the damn cancer finally had the last word, and I didn't get a chance to say goodbye. I immediately start hating myself for coming to see Blue when I should be spending time with her.

Before it's too late.

But then I realize Dad wouldn't be texting me photos of himself chowing down on corned beef and cabbage if Audrey were in trouble. I take a deep breath and let it out slowly.

My phone buzzes again, but it's not from Audrey. It's a text from Jensen. Ever since he insisted we were friends a few months back, a day hasn't gone by without a text from him.

hws yr trip?

I smile to myself at his relentless use of text speak and send him a picture of my coffee in my gloved hand. *It's goin. But it's soooo coooold. Good coffee tho. :)*

whr u at?

I turn around and take a photo of myself making a silly face with Buckingham Fountain in the background.

hawt! :D

I laugh to myself and send, *No! Coooooold. brrrrrrr*

We text back and forth for a while, and for the first time today, the minutes seem to fly by. No tumbles and rolls in my chest and stomach. But as soon as Jensen says goodbye for the night, heading to a party with his basketball buddies, the nerves are back.

I round the fountain for the fifth time, obsessed with finding the right red nose in the right winter coat. I weave in and out, the crowd growing as thick as brambles in the woods behind Gran and Pops's old barn. I push my way through the coats now. I bounce from one side of the fountain to the other, always thinking I've spotted Blue, but when I get closer the red nose is never his.

Just before midnight, the crowd is almost too thick to move through. Everyone is a shadow in the deep darkness. I pull my hood up and tie it tight under my chin. It muffles the sounds of the crowd, the laughter, the shouting, the squealing, the general excitement of being out under the stars to kiss the one you love as the clock strikes twelve. I stake out a spot beside the railing where Blue and I climbed over and stay there, hoping he'll remember which side we were on.

Music begins to play over loudspeakers across the park. The crowd cheers. A man beside me grabs his partner, and they sway and dance. The twinkle lights on the fountain shiver in the wind. Camera flashes ripple across the crowd every few seconds. The atmosphere is electric, just like it was in 1927.

But I still can't find Blue.

A few minutes before the countdown, colored spotlights flood the fountain. The crowd cheers again as fireworks shoot from the top tier in time with the music, whooshing into the sky right in front of me. Pinwheels of sparks ignite all around the perimeter, and the camera flashes come in droves.

Everyone's clapping. Everyone's cheering. Everyone's *oohing* and *ahhing*.

I use the strobing lights to scan the crowd one more time. My eyes dart from face to face, nose to nose, until at last I see him.

Blue.

CHAPTER 2

ASSHOLES AND SAVIORS

Blue is standing by the railing, about thirty feet away, his face lifted toward the sky, watching the fireworks.

At first I can't move. My boots are rooted to gravel. My palms are sweaty, and I'm shivering, but not because of the cold. The crowd starts chanting, counting down from ten, and I burst forward. I push my way along the railing, elbowing bodies out of my way. I have to get to him before midnight.

Six.

Five.

Four.

There's a stroller in my way, and I swerve around it. Just a few more steps and I'll be at his side. Just a few more winter coats to push through.

Three.

Two.

I can still see him, the light from the fireworks flashing on his face. Why isn't he looking around for me?

One.

Happy New Year!

The crowd closes in tighter as everyone embraces, and for a moment I'm stuck between couples. More fireworks explode like machine gun fire, filling the sky over Lake Michigan with blasts of color. Noisemakers erupt all around me. The cheering is deafening.

When two people in front of me stop making out long enough to come up for air, I shove my way between them and reach for Blue's arm. "Blue." I snag his sleeve, a black hoodie with a red stripe down the arm. He turns to face me, surprised.

Within seconds all that elation, all that relief, all that longing to be in his arms dissolves. This boy isn't Blue. He has the same build, the same profile, but it isn't him.

I let go of his arm, embarrassed for snatching onto a complete stranger. "I'm sorry," I say. "I thought you were someone else."

I turn to push my way back through the kissing couple, but the boy grabs my elbow. "Alex?" he says.

I whirl around at the sound of my name.

"It's me." He smiles and takes both my elbows in his hands, gripping them tight. "It's Blue."

For a moment I believe him. Who else would know to meet me here? Who else would know my name? But one look in his eyes gives the truth away. He's not Blue. He can't be. I feel no connection to him. No attraction between our souls at all. No tug at the edges of my memory.

"No," I say, trying to pull away from him. "You're not."

But he doesn't let go. His grip tightens. A man bumps into me from behind, flattening me against the boy's chest. I'm stuck between the two bodies. They're crushing me, and I can't move.

"This her?" the man behind me says. At least I think he does. The adrenaline pumping in my ears makes it hard to hear anything at all.

"Definitely," says the boy. "She called me Blue."

Once I realize that they're pinning me on purpose and they're not going to let go, I shout for help, but I can barely hear my own voice over the percussion of the fireworks, the music from the speakers, the noisemakers, the cheer of the crowd. No one is going to hear me. Not Micki, not the other chaperones, not the other students.

Something sharp presses into my ribs, and I suck in a breath.

A gun.

"No more of that yelling now, sweet stuff," the man behind me says.

Fear slicks my spine. The only person to ever call me *sweet stuff* was the Descender I met in 1876. The one who tore holes through my flesh and painted a cliffside with my blood. I bite my tongue, forcing myself to stay quiet. If it's the same Descender I battled in 1876, then I know he won't hesitate to pull the trigger. Not with a hundred fireworks blasting above to muffle the sound.

How did they find me? How did they know I'd be here?

The boy, the decoy who pretended to be Blue, pushes my head down and shoves me through the crowd. The two of them cling to each side of me as we make our way through the throng. The gun bites into my side. I keep my face down, watching shoes shuffle out of our way. The fireworks light up the pink gravel beneath our feet.

The crowd thins, and soon we're no longer on gravel but on cold, frosty grass. We've passed through the evergreen hedges that surround the plaza, and we're hidden in the dark within a grove of trees. Bare branches are woven overhead like fingers laced in prayer. The Descender pushes me to my knees. The barrel of his gun kisses my temple.

No one will hear me if I cry out. We're too far away from the crowd. No one will hear the gunshots over the blasts of fireworks.

I slip my hand into my pocket and fumble for my cell phone, but Decoy Boy seizes my wrist and rips the phone from my hand. The Descender makes me link my hands behind my head, elbows out, and Decoy Boy walks off with my phone. I hear him crush it against a tree trunk a few seconds later.

"You survived," I say to the Descender, still looking down. The frost beneath my knees melts and soaks into my jeans. A cold shiver works its way up my skin.

"What was that?" he asks, bending down.

I dare to look up at him, to see his face, but he pushes my head down again. It's too dark and I can't get a good look. "I crushed you in Limbo," I say. "I crushed your soul. Your little smoke monster friends had to come rescue you."

The Descender sniffs like he's amused.

"Where are your friends now?" I say. "Who's here to save you this time?"

He stoops down further to whisper in my ear. "Who's here

to save *you*?" He laughs, and Decoy Boy laughs too, as he walks back to us.

Somewhere in the back of my mind, I know of at least two ways I can knock the gun out of the Descender's hand. Call it a residual from my past life as Shooter Delaney, the sharpest shooter west of the Mississippi. If it were just me and the Descender one-on-one, I could kick his ass, gun or no gun. But Decoy Boy keeps getting in my way. He rips off my hood, scarf, and coat, leaving me cold in my thin plaid collared shirt. He kneels in front of me and pats me down, paying extra attention to my chest. His hands rake and paw over me.

I glare at him, anger pulsing through me. "Why don't you rip my shirt off, asshole? Get the full experience?"

He pauses and looks at me with a snarl-like grin. His face is too elongated, too sharply featured to be Blue. And he's older, too. I can see it now. I'm such an idiot.

"Plenty of time for that after we throw you in the van," he says, lip curled.

That's when I take my chance. I spit in his eye, and his hands fly to his face, giving me time to act. I grab the Descender's gun with both hands, twisting it away from my face to break it free from his grip. The Descender stumbles back, but he's still clinging to the gun, so I use the momentum of his stumble to pull myself to my feet. I slam a boot into his groin, and he doubles over. We both clutch the gun as I try to keep the barrel pointed away. Decoy Boy tackles me from behind, and all three of us collapse into a heap. The gun fires twice into the treetops beside my left ear. Sharp ringing pierces my skull. I sink my teeth into the Descender's hand, his blood coating my tongue, and he writhes beneath me, yelling out, but doesn't let go of the gun. Neither do I, until Decoy Boy drives an elbow against the side of my head, splitting my ear. Warm blood seeps down my neck and into my collar.

Everything becomes a blur.

From behind, Decoy Boy yanks me off of the Descender. I grapple for the gun, but the Descender's hand is too slippery, too dark and slick with blood. I scrape at his skin but can't hold on.

Two more gunshots shatter the air. Decoy Boy slumps on top of me. My arms give out and my face smacks into the hard, frosty ground. My fake glasses snap into two jagged pieces, digging into my cheek.

The Descender scoops me up under my arms and drags me to my feet. I can barely stand without his help. The gun returns to my ribs. My head feels swollen and hot; my broken glasses hang from my ears. I have sticky blood all over my mouth, all down the side of my neck. Decoy Boy is lying facedown on the ground, unmoving.

"Not another step," the Descender says, but he's not talking to me. He's talking to someone else, someone in the darkness. Someone I can't see.

"Drop the girl," a voice says from the shadows, "or I'll drop you."

I recognize the voice. Female, dark and smoky. But I don't understand.

"My orders are dead or alive," the Descender says. "I'll put her down if I have to. Don't think I won't." The gun digs deeper into my ribs, and I let out a yelp.

Two shots. *One. Two.*

I squeeze my eyes shut, wincing, prepared to feel the bullets tear through my side. I remember how it feels, to have a hole torn into your body. It's not something you forget.

But I feel nothing.

At first. Then the Descender releases his hold on me and sinks to his knees. He sways for a moment, a gurgling sound in his throat, eyes wide, then collapses nose-first into the grass.

My hands find their way to my mouth, and I stumble backwards, fingers shaking. My broken glasses fall to the ground, but I don't reach for them. I want to scream, but I don't remember how.

Not even when Micki steps from the shadows, calmly, a gun in her leather-gloved hand.

"You all right?" she asks me, stepping up to the Descender and giving him a nudge with the toe of her high-heeled boot. The kind, concerned chaperone is long gone, like a disguise she left back at the fountain, dropped in the pink gravel like a candy wrapper. Now she's all business, with a serious frown and purpose-driven brow.

"You killed them." It's all I can say. Both bodies lie flat in the dirt, souls snatched right out of them, ascending to Limbo. To Afterlife.

"They were going to kill you." She squats over the Descender and pats at his pockets. "Either that or hand you over to Gesh. I'm not sure which is worse. And I couldn't risk letting them go. They saw your face."

"Who are you?" I'm shivering more now. How could she know about Gesh? How could she know about me? My head swims. From confusion, from being elbowed in the head, from my busted ear and the blood oozing down my neck.

From everything.

"I'm Micki. I told you that. Or do you want my call number? That would be MCI." With one swift, fluid movement, she flips the dead Descender over onto his back, so easily and casually she must have done it a hundred times before. The Descender's eyes are open and vacant. Dirt and blood are smeared on his cheeks. Micki pats him down like she's rifling through a duffle bag. Like her hands aren't slipping into the pockets of the dead.

I've never watched someone die before. Not unless you count Gesh shooting Blue in our most recent past life, but that was different. I ascended to Limbo before Blue took his last breath. This feels like part of my soul was snatched out of me, too, right along with theirs. Even though both of them were vile dickheads of the highest order, working for Gesh, they were still human. They had breath and a beating heart.

Now they don't.

"Who do you work for?" I manage to ask.

Micki picks up the Descender's gun, pops it open, and checks the bullets. So casual about everything. She doesn't seem worried about anyone finding her kneeling over two dead bodies with a gun in her hand.

She looks up at me, her eyes dark, black in the shadows.

"Number Four."

My muscles tense. Number Four, IV, was my name, my call number, in my most recent past life, when I worked for Gesh and Porter. Porter and Levi gave me the nickname Ivy. Gesh was the only one who called me Number Four. He spoke it in Danish, *Nummer Fire*, but still. Hearing Micki say those words brought back a host of nasty memories from when I met Gesh face-to-face, when I went back in time and rescued Blue. It made me feel like Gesh was here, standing in front of me. Barking at me, ordering me around, having his henchman hold me down so he could run his hands over me, his property, his creation.

I take a step back from her, my fingers curling into fists. I want to run from her, get the hell out of here, but my head's too swimmy and I don't think I could make it two feet. "Why would you call me that?"

"You asked who I work for. I work for Number Four." She stands up, both guns in her hands now. "I work for you."

I try to reply but my body won't let me. My knees wobble, then I slump to the frosty grass. Micki dives to catch me before I smack my head. She eases me to the ground.

"Shit," she says. "Your ear." She smooths my hair from the side of my face, dabs at the blood with her sleeve.

My eyelids flutter. I can't hold on to consciousness. It's slipping away.

"Hang on, Four. We'll get you out of here. They'll be here any minute."

I want to ask who, but I can't form the words.

Sleep. I just want to sleep.

The next thing I know I'm lifted by strong arms. Hauled through the dark trees. Slid into the backseat of a car. Leather squeaks beneath me. Streetlights shine through the rear window. I smell pipe tobacco and something earthy, like tea. Doors slam shut and the car takes off, the gears shifting, faster, faster.

"She's delirious," a man's voice says over me, deep and gentle. Two large, warm hands cup my face, turning it back and forth. Two fingers press against the hollow of my neck, checking my pulse.

"A concussion, I think," says Micki.

Nausea comes, up, up, and I sit bolt upright. "Heyyy, Micki," I say, my voice slurred, my eyes still squeezed shut. If I open them, see the city rushing past outside the car windows, I know I'll puke. "You said to let you know if I had to barf. Well, the time has come." And then I laugh, a sputtered, tiny thing, as I slump back into the man's arms.

"What did she say?" A second man's voice, this one from the front of the vehicle. It sounds fatherly. Familiar.

"Porter?" I say, too softly for him to hear.

"Shit," says the man holding me. "I think she got hit."

"You *shot* her?" That's Porter. I know it is.

"Of course not," says Micki.

The man holding me unbuttons my shirt. Spreads it wide, pats my ribs, my stomach. "There's blood all over her." Panic and concern. It's a voice I swear I recognize, like I recognize Porter's.

I try to say I'm OK, that I didn't get shot, it's not my blood, but my throat is raw.

"Alex, can you hear me?" the man says.

My eyes flutter open, but they can't focus on the face looming over me. I close my eyes again, my head cradled in his palms.

"Are you hurt?" he asks.

It finally clicks, where I've heard his voice before. The last time I saw him he was in the backseat of a car like this, racing away from AIDA Headquarters an entire lifetime ago. The air was tinted red with blood then, too.

"Levi?" I force myself to say, all raspy and breathless.

"It's me," he says.

I manage a smile, small and weak. "We really have to stop meeting like this."

And then I pass out.

CHAPTER 3

BRAIN FREQUENCIES AND PANIC ATTACKS

Within the deep, deep of my unconsciousness, thoughts and memories swim and swirl. I don't have the strength to drown them out, so I drown in them.

The Descender. Decoy Boy. The flashes of firework light, the cheers ringing in my ears, grubby hands pawing at my chest, gunshots, Micki with the gun, two bodies slumped and bleeding out. Levi pulling me to safety.

Blue not showing.

I had plans. We were going to take one of those stupid horse-and-carriage rides, huddle next to each other under a blanket, and let the snow fall around us. We were going to eat greasy burgers at Billy Goat Tavern and wear the stupid paper hats they give you. We were going to stand on the shore and watch the sunrise. We were going to try to find Peg Leg, the speakeasy Blue took me to, see if the building still stood. See if we could climb up and sneak inside.

Stupid, stupid.

Where are you, Blue?

He has to be safe in Base Life. It's the only way I can cope with not finding him at the fountain. He's with a loving family. He didn't show because he doesn't remember descending like I do. Maybe once he returns to Base Life he has no idea he's been traveling at all. Maybe he only remembers me when he's in the past.

And if that's the case, I may never find him in Base Life.

Maybe I shouldn't even try.

How did they know?

How could Gesh's Descenders know I'd be at the fountain?

There were only four people who knew my plan to meet Blue.

Blue knew.

We made the plan together. Whether he remembered was still a mystery. I thought he was a traitor once before, but I proved myself wrong. I was the traitor. I told Gesh I was traveling again, that I was fighting against him. If Blue were working for Gesh, then his memory would have to be working. He'd have to remember our plan in order to tell Gesh about it. It was possible. But I didn't want to believe it.

Levi knew.

He was standing there when I made the plan with Blue. He overheard us. It was only two months ago for me, but it's been almost eighteen years for Levi. Who knows what he's gone through in that time. Who knows who he's become. Who he's been working for. But if he were working with Gesh to capture me, then why would he be in the car, helping me escape, making sure I wasn't hurt? It didn't make sense, but then again, I barely knew him. He used to love Ivy, my past self, but he doesn't love me, Alex.

Porter knew.

I told him because I needed his help getting here. His protection. Could he be betraying me? Lying to me this entire time? Leading me on some wild-goose chase? Training me so I'm of use to Gesh? Porter was the one who created me. He made me into what I am. He used to be partners with Gesh. He says all that changed, that Gesh is his enemy now. But is that true? My trust in Porter wavers from day to day, it seems. If only he'd been honest with me from the beginning, I wouldn't have so much trouble trusting him now.

Micki knew.

Porter or Levi must have explained everything to her. They must trust her, but I don't even know her. She said she works for me, but what does that mean? And if she's lying, and she works for Gesh, then why would she murder his Descenders?

None of it makes sense. None of them seem like traitors, not after rescuing me. They all seem on my side. So how did Gesh know?

I pull myself from the incoherence of sleep and open my eyes to a small, shadowy bedroom. A large window across from me frames a barren, frosty field, tinted blue from moonlight, and a line of evergreens in the distance.

I have no idea where I am.

I shift under blankets that smell faintly of cologne or aftershave, some kind of earthy boy scent, which means I'm in a boy's bed, tangled in a boy's sheets, my head heavy on a boy's pillow.

Sharp pain courses through my skull when I sit up. I pat my face with my fingertips, gingerly assessing the damage—two tender spots on my cheekbone, and my right ear feels like it had a run-in with a potato peeler. My nose is puffy, like it's grown a size. I glance around for my fake glasses out of habit, even though they were broken during the fight, but they're nowhere nearby. There is, however, a small chair in the corner with my parka and scarf draped across it. My luggage sits on the floor beside it, the bags I brought with me to Chicago.

Gently, I pull myself out of bed. Stand on weak legs. I'm still in the clothes I wore last night. My jeans and shirt smell, but they're not horrible. It's too dark to see how badly they're bloodstained.

Murmuring voices tug me from the bedroom and into a dark hallway with a bright light at the end. Down the carpeted hall I move on socked feet, quietly, toward the voices and the light. At the end, I turn the corner into a living room turned medical examining room. A couch and end table are to my left. There are windows and a front door across from me, covered with blackout paper. Bright white surgical lights on portable stands pour over two exam tables with two bodies lying facedown. The Descender and Decoy Boy. I can tell by their clothes. The black hoodie with the red stripe.

Micki and Porter are bent over one of the bodies, tools in hand.

I see blood.

I smell blood.

I step closer.

The back of the Descender's head is cut open, gaping wide, the white light spilling across the folds of his grayish-pink brain. Porter wiggles a shiny pair of pliers inside it.

I feel like I might puke from the sight of it, from the shock of it, but words tumble out instead. "What are you doing?"

Porter and Micki lift their heads, their faces obscured by medical masks.

"Alex," Porter says, reaching for me with a gloved, bloody hand. "It's OK."

"They're just Subs," Micki says, seeing the disgust on my face. "They were Gesh's drones. They no longer had a will of their own. Think of them as robots. Synths."

"But they weren't. They were human." I look to Porter. "I thought you didn't do this sort of thing anymore. I thought you were finished experimenting on people."

"I am," Porter says. "And Micki is right. They were only Subs. Gesh stripped them of their humanity long ago."

I shake my head, not understanding. Maybe not wanting to understand.

Micki pulls her mask down. "These aren't innocent people, Number Four. These are Gesh's soldiers. Do you know how many people they've murdered? How many innocent people?"

"Doesn't matter." I'm shaking, fists at my sides, not only because of what they're doing but because she insists on calling me Four, reminding me I'm a number, not a person.

"It does matter, actually," Micki says, her voice flat, her dark eyes cold.

Porter steps toward me. "You have a concussion. You should be lying down, not dealing with something like this. It's too much to process right now."

I step away from him, but my heels hit the couch and I fall onto the cushions. Porter reaches out and grabs my arm to steady me, but I yank it away. They watch me for a moment while I stare at my feet. Socks on worn, stained carpet.

"You have to trust me, Alex." It's one of Porter's favorite lines. It's a damn catchphrase at this point.

"You know me well enough by now," I say. "I'll trust you when you explain. So start explaining. Where am I? Why are you dissecting brains in the living room?"

"We'll tell you everything, I promise, but there has to be an order to the information. I don't want to overwhelm you with a lifetime of knowledge crammed into a few hours."

"I can handle it."

He smiles sadly, like he knows I can. Maybe he's always known. But he thinks keeping me in the dark keeps me safe. I wish he understood that it does the opposite. It leaves me vulnerable. Unprepared.

He sits beside me, knees turned toward mine, and pulls his mask down. "We're a team, you and I."

"I used to think so."

"For the past seventeen years I've been watching you grow. But that's not all I've been doing. And I'm not the only one who's been protecting you. Levi and Micki have, too."

I glance at Micki. She doesn't look like the kindly chaperone I met a few days ago, urging me to make friends, buying me coffee. She looks fierce. A tiger ready to pounce.

"I don't understand."

"They've been working with me this whole time. Working against Gesh. Waiting for you to grow up and join the team."

"Working against Gesh how?"

"Battling his soldiers." Porter glances at the two bodies on the tables.

I glance at them, too. "You mean going around murdering his Descenders?"

Micki steps around the exam table. She's still wearing heels, if you can believe it, even after all that's happened. Even while digging in a dead guy's brain. "If we don't want Gesh to tamper with time, if we want to diminish his power in Base Life, then we have to take his Descenders out. Take out his Subs, too. This is reality, Number Four."

"But you told me it was just us," I say to Porter. "We were going to smoke Gesh out of his hole by screwing up his treasure hunts. We were going to steal all his funds so he couldn't control the government anymore. You never told me he had soldiers, or that we're killing them."

Porter's red-rimmed eyes are solemn. He rubs circles around his pinky knuckle with his thumb. "Gesh's funding is only one way he maintains power. Another is the use of his Subs. They're everywhere. Ready and waiting to do his will, like sleeper agents. They're in the White House, the Supreme Court, the CIA, the FBI. In our universities, our police forces, the army, navy, you name it. That's why we take them out. If we can't cut off his head, we cut off his feet."

"You keep saying Subs. Isn't Levi a Sub? That's what he told me when we first met. He said he was a Sublunary, someone who couldn't ascend to Limbo, someone who works for Gesh on earth, in Base Life."

"He was a Sub," Porter says. "He's not anymore."

"What do you mean? He's a Descender now?"

Porter shakes his head and looks to Micki to answer the question.

"Ever heard of Nikola Tesla?" Micki asks, folding her arms.

Her change of topic knocks me off guard for a second. "Of course." Tesla was the father of electricity. When most people think of electricity innovation, they think of Edison, but Tesla was an unsung hero. Most of what he developed was used by Edison, attributed to Edison, while Tesla was forgotten. But I know better. I admire Tesla, because I know electricity inside and out.

Micki taps her red fingernails against her arm. "Ever heard of his brain manipulation theory?"

I scrunch my nose. "He worked with wires. Connections. Electrical impulses. Not brains."

"Brains run on electrical impulses. Our nervous system is a tangle of wires. Connections. Everything on the planet, in the solar system, runs on bioenergy, and that energy is composed of distinct frequencies. We all function in harmony, in balance, because of the way our frequencies interact. If you controlled those frequencies, though, if you altered them, as Tesla theorized, you could control the human race."

Now that she mentions it, I remember reading about that theory. It was part of the reason Tesla fell into obscurity. A lot of his ideas, his limitless thinking, made him sound like a madman. "It was just a theory. He never tested it on humans."

"He didn't, but Gesh did. And he developed this." Micki nods at the Descender's brain, beckoning me to take a look. I stand and move toward the body, feeling sick.

I lean over the Descender, peering into his brain. Something small and shiny is lodged there, tucked between the fleshy pink wrinkles.

A microchip.

"Gesh surgically implants them in the brains of his Subs. It controls the resonance of the brain's frequencies, which induces an altered brain state, sort of like the sleepwalking phenomenon. Enough for the person to function normally on the outside, but their impulses, their desires, their inherent free will are subdued. Their need to follow, to worship, to do what they're told, is heightened. They no longer think for themselves. They're glorified robots, slaves programmed to follow orders."

"Gesh's orders," I say, peering closer at the chip. "So he turns them into the Illuminati? Russian spies? The Mafia?"

"Sort of, only Subs are much more lethal. They pull silent strings. Keep the flow of power aimed in Gesh's direction. It's all very subtle. Very sleight of hand. But effective. You never know it's happening."

"So this chip brainwashes them."

"It's more than brainwashing. It's reprogramming to the point that they're no longer human. Gesh wants soldiers who are deadly but submissive, soldiers who will walk into the face of death without question. Humans as good as machines, stuck on autopilot."

I glance at the Descender's hand, lying on the table, limp and cold. "But why kill them? Why not just remove the chip?"

Porter moves to my side. "Removing the chip kills them instantly. It's far more humane to put them out of their misery."

It makes me sick, hearing Porter talk like that. Like they're rabid dogs that have to be put down. And it makes me sick to think I'm part of it, up to my neck in it.

He should've told me. I would've never agreed to this.

I want to say it out loud, shout it, but no sounds make their way to my lips. Just air, rushing past as my concussion sends a wave of nausea over me, and an asthma attack sets in. Gasps, again and again. Short, sharp breaths going in, but no breaths going out.

"Levi," Porter calls out.

Spotty darkness closes in at the edge of my vision, and everything fades.

CHAPTER 4

A CHOICE

A door opens down the hall, closes, and then Levi is here, swooping in from my right, holding me under the arms, and ushering me into a kitchen. Small, windowless, with ugly yellowed linoleum and sagging oak cabinets. The faucet drips. The light overhead flickers. *Tink, tink, tink.*

He lifts me onto the counter by the sink and hands me an inhaler. I suck in deeply, letting it open my airways. Two puffs. The albuterol floods my body, and I start shaking. I'm not sure if it's a reaction to the meds or if it's just anger coursing through me.

I haven't had an asthma attack in months. Not since I began descending into my past bodies. I drew strength from those bodies. They made my lungs stronger, my courage sharper. But now? The concussion makes me feel like a puddle of little-kid goo, too weak to stand on my own two feet.

I squeeze my eyes shut. I need to get a handle on my breathing. Calm down. Focus on something small, something that doesn't make me so angry. So I open my eyes and zero in on the person standing in front of me, the one running cool water over a washcloth, then pressing it to the back of my neck.

Levi.

He looks just like I remember, only older. Eighteen years older. Dark blond hair. Round glasses, tortoiseshell this time instead of wire. Concerned crease between sad brown eyes.

"You changed your glasses." Those are the first words my muddled brain strings together. Two months ago, Levi was my age.

Two months ago.

"Don't talk," he says in that same deep voice from the backseat of the car, gently, quietly. "Catch your breath."

Rivulets of cool water run from the cloth down my back. It helps. The inhaler, the washcloth, the heaviness of Levi's hand resting on the back of my neck. It's comforting.

The grown man standing before me isn't the same teenage boy I woke up snuggling with in his bed at AIDA Headquarters two months ago. Nor is he the same little blond boy with the wire-rimmed glasses I remember playing Polygon with from my days as Ivy. He's still cute. Really cute. Tall now, taller than Porter. His features are sharper, his jaw squarer, his build no longer lanky but strong and muscular beneath a heather-gray sweater and black jeans. The tip of a tattoo peeks out of his collar on the side of his neck. I can't tell what it is. His jaw is shadowed with a few days' worth of stubble.

He runs a hand through his light hair. It's short on the sides but long on top, and there's product in it or something that makes it stand up tall in the front, then slope backwards like an ocean wave. With the round glasses, he looks like he belongs on a street corner busking in Portland, or as a frontman in a hipster folk band.

He looks cool the way Micki looks cool. I want to say something else, something more eloquent and mature than the glasses thing, but I'm too struck by how grown-up he looks. And the more I look at him, studying his style, his stance, his downturned mouth, the more I realize I was wrong. He's not cute. He's captivating. Handsome and timeless and a little bit wild. If Micki is a tiger, Levi is a lion.

"How old are you now?" I ask because I never knew how old he was when we worked at AIDA together. When he and Ivy were a couple.

When he and I were a couple.

So weird.

"Thirty-six." His voice is still gentle. Steady.

God, that's old. But he doesn't look it. He looks only a few years older than me. Like a college guy. His youthful features are still there, he's just filled out.

"Levi, I'm so sorry."

He lifts an eyebrow. "About my age?"

"No." I let out a half laugh despite how I feel. "I'm sorry about Ivy." The last time I saw him, he was so angry with me, angry that Ivy would be dying soon to make way for my reincarnation.

He runs the cloth under cool water again, wrings it out, and returns it to my neck. "We don't have to talk about that now."

"I barged in and took her from you. I am so, so sorry."

"Alex, listen to me." He places his hands on my knees. "You have nothing to apologize for. Nothing at all."

I shake my head, but he continues.

"You saved me when you traveled back to AIDA. If you hadn't come that night to see Tre, I'd still be one of Gesh's brainwashed kids. I'd be the one lying on that table right now, a chip implanted in my brain. You didn't just rescue Tre. You rescued me. Micki. Porter. You rescued Ivy. You released her from that worthless life as one of Gesh's lab rats. You saved us. I need you to know that."

I laugh again, one of those dry, bitter laughs. "Funny how you can save someone one minute, then be the cause of another's death the next."

Levi's frown deepens, and his brow darkens.

Tears sting my eyes, the kind that show up when you're trying to be brave but they betray you and make you feel like such a wuss. And there's a lump in my throat, making it ache. "I didn't sign up for this. I thought I was slashing tires. Making things difficult for Gesh by screwing up his missions. I didn't sign up to kill people. I'm just a kid."

"No one expects you to do what we do." Levi looks me square in the eyes. "Micki and I, we weren't going to reveal our true identities to you unless there was an ambush and it couldn't be avoided. We were going to continue doing what we've been doing all this time. Taking out Gesh's Subs. You were going to keep working with Porter, descending, funding our work. Doing what you do best."

"Funding?" I sniff and wipe my nose with the washcloth.

"The money from the lost Rembrandt isn't sitting in a

bank somewhere. We use it to pay for our missions. Hideouts like this one. The tools we need. We'll continue using it if you continue descending."

"What do you mean 'if'? Porter already has missions lined up for me. He wants me in the Middle East to find the treasure of the Knights Templar. He wants me off the coast of Costa Rica to find the Treasure of Lima. I've been studying for weeks."

"Doesn't matter. You don't have to continue after tonight. After what you've seen. You have a choice. You can choose not to be a part of it. You can choose to move on, live this life out to the fullest. We'll be here when you're born again. We'll pick back up then. You'll have a chance to grow up with us training you. You'll never be blindsided again. You'll be prepared."

I shake my head, clinging to the washcloth in my lap like a security blanket. "That could be decades from now. There's no telling what Gesh will accomplish in the meantime. I can't ask you to wait for me to die and be reborn when you need me right now."

Levi frowns. Doesn't say anything.

"Why didn't Porter do that this time around?" I ask. "Why didn't he raise me instead of my mom and dad? Raise me as his own, mold me into a weapon?"

"He wanted to protect you. We didn't know it would go this far. We didn't know Gesh would use these microchips on his Subs. All we knew was that Gesh would come looking for you, so we hid you, kept you safe. We wanted a normal life for you. And you can still have it. The choice is yours. No one's forcing you to continue."

"But you'll continue. It doesn't feel right to leave and let you guys fight Gesh all on your own."

"We've been fighting him on our own all this time. Don't worry about us. Make the right choice for *you*."

He makes it sound so easy. Like walking away from time travel, from treasure hunting, is something I can flip a coin over. Flip a switch, turn it off. Say goodbye to the past, to Blue, to the purpose I thought I'd found for my life.

I sniff again, my breathing at last returning to semi-normal. "I don't know. I need to think about it."

Because I don't think I'm strong enough to let go, even after all I've witnessed, all I've learned.

"Take all the time you need." He squeezes my knees. "I'm here to help you. We all are. You are not alone in this."

Oh, but I am.

He doesn't know it, but I am.

CHAPTER 5

DIRTY WORK

They told me I didn't have to help, but I felt compelled. The deaths were partially my fault. Burying the bodies felt like penance.

Digging a grave is harder than it looks in the movies. Every inch of you receives a coat of dirt. Every muscle in your body grows fatigued within minutes. Your hands grow stiff, cramped around the handle of a shovel. And it's worse dealing with the cold. The ground is hard, frostbitten. My hands are gloved, but they're frozen to the fingertips. With the four of us, it takes a few hours to dig two holes deep enough for the Descender and Decoy Boy. Levi got started earlier, while I slept, so there's decent headway to work with, which helps. Levi and Micki have shovels, pickaxes, and tools that slice through roots. They're so prepared for this kind of thing, and it makes me feel uneasy.

And a bit scared of them.

The old, rundown safe house sits behind us, across the barren field, beyond the little stand of evergreens that will become our makeshift graveyard. Early morning sunlight shines through a ceiling of thin clouds, trying in vain to burn away a layer of fog. We're two hours outside Chicago. Levi and Micki have used the house for years, way out in the middle of Farmland, Nowhere, as a hideout while tracking down Gesh's Subs.

"You knew I'd get ambushed," I say to Porter, taking a break and sitting on the edge of the grave he and I are digging together. "You knew, and you didn't warn me."

"Of course we didn't know," Porter says, hefting a chunk of black, frozen dirt out of the hole.

"But you suspected." I stare down into the grave, no longer feeling angry, just numb and empty. It's the only way I can dig this hole. I turn off all my emotions and become a robot like Gesh's Subs. Deadened, like the bodies wrapped in a tarp on the ground behind me.

An hour ago, I hit Porter with a barrage of questions about the bodies. How they got them out of Grant Park without anyone noticing. (They dropped Levi off near another stolen car while I was passed out, and he went back for them.) Why Porter and Micki removed the microchips from their brains. (Bodies decompose, microchips don't. They didn't want anyone to find the chips, should they stumble across the dead bodies.) What happened if someone *did* stumble across them. (Unlikely, since this is private property. And at this point they got tired of answering my questions.) I asked how Micki explained why we didn't go back with the other chaperones and kids after the fireworks. What they told the workshop leaders about my early departure from the group, and how they managed to get my luggage from my hotel room. Porter assured me they had it covered, and I didn't have to worry about it. It pissed me off, but I figured details and logistics were just another thing I couldn't fit on my sanity plate at the moment.

When Porter says he's got it covered, he usually does. But my trust is paper thin at the moment, and after this, I'm leaning toward taking Levi up on his offer to retire.

Porter leans on the end of his shovel. Wipes his forehead with a handkerchief pulled from his back pocket. His khakis are streaked with dirt, his boat shoes caked with it. "We have to be prepared for every outcome," he says. "I wouldn't let you walk into a trap by yourself. I told you, we've been protecting you your entire life. We're not going to stop now. If I had told you about our suspicions you might not have gone along with our plan."

I make a grumble in my throat because he's probably right. "So what was your grand plan?"

"We foresaw three possible outcomes, and we were prepared for each one. If Tre's memory was intact, and he met you at the fountain, we'd bring him aboard the team. We'd help him acclimate to being a Descender and give him the guidance we've given you. If he didn't remember and was a no show, then we'd know his memory defects still persist. And if there was an ambush, then we'd know for sure that Tre..." Porter trails off, glances at Levi, who's working on the second hole with Micki.

"That Tre what?" My stomach clenches. Both Porter and Micki are staring at Levi, so I look to him too.

Levi sighs, stops digging. He looks pained to have to be the one to tell me. "That Tre is working for Gesh. That he told Gesh where to find you."

A nervous giggle bubbles in my throat. "You're joking."

Except Levi doesn't look like he's joking. I've never seen him look anything but serious and somber, and he looks more serious and somber now, if that's even possible.

"Don't do this to me right now," I say to Porter. My voice comes out breathy, shaky, and I hate it. "I haven't seen Blue since October. I'm worried about him. If he's safe. And I'm worried I'll start forgetting what he looks like." *Smells like. Tastes like.* "Don't take away the one thing that's firm in my memory." *Blue's loyalty. His goodness.* "Blue is as good as they come. His heart is good. Always good."

"Always good?" Micki scoffs, thigh-deep in her hole. She finally traded in her heels for a pair of Wellies. "And how do you know that? You've only seen him, what, a handful of times?"

My fingernails dig into my palms through my gloves. Micki's right, and it makes me even more defensive. "I know him better than I know you."

Her eyes go darker, sharper, under the hood of her black puffer coat. The fur lining shivers in the breeze. She looks even more like a wild animal now than ever.

I turn back to Porter, who hopefully will hear me out. "We've been through this. We thought Blue was working for Gesh before. That's why I went back to Headquarters in my most recent past life. To confront him." Back to Micki. "He didn't betray me. He wasn't the one who told Gesh I'd be his enemy in the future. *I* did that. I was the snitch. I created the Variant."

Her eyes are tight. Angry. "That doesn't mean he's not working for Gesh."

"Yes. It does."

"No, it doesn't, and Porter agrees with me." Micki gestures for Porter to back her up.

Porter draws in a deep, shuddering breath, then frowns and looks at me with his pale, watery eyes. I know what he's going to say, and I don't want to hear it.

Micki doesn't care about sparing my feelings, though. She barrels right through. "If Gesh has Tre in Base Life, if he's had him since your last reincarnation, then he's had seventeen years to work on Tre's memory defects. He's bound to have made progress. All Tre would have to remember are two things: New Year's Eve and Buckingham Fountain. Suppose he *did* remember. Those two things are all Gesh needed to capture you. Tre would've finally served his purpose."

"If Blue is working for Gesh," I say, "then they would've sent *him* to meet me. Not some decoy. Blue wouldn't need those other guys to do it for him. I would've gone with him. I would've gone anywhere he asked me to go. I wouldn't fight him."

I'd have gone willingly. I wouldn't have bitten at his hands and torn at his skin. I wouldn't be burying him beneath an oak tree, in the frosty ground.

"Not necessarily," Levi says. "Gesh would assume you'd come with protection. And if Tre is his asset, his greatest asset apart from you, then he wouldn't put that asset on the front lines. Not unless he was certain he would win."

"So he sends two Subs instead. And the fact that he only sent two means he thought it would be an easy snatch." Micki smiles to herself as she scoops a load of dirt. "He didn't count on me being there." She looks proud as she digs a grave for one of the two men she's killed.

"That's it?" I say. "You're just going to believe Blue's a traitor?

Without any solid evidence? How do we know Blue didn't get captured at the fountain like I did? What if Gesh had other Descenders there? Maybe that's why Blue didn't show." Porter shakes his head, but I don't let him speak. "He could've been taken, Porter. He didn't have a team there to protect him like I did."

Both Levi and Micki shake their heads too. Obviously they know something I don't.

"How can you be certain?" I demand.

Micki narrows her eyes at me. "It has to be Tre. How else would Gesh have known about the fountain?"

You could've told him, I want to say, but I stop myself.

"Hell, it could be me," I say. "Somehow. I've been the traitor before. Maybe I haven't even done it yet, but I will. I could let something slip in the past that could change the future. How can you dismiss that possibility?"

"It's Tre," Micki says, going back to her digging. "Gesh has him, and he's using him to track you down. We all know it. You're in denial."

"If you're right, then we can't let him rot in Gesh's hands. We have to find him in Base Life."

"Why?" Micki says, slamming her shovel into the dirt.

"Because he's my partner." I look at each of them, expecting at least one of them to understand. "He's my partner, and obviously that doesn't mean the same thing to you as it does to me. If he's with Gesh, there's no telling what kind of torture he's going through. I can't leave my partner behind. I have to rescue him. Give him a chance at a real life."

"You're worried about his *life*? Are you kidding me?" the tiger roars, ready to dive at me. "Your lives are renewable resources. If this life isn't what he expected, he'll get another. And another. Don't you get that? His life, your life—they aren't your own, no matter what kind of Kool-Aid you've been drinking the past seventeen years. You and Tre are tools. Weapons." She points in the direction of the safe house, the driveway, the little road leading back to civilization. "Those people out there? The ones living actual lives with actual expiration dates? They're allowed to be human. They're allowed to fuck up because they don't have another life waiting for them. They don't get a do-over. You do. Tre does. So I'd stop sniffling over Tre's life and how miserable it might be. I'd focus on your job. Your mission. The team that's right in front of you. Forget him. He's only going to be an obstacle for you, and that makes you an obstacle for us. And I don't do well with obstacles. I tear them down. I crush them to dust. Got it?"

Screw you, I want to say. She doesn't know me or my motivations. She doesn't know Blue the way I do. None of them do. She never saw his eyes, scared and worried, not understanding why his memories change from moment to moment. Holding me tightly when he was dying in my arms, smiling, always smiling, even in the face of death, telling me that death is what we do. It's what we're meant for. Just to make me feel better. To dry my tears.

I want to help him if I can, help him understand. I don't think it's fair for him to be subjected to some awful life somewhere, even if he does get another one.

My anger bubbles, and I'm shaking, shaking, until I can't hold it back any longer. I climb out of the grave and stand over them, hands fisted. "Why are you being such a jerk to me all of a sudden?"

She shakes her head. "That sweet chaperone you met in Chicago? It was an act. I was playing a part. It was my job."

Even though I figured that was the answer, hearing her say it out loud hits me in the gut, brushes against an old wound. The deep cut caused by countless rejections at school. "I actually believed you cared about me. Now I know you're just a damn good liar. So how do I know you're not the one working for Gesh?"

I expect her to roar at me again, but she doesn't. Instead, she smiles, barely, ghostlike, at the corners of her red lips, like I finally said something that impressed her. Like she approves of me showing some fire under my skin.

Her grin broadens. "Finally," she says, looking at me over her shoulder, "you're asking the right questions."

I try not to act like her change in demeanor totally throws me off. "Then who the hell are you? How do I know I can trust you?"

She keeps digging while the rest of us stand there, Porter and Levi looking uneasy, like they can't decide if they should step in or let us duke it out. Micki's hands must be blistered and aching, but she keeps going. It makes me wonder how many bodies she and Levi have buried in the last seventeen years.

"I was your Sub at AIDA," she says. "I was assigned to you."

I glance at Levi and Porter, and they nod.

"What does that mean, you were 'assigned' to me?"

"I was your record keeper. I kept track of your past-life data. When you went on a mission, I was the one behind a computer making sure everything went as planned. I was the voice in your head, directing you where to go, what to say, how to navigate your surroundings. I'd train you beforehand on what you'd encounter. I was the reason Gesh's missions were a success. That *you* were a success."

I don't quite believe her. She doesn't look old enough to have had that kind of responsibility seventeen years ago. "You were only what, fifteen years old? How could you possibly be in charge of all of that?"

"Kids can master anything if you train them well enough. Gesh was training me to be your Sub since before I could stand on two feet. He said it was my purpose."

"And now?"

"It's still my purpose, as far as I'm concerned."

"Why?"

This is when she finally stops digging. When she finally faces me. "Because you saved my life when you traveled back to AIDA. Because of you, I got a chance to escape that shithole with Gesh. I owe you, and to me that means a lot more than whether or not I like you. So that's why I'm here. That's why I stay."

Her eye contact and the sincerity in her words make me feel childish for standing over her. I drop back down into the grave with Porter. "You saved my life at the fountain. Doesn't that make us even?"

She grins and scoops another shovel of dirt. "Not quite. But I wish."

If that's how she feels, then she must have some sense of honor. It makes me respect her, if only a little. I pick up my shovel and stab it into the ground. "How about this? We can call it even if you stop being such a hardass."

She grins, ear to ear, and I see a glimpse of the chaperone she pretended to be in Chicago. "Only if you stop being such a whiny teenager."

"I make zero promises."

It takes another hour before we're ready to bury the bodies, and just like I imagined, that part is way worse than digging the graves. I stand off to the side by Porter, watching, huddled in my parka, rubbing my sore hands, while Levi and Micki drag each body into its respective hole. Sprinkle them with lye to speed up the decomposition process. The piles of black, frozen soil we made grow smaller and smaller, the holes filling in, the bodies becoming one with earth, until there's no sign of flesh and bone, only gentle mounds of dirt in a silent, shadowy wood.

Snow begins to fall, and I brush the flakes from my eyelashes.

SO THIS IS MY TEAM

Later, as Porter drives me to the airport for my flight home, I slide my new pair of fake glasses up the bridge of my nose and ask him about Micki and Levi. "Why didn't Gesh put a chip in their brains? If they were Subs?"

The snow is heavier now, thicker, and Porter has to squint to see through the wiper blades. "You have to be an adult to undergo the surgery. The brain has to be developed enough to withstand the change in frequency. Levi and Micki were kids when they escaped. But had they stayed, had you not come back and saved Tre, they'd have the chip."

For a long while I think about that, until one question keeps rising in the back of my mind. "How did he know it couldn't be implanted in children?"

Porter fidgets with the steering wheel. I can tell he wants to rub his pinky knuckle with his thumb. "How do you think?"

"He tried it out on kids."

Porter frowns, grips the wheel harder. "Micki had an older sister when she came to AIDA. She was twelve years old when Gesh performed the surgery on her." Another swallow. "She didn't survive the implant."

The snow slaps at the windshield, becoming more like slush by the minute. The wipers swat it away. I fist my hands on my lap. "How many kids did he kill before he stopped trying?"

"Too many."

I wish I had another chance with Gesh one-on-one. I wouldn't screw it up this time, wouldn't be afraid. I wouldn't let Porter smash his face in. I'd do it myself. "So not only does Gesh like experimenting on kids but he kills them too, all in the name of science." I clear my throat, and it takes a minute before I have the courage to ask, "Were you a part of that, Porter?"

I knew the answer. He didn't have to say anything. Blue and I were kids when Gesh and Porter started their experiments on our brains, trying to fix our memory defects, but I had never let myself fully picture Porter being involved. Now, in my head, I imagine him standing over a little girl, the same age as my youngest sister Claire, and cutting her open. Attaching a chip to her brain. Watching her die because of it.

An acceptable loss. Isn't that what they call it?

So this is my team. Hunters. Murderers. Child abusers.

Monsters.

I know I can't fully trust Micki or Levi. Not yet, at least. But I still had a shred of hope that Porter was on my side. Now I can't stop the images from coming, flipping before me like a slideshow.

I can't trust him either.

I can't trust anyone.

CHAPTER 6

THE LIAR

After a delayed flight due to snow, and dinner out of a crappy airport vending machine, I'm finally at baggage claim waiting for Dad, turning my new phone over in my hand. Decoy Boy destroyed the original, but Levi was able to clone the SIM card and set me up with a new one. While I slept, Levi texted back and forth with Dad and Audrey, pretending to be me. Telling them everything was all right, that I couldn't wait to see them, that the fireworks and the workshops were awesome. Lying to them, just like I would've done, had I been awake and concussion-free.

He's brilliant, Levi. Always thinking five steps ahead.

I turn it over in my palms again and again, like my thoughts, wanting to trust them all, wanting to believe everything they say. Believe they are the good guys, even if they've done bad things. Because if I can't trust them, then I truly am alone, like I told Levi. And the only person out there who could possibly know what I'm going through is lost. I could find him in the past, but would he remember me? Would he remember what it's like to be a Descender in Base Life?

"Bean!"

Dad jogs toward me, beaming, arms outstretched. His dusky hair is shaggy and disheveled, and his gray eyes sparkle behind his glasses. He's so happy and proud and everything he shouldn't be as he approaches his Massive Liar of a Daughter. A daughter who's at the center of an invisible war between rebels and brainwashed drones. A daughter who hides a busted ear behind her hair. A daughter who still has flecks of a dead man's blood under her fingernails.

No matter how hard I scrub, the red stains remain.

Dad pulls me into a hug, and I feel rotten to the core. I hate lying to him, and I hate that I've gotten so good at it. I've treated him like the people I meet when I descend. I con those around me, letting them believe I'm the same person they know and love, when I'm not. I'm a stranger in their loved one's body. Wearing another pair of fake glasses.

"Have fun?" He takes my bag, and we walk through the parking lot, heading to Mom's old Civic. The snow is even thicker here than in Chicago. We pull our hoods up to keep the slush from gathering at the back of our necks.

"Yeah. I had a good time." I try to put some cheeriness behind it, but I'm not sure it works.

Dad lifts my bag into the trunk. "Digging the independent life already?"

I let out a halfhearted laugh. "Yup. Can't wait to graduate."

He opens the passenger door for me. "Don't rent a moving truck yet. I've still got you for another year, remember?"

On the drive home, wipers on full blast, Dad asks about my trip, but I turn the conversation back to him every chance I get. I peruse his phone for pictures of any family shenanigans I missed, interrogating him on each one.

Dad smiles as he navigates the expressways, answering my questions. He's so happy to have me back, I can tell. I smile too, because there's no place I'd rather be, but the lies are everywhere I turn. They blanket me like the snow blankets the world outside my window. They stick to my skin, piling up until I'm buried, never melting, never letting me forget their presence.

MY GREATEST FEAR

Almost two hours and four expressways later, we pull into our street, and it hits me, how much I've missed home, the faces there, my own bed. But something's wrong.

All the big-picture things, all the things I've been through—the fountain, the fight, burying the bodies, finding out what I know about Gesh and his Subs, whether or not I'll keep traveling—it all disappears. It shrinks and narrows until there's only the here and now.

Right now. The snow, the beating wipers, and the flashing red lights.

Dad slows the car. I know his heart is probably racing like mine. I can feel our collective held breath, our fear filling the air as we pull up in front of our house.

Two police cars are parked by the curb. An ambulance sits in the driveway, engine rumbling, back doors flung open.

Before I know it, I'm running through a half foot of slush, squinting through the snowfall as blood-red lights dance in the darkness. My shoes and socks are soaked through. My breath is ice. But I don't feel the cold.

Crippling fear helps you overlook things like that.

It helps me forget to put on my parka when I stumble out of the car, calling Audrey's name as two EMTs haul her down the driveway on a stretcher. It helps me forget to be calm and hope everything's going to be all right. It helps me ignore my dad as he shouts and runs after me. It helps me forget myself, lose myself entirely. Fear is the only thing left, staring me in the face, punching me in the gut, harder.

Harder.

"No, no, no," I say, slipping in the slush and slamming into Audrey's gurney with my hip. A thin dusting of snow has already gathered on her white face. On the oxygen mask over her mouth. On her closed eyelids.

She can't leave like this. Not when I just got back.

I grab her hand and lock our fingers together, but one of the police officers strong-arms me away from her. Our hands slip apart.

"I want to go with her," I say, but the officer won't listen. I'm still being pulled away. "I want to go with her," I shout, struggling against the arms holding me back, my feet sliding in the slush.

The officer grips my shoulders and stoops to look me square in the face. Her eyes are stern. "Listen to me," she says, giving me a firm shake. "If you get in their way, if you delay them even one minute, it could cost your sister her life. Do you understand me?"

It's enough, hearing those words. I stop struggling, Dad pulls me away, and the EMTs finish loading Audrey into the ambulance. Mom rushes past, moving as fast as she can through the ice and snow, her coat and purse clutched under her arm. Snow clings to her long hair. She climbs into the back with them.

Dad gathers me against his side. His arms are iron bars. Gran, Pops, and Claire join us, and we watch, standing in a line like sentinels, blinking back tears. The ambulance drives away, blaring its sirens, its lights dancing like scarlet ghosts through the white curtain of snow.

And just like that, they're gone. All is quiet. Finally, finally, the fear stops gut-punching me. It fades with the sirens into a dull roar in my ears. Hope whispers things like *she'll be OK. They'll save her.* My body registers how cold it is. It tells me to go inside, change into warm, dry clothes, and head to the hospital with the family.

I move like a zombie, not quite alive, not quite dead, replaying the scene in my head over and over. Her hand was so weak and cold. I don't ask questions, just listen to Gran relaying everything to Dad.

They were watching a movie. Audrey was laughing one minute, then the next, she wasn't. Her breath went shallow, she started coughing, then her lips turned blue, and she collapsed. They have no idea what happened. Why she couldn't breathe. It doesn't make sense.

The dull roar in my ears lasts the entire drive to the hospital. It lasts during the ride in the elevator up to Audrey's floor. And it doesn't let up until I'm sitting in a waiting room next to Claire, Gran, and Pops, with nothing to do but wait. It reminds me of waiting at the fountain, the worry, the what-ifs tumbling in my chest as I searched for Blue. Death came that night.

What if it followed me here?

It takes two hours for a doctor to appear and explain what happened. She takes Dad aside first, then lets him break the news to us.

"There was a blood clot," he says, running a shaking hand through his hair. "Caused by the chemo. None of her doctors caught it. It moved to her lungs. They're trying to stabilize her."

I don't know if he says anything after that. All I can hear is the rush of blood to my head, my ears, only my heart thudding in my throat. The dull roar is now a thundering avalanche.

"Is she..." I start to ask, but my throat's too dry, and I have to swallow before I can continue. "Is she strong enough to fight something like this?"

But we all know the answer.

And I'm already blaming Audrey's doctors, the ones who see her every day, who are supposed to be watching out for things like this.

If someone had asked me what I feared the most, I would've said this very moment. The moment there's a complication and the cancer makes her body too weak to fight back. The moment she's taken from us. The imminence of it, the looming shadow it has cast over our home for years.

We acted like it wasn't coming for Audrey. Like she'd sidestep it somehow. But we were just biding our time. Holding our breath. Because it hurt too damn much to think about *what if*. We've all been dying right alongside Audrey, alone in our beds, screaming into our pillows. We kept it together on the outside, for Audrey's sake, so she didn't see it was killing us, watching her die. She didn't deserve to watch us fall apart while she was in so much pain. She didn't deserve that guilt. So we hid it. We acted hopeful when in reality we were crumbling beneath the surface. Decaying beneath our glowing smiles.

We knew one day our facades would come down.

Today is that day.

How cruel is fate, to give me fifty-seven lives when Audrey only gets one brief moment on this earth?

Dad slumps into a chair next to Pops. He takes his glasses off and rubs the bridge of his nose, his temples. I walk over to him, my feet heavy, my legs sluggish, and lay a hand on his shoulder. His hand engulfs mine, warm. Secure.

"How long before we know anything?" I ask.

"Shouldn't be too long now."

I give his hand a squeeze, as much to comfort me as him. "Coffee?"

"Dear Lord, yes, please."

The labyrinth of hospital halls is a welcome change. Anything is better than the stagnation of the waiting room. You sit for hours, staring at your hands, wondering what to do with them, while doctors and nurses sweep past, muffled voices float down halls, and some nightly news guy stares down at you from the TV on the wall. You could change the channel, but there's never anything good on. You could flip through the magazines, but they're all ads anyway. You could stare at your phone, but you'll never find a distraction strong enough to silence the whispers in your head. The ones that say, *She could be dying right now, right this very moment, and there's nothing you can do about it.*

A few floors down, I find a coffee vending machine and shell out two bucks for two Styrofoam cups filled with black sludge. It smells burnt, but I don't care. It's caffeine. It's warm.

By the time I get back to my family, Dad's gone. I sit next to Claire and sip my coffee, leaving Dad's on the end table next to me. Claire stares at her feet, her long, pencil-straight hair hiding her face. Her feet sway back and forth, not quite touching the floor.

Gran leans over. "Your dad went back to talk to your mom and check in on Audrey. Nothing to report yet."

I draw in a deep breath, steadying myself, wondering if I should be preparing for the worst. For Dad and Mom to come through the double doors, arms around each other, tears streaming.

What would I do? What would I say?

"Why are you drinking coffee?" Claire says, frowning up at me. She's annoyed with me. Even more than usual.

"It calms my nerves," I say, but in reality, it's a residual I picked up from one of my past lives. I used to hate the stuff until I walked in Susan Summers's shoes and came back with her addiction to coffee. My thoughts flicker back to 1961, when I stood on the side of the road talking to Blue, leaning against my turquoise Corvette. The setting sun on his skin. His dark hair in his eyes.

I push the memory away and take another sip.

"But you hate coffee." Claire's scowling at me now.

I'm not in the mood for one of our regularly scheduled arguments, so I say, "People change."

Her eyes fall and search the scuffed tile floor; her hands grip the edge of her seat. What she says next is strained, like she can barely get the words out. "I don't like when people change. One minute they hate coffee, the next they're drinking it black like Daddy. One minute they're laughing, the next they can't breathe."

She looks at me like she expects me to say something, to comfort her somehow, but I can't find the strength to respond. There isn't any air in my lungs.

She stalks over to the windows on the far side of the waiting room, her hands fisted tightly at her sides like she's trying to keep everything in. All the raging emotions clawing at her from the inside. I recognize the agony she's going through. I feel the same way. But I've never been able to open up to Claire. I'm not as close to her as I am with Audrey.

I've never regretted that distance until now. The moment Claire needs me and I've got nothing to give.

Gran follows her and wraps her in her arms, both of them going blurry as my eyes fill with tears, their bodies bleeding into each other under the fluorescent lights.

"What if we never get to see her again?" I hear Claire whisper, her face pressed into Gran's cardigan. "What if she never comes out of that room?"

I set my coffee beside Dad's. I can't stomach anything now.

After another hour, Dad and Mom emerge from the beyond the double doors. Gran, Pops, Claire, and I stand and try to gauge their expressions. They look tired, but that's all. Not tearful, and that gives me hope. Claire runs to them, and they pull her into an embrace. I walk forward, slowly, hugging my arms across my chest.

"How is she?" I ask. Gran entwines her arm with mine

and squeezes.

Mom's smile is warm. "She's all right, for now. They have her on blood thinners."

"Praise the Lord," Pops says with a sigh.

"But she's weak," Dad says. "They want to transfer her to AIDA West so her regular doctors can keep her under supervision for a while."

"How long?" Claire asks.

Dad takes in a deep breath before he answers. "Could be weeks, Bear. Months. This has been really hard on her body. She's going to be weak for a long time while the blood thinners do their work."

"Can we see her?"

"She's sleeping, but you can peek in for a minute."

I'm the last one in the room. I'm almost too afraid to go in. It's been three years since I last saw Audrey lying in a hospital bed, when she got so sick and the doctors told us it was leukemia. That night seemed like the hardest thing I could endure.

This is harder.

The room is small, and we all huddle together at the foot of Audrey's bed. Only the light from the hallway stretches in, faint and yellow, but I can see her well enough.

So thin. Like she's gotten thinner in the past few hours somehow. Her skin almost fades into her stark white bed linens. Her bare head on her pillow makes me shiver some more.

"Isn't she cold?" I whisper. "Where's her stocking cap?"

Mom's hand finds my shoulder. "She's fine," she says, her voice low and reassuring. She rubs my arm. "They'll take good care of her." She adds that last part because she knows my question has more weight than just wondering if Audrey's cold. It's fueled by worry. More what-ifs.

What if they miss something again, like they missed the blood clot? Even the best, well-meaning doctors make mistakes. Even the ones Mom and Dad have faith in at AIDA West.

Why isn't their faith shattered like mine? Why are they still putting their trust in the very doctors who could've prevented this from happening?

If only I could go back in time and save her. Travel to a few months prior and give her doctors the heads-up to look for a clot. They could've prevented all of this. But that's not how descending works. I can only travel back in time to my past lives, jumping back decades at a time. Not days, not months, but lifetimes.

My hands form into fists, and I turn and walk out. If I stay any longer, I'll punch a wall, or worse, fall apart, and I can't fall apart. The last time I did that, with the EMTs in the driveway, it could've cost Audrey her life. I can't lose control like that again. I have to keep it together. For Audrey. For the whole family.

CHAPTER 7

DEAD SEXY

In the car on the way home, I text Porter's number. It fails to send, which means he has a new burner cell, and I don't have a way to reach him. I have to wait for him to make contact.

The last few days of holiday break are restless. I pace the house and busy myself with the fix-it projects I have on my schedule, like turning a vintage Peavey amp into a smartphone speaker and building a GoPro mount for a dirt bike, both for kids at school. Still, it doesn't help calm my nerves or get my mind off anything. Mom and Dad spend most of their days at the hospital and Gran and Pops are left to entertain Claire and me until the doctors say it's OK for us to visit.

Gran tries to keep the mourning at bay. "It's too early for that," she says when she sees us frowning off into space. We have movie night with pizza. We have hot cocoa by the fire. Gran even tries to stretch the Christmas spirit into January by playing her old Andy Williams holiday records while we put away the hot-glued ornaments and frayed burlap garland Audrey and I made as kids. Afton bats at the decorations and pounces in and out of the boxes. Claire and I try to be upbeat and positive, but it's tiring keeping up the act. So after a week of Audrey in the hospital, the attempt to pretend all is well was abandoned. Now we're keeping to ourselves, and the house is almost silent, save for a few creaks across the floor as we move from room to room like shifting shadows.

I wait for news from Mom and Dad about Audrey. I wait for contact from Porter. And I darken from the inside out, becoming nothing but a shadow myself.

It's Wednesday afternoon when I get a text, but it's not from Porter.

outside, yo. prepare 2 b amazed

A smile breaks across my lips. If anyone can distract me from death and destruction and cancer and blood clots and silent soldiers no one realizes we're fighting, it's Jensen Peters.

I slip on my Chucks and parka and head outside. I find Jensen in our driveway, wearing a grin, a black winter jacket, and a slouched gray beanie, leaning casually against the most hideous car I've ever seen. His ankles are crossed. His smile is infectious. With his honey-blond hair swept across his eyes, he looks like something out of a J. Crew catalog. But the dilapidated hatchback behind him ruins the effect.

"What is that?" I say, eyeing the car.

"A 1980 Toyota Corolla."

"It's powder blue, Peters."

"And pink." He grins wider and points to the horizontal pink pinstripes along the body.

"And rusty." I nod at the driver's-side door. The bottom half is almost completely corroded away.

"Yeah, don't look at that. Look at *this*." He opens the door, slides onto the passenger seat, and twirls a pair of pink fur dice hanging from the rearview mirror.

"Sexy," I say, stepping closer and draping an arm on the top of the doorframe.

"Dead sexy."

I laugh and shake my head. "I'm not sure the kids at school are going to see it our way, though."

"You think I bought this beauty just to have her rot in some high school parking lot?" He slides out and opens his arms wide. "She's meant for bigger things, Wayfare."

I glance at the little hunk of blue and pink and rust again. "Like?"

"Autocross."

"Autocross?"

He nods. "Autocross."

OK, I'll give him this one. Little cars are pretty perfect for an autocross competition. They're nimble enough to plow through the tight turns of any mapped course without fishtailing out of control and eating a bunch of orange cones. It's a timed trial, so speed is key. "Is she race ready?"

He squints in the winter sun with a half grin. "I was hoping you could help me out with that."

A tiny shiver of excitement sparks beneath my skin. What did I say? Jensen's always good for a distraction, even from events of the catastrophic, world-ending variety. My fingers have been itching to work on something new for weeks, something bigger than replacing the heating element on the toaster and figuring out why Claire's tablet can't hold a charge. "You want me to help fix her up?"

"Oh, I want much more than that. I want a commitment, baby." He drops to one knee, right in the snow, soaking his jeans straight through. He looks up at me, holding the keys out in his palms. "Alex Wayfare, I want to make sweet engine music with you. Will you be my mechanic?"

Two of my neighbors walk by with their dog, staring and grinning, and I yank Jensen to his feet. "Get up before someone thinks you're proposing, you goof."

"Is that a yes?"

I take the keys in one hand and slap his arm with the other. "Yes," I say with a laugh. "Now stop making a scene." I start up the driveway toward the garage. "Want to leave her here? We've got room. And all my tools are inside."

"Yeah, that would be awesome." He follows behind me. "If it's OK with your parents."

I slide the garage door open and Jensen walks in, looking around, stepping on grease spots. He flashes me an approving smile. "I'll come by after school when I don't have practice and help."

"Sounds good," I say, because it does sound good. I need a project while I wait for Porter. Maybe getting back under a hood will help ease the raw feeling in my stomach, the feeling that says Porter's gone, he's not coming back, he thinks the situation is too much for me, so he's going to spare me any further pain and burden and take it away.

I want that to be my choice, not his.

My phone buzzes in my pocket, and I pull it out as my heart leaps into my throat, but it's only Claire asking when I'll be done with my "makeout sesh." I stare at the screen, trying to think of a biting reply, but dammit, nothing comes to mind. Not with Jensen standing there watching me.

"Do you need to take that?" he asks, tucking his hands in his jacket pockets, shrugging his shoulders against the cold.

"No. It's nothing. Just a text."

"From your boyfriend?"

I let out a laugh. If only things were that simple. "Yeah, right." I lean a shoulder against the garage door.

Jensen furrows his brow. "He doesn't text you?"

"Texting isn't exactly his style."

"Oh. Old school, huh?"

That's an understatement. "Something like that."

Jensen toes at one of the grease spots on the floor. "So, you guys are doing good, huh?"

"Yeah. Good."

He laughs. "That sounds convincing."

"It's just…he's been sort of…" I pause, looking for the right word. "Distant lately. I haven't talked to him in a while."

"Why? He's too busy or something?" Jensen takes a step toward me, frowning. "This guy sounds high maintenance, Wayfare."

I smile, because he has no idea. "You think?" I nudge my glasses up my nose.

"I mean, it wasn't that long ago you were pissed at him and thought he was lying to you. Messing with your head."

I remember. How can I forget the moment that caused me to create this Variant timeline? "It's complicated," I say, wondering if Jensen and I would've become friends in that alternate universe, the one we'll never get to see play out.

"You don't want complicated. Take it from me. Tabitha

was complicated."

I nod just to appease him. Blue isn't complicated in the way Tabitha is complicated. Jensen doesn't understand, and that's OK. He doesn't have to.

He takes another step forward, closing the gap between us, and suddenly I feel fidgety. Nervous.

"You deserve to be with someone better," he says.

"Someone who texts me?" I let out a laugh, trying to disperse the tension that's suddenly wrapped around us, linking us at the ankles.

"I'm serious. You should be with someone easy. Someone you can be yourself around, no strings. Someone you can't think about without getting a stupid grin on your face. Someone you want to do everything with, try everything with."

I lift an eyebrow. "*Everything*, everything?"

He laughs. "Well, yeah. Especially *everything*, everything."

I want to tell him I have all that with Blue, except I don't. I feel like I can be myself around him, but does that count when he doesn't know the real me? The real Alex? How long am I going to keep pining for him in Base Life, hoping to find him here?

What if I never find him? What would I be passing up?

Jensen's standing so close now I can see flecks of gold in his hazel eyes, how long his lashes are. A few months ago, I would've killed to be standing somewhere, anywhere, alone with him. Close enough to kiss. I used to think about kissing him all the time.

Maybe I'm thinking a little about it now.

Damn those seeds of doubt about Blue being our enemy. Damn Levi and Micki and Porter for planting them. They're creeping up now, through the soil, reaching for sunlight.

I need to find Blue. Spend more time with him. Prove Micki and Levi and Porter wrong, prove Jensen wrong. Prove to myself that Blue is the one I want, not just in the past, but in the present.

I'm not wrong about Blue, or my feelings for him. It's complicated, but I'm not wrong.

"Anyway," Jensen says, taking a step back and breaking the spell his closeness has over me. Snapping the tension. "James, Tyler, and

I are going to hit Chick and Ruth's later and see if we can slam the Six-Pound Shake. You should come with us."

My mouth goes dry at the thought. Not at the idea of going somewhere with Jensen. I've gotten pretty used to hanging out with him the past few months. But hanging out with him in public, with his friends, is another story. I'm not ready for them to disapprove of me. To make fun of me and make me feel unwelcome. Talk about me when I'm gone. And I don't want Jensen to have to defend me when they ask him what the hell he's thinking.

"I can't," I say, my voice small.

His hopeful shoulders fall.

I want to tell him that I finally get to visit Audrey tonight, but I don't want him to know about that yet. I don't want him to feel bad for coming over, asking me to work on his car, asking to hang out with me, when my sister almost died. He'd feel awful, I know he would. Besides, I don't think I can form the words without breaking down. And I'm definitely not ready to let Jensen see me like that. "But I'll see you Sunday at church, yeah? And we can start on the car on Monday."

"Sure." He steps past me, hands still in his pockets. "See ya, Wayfare."

"You need a ride?" I call out as he reaches the sidewalk.

He squints up at me with his half grin. "Nah. I can walk. Have fun, whatever it is you're doing tonight." He lifts a hand to wave, then he's off, his long legs carrying him around the corner and out of sight.

NOW AND LATER

Audrey's hospital room is dark and shadowy, with only the light from a table lamp spilling across the floor. Her signature black stocking cap is pulled over her ears. Mom must've brought it from home, and I'm glad she did. I didn't like that Audrey's head was bare. It made her look cold. Always cold.

She's curled onto her side, hands fisted, clutching the threadbare quilt Gran made her when she was twelve, the well-worn satin edging pressed against her chin. Mom must've brought that for her too. As a kid, Audrey used to suck on the corners of her favorite blankets. I can remember how she looked as a toddler, curled up in a ball, her beautiful dark blond mop of hair swept over her sweaty forehead, her blanket tucked between her lips, her eyes squished tight so her dreams wouldn't escape. I used to climb into her bed and curl up behind her. I always seemed to find sleep easier that way, with her breath keeping pace with mine.

I often wonder what her life might've been like if I hadn't created the Variant. What if in that other reality Audrey never had leukemia, never felt this kind of pain and exhaustion, never missed out on taking the stairs two at a time? And if so, does that make her cancer my fault?

I'm too steeped in those thoughts to notice I'm crawling in behind her like I used to, wanting to curl up next to her. The mattress squeaks. I snap out of it and realize what I'm doing. I shouldn't disrupt her sleep, I shouldn't chance hurting her. There are tubes snaking across her arms, held on with tape. But before I can stand, she stirs and turns over.

"You're back from your trip." She stretches her arms over her head and coughs.

I frown at the sound, wishing I hadn't woken her. "Go back to sleep," I whisper, moving to leave, but her slim fingers find my wrist, and she pulls me down onto my back so I'm lying next to her.

"No, I was hoping you'd come see me." She smiles, her soft gray eyes creased at the edges, her lids heavy with sleep. "Tell me everything."

I shake my head before images of the last week resurface. I don't want to think about my trip, and I especially don't want to think about the hand she's holding, and how it helped bury two dead bodies. "Later," I say, staring up at the sphere of soft lamplight on the ceiling tiles. "Tell me about your week. What did you do while I was gone?"

"Besides almost dying?"

The ghostly red ambulance lights. The snow. My frozen feet. I press her hand between both of mine, holding on tight. "Besides that."

She sends a short, low laugh floating above us. "It was fraught with drama, my dear, let me tell you." She uses a smoky, dark voice, like an old Hollywood starlet's. "Let's see. Gran found raccoons sneaking into her greenhouse and declared war. Pops lost his pipe and found it in the dishwasher, of all places. It's still a mystery how it got there, but I suspect the Anti-Tobacco League had something to do with it. Hmmmm. What else? Claire lost a tooth so she got dibs on picking the flick for movie night."

I roll my eyes. "How fun for you."

"Wasn't that bad. Some new Cinderella retelling with a lot of twirling and singing. The main guy was hot and made me forget the crushing agony flowing through my veins for an hour, so there's that."

I smile to myself, knowing full well the healing powers of Hot Guy Distraction. "What about you? What did you do?"

"Me?" Audrey looks down at her blanket, rubbing the satin edge between her fingers. "Same old. Napped. Puked. Napped some more. Oh, and I decided to quit school."

I sit up. "What?"

She sits up too and folds her legs. Our knees touch. "I quit the homebound program. Mom said I could. I couldn't keep up, what with all the napping and puking, so I quit."

"But," I say, my mind whirring as the circuits scramble to connect, "you can't quit high school."

"Yes I can. It's one of the universal perks of having cancer, you know. I can do anything. Quit school. Have ice cream for breakfast. Cancel our Scotland trip."

"Wait, what?" She hands me all this new, huge information so casually, like it's nothing, and it feels like she jumped onto a moving train and I'm running alongside, reaching, stretching, unable to catch up. "Why would you cancel? It's your dream to go to Scotland."

She shrugs. "Doesn't matter. I can't go with this stupid clot. Too risky. I have to take it easy."

"OK. The trip can wait. We can postpone it until you're better. But what about school? Will you pick back up in the fall?"

She tilts her head to the side with the same expression Levi gave me when he told me Blue was a traitor. Half sympathy, half pity. Like I'm missing the huge, glaring point, but I'm not. I know the point. I just don't want to face it yet.

Facing things makes them real.

"There's no guarantee I'll get a fall," Audrey says. "I've got what I've got now, and that's what matters. I want to make the most of my now. There may not be a later."

And there it is. Making things real.

My throat tightens. I'm shaking my head, trying not to hear her words, trying to hold back a sudden threat of tears.

How can she say that? That she may not have a fall? Like she has an expiration date stamped across her forehead. Like, hurry up and do everything now because Audrey won't last until August.

She takes my hands. "I'm all right, Allie. I've been preparing for this. Everything's going to be all right. All right?"

I nod because I'm a liar. I pat her hands and turn away, sliding my feet to the floor, because I can't have this conversation right now. "Get some sleep." The words scrape against the knot in my throat. "I'll come by and see you in the morning." I don't look at her because I can't start crying.

I may never stop.

I try my best to push the sobs down, keep them silent and trembling beneath the surface. I need to disappear, go to a place where I can let all these emotions out, or else I might self-destruct.

Most people—when their worst fear comes crashing into their lives like a freight train, ripping their entire world from their hands—have to face those tragedies head on. Excruciating minute by excruciating minute.

Or die trying.

But I'm not most people.

I have an escape. I can travel to other worlds, slip into another pair of shoes. Time travel, as much hell as it's given me, provides some relief. It gives me time to regroup, recharge, and resurface once I've processed things. And when I return to Base Life? The present day? No time will have passed at all. I get to disappear for a while without anyone noticing I was gone.

I'm thankful for this gift, this power, because as crazy as time travel may seem, it's the only thing keeping me sane anymore. The only thing keeping me from falling to pieces and scattering across the floor.

I want to talk to Blue, tell him what I'm going through, have him wrap his arms around me, but I can't risk going back in time without Porter there to make sure I don't mess up. I'm still new at this. Still green.

But there is one thing I can do. I can disappear into the Black. I can ascend to Limbo and rest there, for as long as it takes, before I come back down and face what's before me.

Death and more death, everywhere I turn.

In the pocket of my jeans, my fingers close around my Polygon stone, my little piece of déjà vu that helps me ascend. My soul crawls out of my skin and reaches for Limbo. The billowy, familiar ribbons of the Black slink and roll into Audrey's room. It swirls and wraps around me, taking me as its prisoner. It pulls me into its arms, and I am gone.

CHAPTER 8

LIMBO

The deep Black of my garden surrounds me. It's a comforting kind of darkness, like your bedroom at night when the moon filters in. My soulmarks sway gently before me, glowing, pulsing white-blue in the black expanse.

There are no walls in Limbo. No ceilings, no floors, although there is a perception of standing. On what, I couldn't say. Endless Black wraps all around. It depends on which level you're on, but there can be an endless amount of soulmarks, too, glittering and dotting the blackness.

Here on my own level, the one Porter created for me, hidden away from Gesh, are the fifty-six soulmarks belonging to me. Like a forest of birch trees, they tower over me, blindingly white, swaying gently. They are the evidence of my fifty-six past lives. My soul made these marks each time I died and ascended, not to heaven, but to Limbo, only to be reincarnated again. Sent back to earth, becoming someone new. My lives have been woven throughout time, each thread tightly secured in history.

And I have the ability to unravel it.

That is why Gesh sent his men to capture me at the fountain. He's been trying to find me since I was reborn. He's scared of me, of what I could do to the world he silently controls. I could bring it crashing down around him, see him kneeling before me, if I wanted.

If I knew how.

The ability is within me. Gesh knows it. Porter, Micki, and Levi know it. That's why they handle me with kid gloves. I'm a bomb, and one wrong move, one miscalculated plan, could cause detonation.

I've done it before.

I made a choice. There's no telling if it was wrong or right. We'll never know. I changed the past, created a Variant timeline. Everything in Base Life is the way it is because of that one choice, that change. And no one's the wiser. No one remembers the way it was before, in that other world, the one I erased.

Maybe it's still out there somewhere. An alternate version living right alongside this one. We'll never know, because we don't remember it being any other way.

At the end of my garden of soulmarks stands the fountain Porter made for me. Tall and slender, standing stalwart in the Black. The water gurgles and I dip my hand into it. It's not a real fountain. Not even real water, just the perception of water. For the past two months, Porter's been teaching me how to create things in Limbo, perceptions of things on earth. Organic matter doesn't exist here, in the Land of Souls, so you have to manipulate the Black to conform into the memory of objects. If you're strong enough to bend the Black to your will, the object comes to life, like magic.

Your body can change, too, into any shape you can dream up, simply because you have no body at all. Just the memory of your body from earth. The Descender I fought at Buckingham Fountain once battled me here in Limbo. He took on the shape of smoke, and you can't fight smoke.

Except I did. I harnessed the energy of the Black and defeated him. But then he brought reinforcements. I couldn't fight them all, and I had to rely on Porter to help me escape. That's why I asked Porter to teach me how to shapeshift, in case I ever needed to battle in Limbo again.

If Porter were here he'd see the body my soul is projecting. It's not exactly what I look like in Base Life, but my perception of what I look like. So I might seem distorted, depending on how I see myself. I'm wearing my parka, jeans, black Chucks, and Gran's flowery scarf I lost in Chicago. The one that got too bloody to clean—Levi had to burn it to dispose of any evidence. At least here, in Limbo, I can see it again. Hold it in my hands. Smell Gran's lemon verbena perfume still lingering on the fibers.

No nerd glasses this time. Ever since I started wearing the fake pair, they don't feel like they're the real me anymore. Just a disguise, like Clark Kent.

My body begins to shift as I remember what Porter taught me. The edges of the Black bend inward, pulling toward me, its energy melding with mine. I let it flow through me. My instinct is to tense up, but relaxation is the key. Total submission to the Black. We must blend and work together as one.

My fingers fade, dissipating into particles that float up and swirl in front of my eyes, followed by my hands, my arms, my chest, until I'm a cloud of smoke, hovering, quiet, still. I hold myself there, in that form, for as long as I can, then let go. I can't explain it. It's like letting out a breath. My body snaps back into its base form, the form I always take on when I'm here, without even thinking about it.

I can't hold onto that other form as long as the Descender could. Not as long as Porter can. I'm not that strong. But it was a good run. Longer than before.

I'm getting there.

LEVEL FIVE CLEARANCE

It's dangerous to visit Polestar while I'm in Limbo, venturing outside of my garden where I'm safely hidden from Gesh and his Descenders, but I want to see it again. I haven't seen it since Porter and I first met, when he first showed me Limbo. I'm not even sure I know how to move levels to get there, but I close my eyes and concentrate.

A feeling like air seeping from my lungs takes hold. A slow leak, then a rush, like the wind's been kicked out of me. My chest constricts and my feet lift me into the air. I remember this from last time. I tried to tell Porter I couldn't breathe, but he reminded me I didn't have lungs. I didn't need air. That's when the tightness, like a rubber band around my lungs, broke. It happens this time too.

Snap.

I drop to what I perceive as smooth ground, look up, and I'm there. Polestar, the center of Limbo, is just as I remember it.

Unlike in my garden, there is a landscape of sorts here. Those who've come before us built hills and valleys and grasses, like Porter built my fountain. The perception is so strong it seems real. The night air feels fresh. The soulmarks glitter like stars in the sky, sway in the distance like glowing trees. Ahead of me, a ruined, shadowy castle sits on a hill. I'm not sure if it was meant to look ruined or if something happened to it, a battle perhaps, and someone tore at its walls and turrets. After my fight with the Descender, I know things can be destroyed here, just as easily as they are created.

At the base of the castle's hill, a river winds around it, a shimmering moat. I make my way to the crystal-clear bridge that arcs over the water, leading to what was once the entrance of the castle. Standing on the bridge, I can see the river rushing beneath my feet, like I'm hovering over it. Soulmarks swim in the water, swirling, spinning, slithering. The marks of those who've passed on, their life stories written on each one. They could belong to anyone. Queens, dignitaries, orphans, aborigines, Anastasia, Martin Luther King, Jr., Julius Caesar, Joan of Arc, Adolf Hitler.

Porter once told me that soulmarks are the lifeblood of Limbo. The energy source. Maybe that's why we can create things out of the Black. They are powerful things, soulmarks. Gateways to the past. Our souls can use them to slip into the past bodies they once inhabited. They give us the ability to wear their skins, assume their lives, if only for a second. And it's a dangerous, dangerous journey for those not strong enough. Once a soulmark is used for descending it cannot be reused. It burns up. Porter says it sort of fizzles into the air, disappearing before your eyes.

Which is a problem, especially if the Descender made an impact on history while they were in the past. To erase that impact you have to do a touchdown. You have to use the same soulmark to go back to the beginning of your journey, like a reset button. I've had to do it twice. Once when I first met Blue, and I kissed him and made an impact on his heart. Then again when the Descender shot me and left me for dead in 1876. That was against the rules. You're not allowed to take a life. So I had to go back, reset the mission, make it so it never happened. I was never shot. I never kissed Blue. For me, touchdowns are easy. My soulmarks don't burn up because my soul hasn't gone to Afterlife. I'm still here. And so my soulmarks wait for me in my garden, and I can use them over and over again. That's why I'm special. An asset to Gesh and whatever he's planning.

Other Descenders must go through several levels of training before they're allowed access to Limbo. The lowest, Level One, are trainees. They study the theory of descending and Limbo, but don't actually get to see it. Level Two finally grants them access to Limbo, but only under strict supervision, like taking a field trip. They practice shapeshifting and moving between the different levels of Limbo. The Descender I battled in Limbo was Level Three. He could access Limbo alone and go on missions, using specific soulmarks that had been carefully researched for him, but his every move was tracked by Gesh's team. If he disconnected from a soulmark it would burn up, but as a Level Three, it meant he had the strength and ability to maintain a connection to a soulmark long enough to do a touchdown.

Gesh and Porter are Level Four. That just means they have free rein. They can maintain a connection to a soulmark in order to achieve touchdowns just like Level Threes, but they answer to no one. They can descend into any soulmark they want. That's how Gesh became obsessed with descending. He had the power to change the past again and again, replaying the same scenarios in different ways, each time upping the stakes, using bodies for his own pleasure and gain. Using people like puppets to bend to his will. And it made him crazy. Greedy. A god who wanted to squeeze the world in his fist until it burst.

He was careful, though, to touch down and erase the hideous things he'd done, leaving no trace in Base Life of the heinous man he truly is. And once he was done with a soulmark and disconnected from it he could never use it again. It was free. Released from his bondage and burned up into the Black.

That's Level Four clearance.

Blue and I are Level Five.

We have free rein too, although Porter tries to give me boundaries. We have the ability to ascend and descend anytime we want, and we can reuse our own soulmarks and benefit from the memories of our past lives during our missions.

The memory thing only works part of the time. Some memories are strong for me, like muscle memory. So strong, in fact, sometimes I have to fight with my past-life body to get it to do what I want. It's like driving a vintage muscle car like the Mustang. Sometimes they have a mind of their own and you have the wrestle them into submission. But other memories, like names and places and dates, are far less clear for me.

I guess that's why I needed Micki in my most recent past life, when I worked for Gesh and Porter at AIDA. She kept track of all those things. Made sure I had all the information I needed for my missions.

I asked Porter once if any newbie Descenders ever made an impact they didn't have the strength to erase. He simply said, "How would we know?"

His answer made the hairs on the back of my neck stand on end.

I'm not sure how long I stand on the bridge, watching soulmarks swim beneath me, thinking about all the impact that could've been made and the ripples that could've been created, before I hear his voice.

Soft at first, so soft I think I may have dreamed it, then louder, right behind me.

A whisper. "Sousa."

I turn, and for a moment just stare, uncertain that what I'm seeing is real.

Blue.

CHAPTER 9

A GLEAMING PALACE

After months of waiting, after holding him in my arms as he was dying, after all I went through at the fountain, he's here. Standing in front of me. And he's beautiful. Even more beautiful here, in Limbo, than I've ever seen him. Maybe it's my perception of him that makes him so breathtaking. Tall and gorgeous. Cropped dark hair, shining blue-green eyes, wool coat draped over square shoulders, like the first time I saw him in 1927 Chicago. Those lips that make me forget everything, everything, except wanting to kiss them.

"Are you real?" I press a palm to his chest.

He places his hand over mine and holds it close. His smile widens. "As real as I can be in this place." He lowers my hand, but keeps it held at his side.

"You didn't show," I say, looking down at our fingers, entwined and clasped tight.

"I didn't?"

"At the fountain. You weren't there."

"I'm sorry," he says.

"What happened?"

"I don't know." He pauses, thinking. "I can't remember."

I'm not sure what else I expected him to say. But I'm not angry. I know it's not his fault if he can't remember. For a long while we're both quiet, holding hands. Silver threads of soulmarks glide beneath our feet.

"Have you ever been here?" he asks. "To Polestar?"

"Once." I lift my face to the castle ruins.

"In *Inferno*," he says, "Dante claims Homer resided here, in this castle, with Socrates and Plato and all the other great thinkers of the world. There are those who believe Christ liberated souls from Limbo after he was crucified. That he ascended here and rescued them—Abraham and Noah and all those believers from the Old Testament. I think he must have rescued Homer and the others, too. I've searched this place from end to end. There's no one here anymore, no souls at all. Just their marks."

I'm glad Blue's the one talking, because I can't find any words. I stare up at him, dumbly, like I'm in a dream. I like watching him speak, how his lips form each word, hearing his thoughts. I feel like I could listen to them for the rest of my life.

"When Dante and Virgil toured Limbo they entered the castle," Blue says. "Dante described it as a sprawling, gleaming palace, with many courtyards and gardens. But I've been inside, and it's no such place. It's dark, and lonely, and cold, and ruined. There's nothing gleaming about it."

"When did you read *Inferno*?" For me it was freshman year, so it's been a while, and even then it was only the summary online. I didn't like reading books before I met Porter, especially ones set in the past, even fiction. I feared they would trigger déjà vu from one of my past lives, back before I knew what my visions were.

"Not sure," Blue says, tracing the lines of my palm with his finger. "Isn't that strange? I can remember the contents of a book but not when, or who I was when I read it." He shakes his head. "Books are powerful things. Our memories may fade, but the written word lasts across lifetimes."

I've never encountered this philosophical side of him. I like seeing it, getting a glimpse inside his mind. "Have you been here a lot?"

He nods. "Every time you ascend to Limbo you pull me here. But I can never find you in Polestar. I've looked. You must ascend to some level I can't access."

The thought of him wandering around Limbo, searching for me, makes me reach out for his arm. Tug him closer. "I'm sorry. I didn't know I pulled you to Limbo with me."

"You didn't?"

"I thought we pulled each other to the past. I knew that affected you, but I never realized my time in Limbo affected you too. Before I knew what we were, when you'd have déjà vu and you'd pull me back in time without warning, I hated it. I felt like I had no control over my life. I hate that I do that to you."

"Our souls are linked. I can't descend without you, and you can't descend without me. We pull each other no matter what. But it's OK." A grin creases the corners of his eyes. "I like it here. I'd rather be here, knowing I'm connected to you, than back in Base Life. I'd rather be anywhere than there."

Hope lifts in my chest like it's caught in a breeze, like the sheets Gran pins to the clothesline in our backyard. "Do you remember something about your Base Life?"

He shakes his head, his grin disappearing. "I can never remember it. I try every time you pull me here, but I can't."

"Then how do you know you'd rather be here?"

His smile is back and he squeezes my hand. "You once said to me, in Chicago, when we were at Peg Leg, you said you didn't want to go back to your old life because it didn't have me in it. That's exactly how it is for me. I don't care what life I leave behind when you pull me back. I don't care because you're not there. You're here. And I'd rather be pulled away from Base Life than not have these moments at all. We're partners. I'd rather be with my partner."

"But you could have a life out there, a real life. You could have a family. A girlfriend waiting for you."

"Nah." His blue-green eyes make my stomach dip. "If there were a girl in Base Life that meant half as much to me as you, I'd remember her. Like I remember you, no matter where I go, no matter what body I'm in. I remember you."

"Just not in Base Life."

"We don't know that. Maybe I do remember you in Base Life. Maybe I just can't get to you. Maybe there's an obstacle."

"If you could remember something, anything, about your Base Life, I could figure out where you are. Follow the clues. I could come to you."

He frowns, thinking hard, his eyes searching the soulmarks in the distance. Then he shakes his head. "It's all black, all of it. It's all black until I see your face again." He winds a strand of my hair around his finger. "Is this what you look like in Base Life?"

I look down, hiding my face from him. For a moment, my trust in this boy standing before me wavers. Loses its balance. What if Micki is right? What if all this, his interest in me, is a scam? A plan created by Gesh to find me in Base Life?

I brush the thought away, because I know it stems from my self-doubt, something I'm trying to overcome. For as long as I can remember, I've questioned my own judgment until I couldn't see straight, depending on others to guide me. Because they were the normal ones and I was the one with the psychotic breaks from reality. It's so easily done when you truly believe you're certifiably crazy. And now, even though I know I'm not crazy, that I'm just as sane as anyone else, my old habits remain. My instinct is to doubt myself, doubt Blue's attraction to me, doubt anyone's. Because why would anyone want me? A socially awkward nutcase?

I can't fathom a reason. Not one.

But I don't want to think like that anymore. I want to give myself some credit, trust my gut. And my gut tells me I know Blue better than they do. It tells me I can trust him. Maybe it's just hope or wishful thinking, but whatever it is, it's strong enough to make me want to prove his innocence.

Prove I'm not crazy.

Blue lets my hair fall, and he traces a finger down my jaw. Lifts my chin. I close my eyes while he takes in what I look like as Alex Wayfare.

"Your perception filter is blurry," he says. "You're not letting me see the real you."

"I'm sorry. I'm not used to holding one form very long," I say, lying, my eyes still closed. Because this is the one form I can hold as long as I want. But I don't want him to know my true face. Not yet.

And I realize now it's not just about my insecurity, whether or not he'll like what he sees. It's what Micki said about Gesh's Subs in Chicago. *I couldn't risk letting them go. They saw your face.*

If Blue is working for Gesh then I shouldn't let him see me. I shouldn't give away all the tiny details that make me Alex. My gray eyes, my freckles, my round nose. I shouldn't give Gesh any way to track me in Base Life.

Find my family.

I need to be cautious, at least until I can prove Blue is innocent. Again.

As if to tell me he doesn't care what I look like, what form I'm in, he pulls my arms up and wraps them around his neck. His hands slide around my waist, and then we're swaying, our bodies fitted together, dancing beneath the starry soulmarks, my head on his chest.

He smells so good, like he did in Chicago. And with my eyes closed, I can almost pretend we're back there, when he teased me all night long, until finally, finally, he kissed me.

I want to make the most of my time with him, even if it isn't real. Even if it's only our perception of each other, how we smell, how we look, how we taste.

I slide my fingers into his hair at the base of his neck. I tuck my nose beneath his jaw and kiss him there, where his stubble fades to smooth skin.

His heart beats quicker.

Mine does too.

His nose touches mine. I can feel his breath on my mouth. "Can I kiss you now, Sousa?"

I don't answer. I kiss him first.

We sink to the bridge, wrapping ourselves around each other. He kisses me faster, hungrier, like I might descend back to Base Life at any moment and leave him behind. And even though this is only my perception of his fingers on my skin, my memory of his touch and not the real thing, I'll take it.

Because it's all I've got.

The energy we produce pulls the Black inward, and the

soulmarks close in until there are stars above us, and stars below, and we're swimming in them, floating in them, becoming tangled up in their light and each other and the Black all at the same time.

THE PATTERN

"How much time do you think we have left?" Blue kisses my fingertips, one, two, three.

We're lying on the bridge, staring up into the Black, his arm around me, my head resting on his chest. "Not long. I can feel the pull growing stronger."

The Black never lets you hang around for long. It kicks you out, return to sender. You have to be strong enough to resist it, like Porter. And I'm not. Neither is Blue. If we were, we could stay here forever. Stealing a kiss whenever we want one.

"I've always wondered," Blue says. "How did Dante know about the castle in Limbo? He describes a dark valley, too, like this one."

"I don't know."

"I think he was a Descender. I think there are many who've come before us, who've entered Limbo, but weren't sure what they were seeing, or how to use it. I think he thought it was all a dream. But it's real. And he could've changed the past with one slip into the wrong soulmark."

It's a scary thought, random people accessing Limbo. If only Gesh had written a poem about his discovery and left it well enough alone, like Dante. But then again, I wouldn't have been created. I wouldn't have met Blue.

"I want to be your partner again," Blue says, pulling me from my thoughts. "I want to help you when you travel, be your backup, like when we worked together at AIDA. When we were Tre and Ivy."

I snuggle against his side, tighter. "I would love that, but I may not be traveling anymore."

I don't see how I can keep going, even if I want to. My team doesn't trust Blue, and I don't trust my team. Plus, it's not safe anymore, not when Gesh is so close, and Audrey is so far away.

Blue sits up, surprised, and I do too. "You can't stop traveling," he says. "It's the only way I exist."

I touch his cheek with my fingertips. "Don't be silly. You exist. And we'll find each other in Base Life. We will."

"What if we don't?"

I open my mouth to argue, but he keeps going.

"It feels like I'm only alive when you pull me back in time. When I'm not with you, everything goes dark. My memory gets put on hold until I see you again, then it starts back up, like the winding of a clock." Blue grips my hand in his. "I don't want you to leave again. Please don't send me back into the dark."

"I don't want to leave either. But the only way we can be together, for real, is if I find you in Base Life. You have to help me find you."

He frowns, the familiar, teasing light in his eyes long gone. Now they're dull and faded. "What if I don't exist in Base Life? What if I'm dead? What if I was never reincarnated with you?"

My stomach clenches at the thought. "Not possible. You said so yourself. Our souls are linked. We descend together. We die together. We're born together."

"Anything's possible. We're reincarnated time travelers, Sousa. There was a time in your life when you thought *that* was impossible, yet here we are."

"If you were dead, how could you travel back in time with me? Your soul would've gone to Afterlife. You wouldn't be here now."

He's silent for a while, frowning. He's so beautiful. Even when he's sad, he's beautiful. "Maybe I'm wandering around Limbo, a lost soul, and Christ hasn't come to rescue me. Maybe my soulmarks are playing tricks. Maybe there was a glitch during our reincarnation. I don't know. All I know for certain is that I can't remember one single thing. Maybe I never will."

The hurt in his voice makes me ache. I'm unable to respond, because now there are more unwelcome seeds of doubt, and I don't know how to organize them into coherent thoughts.

He lies back down, holding my hand to his chest, and I lie down too. Nestle against him. "I'm a ghost." He speaks the words to the dark sky. To the stardust. "That's all I am. A ghost, wandering through time, haunting you."

"That's not true. You're alive. You're real. I'll prove it when I find you."

He kisses the top of my head, sadly, like he doesn't believe me. "We're running out of time."

"Here? In Limbo?"

"In Base Life."

I sit up again. "What do you mean?"

He furrows his brow at me. "We only have a few months before we're reincarnated again. I don't know if we'll find each other before then."

I shake my head. "I'm not planning on dying anytime soon."

"It's not up to you. It's just how it is." When he sees that I don't understand, he sits up too, holding my hand tightly. "You haven't done the math? Our past lives. The years we can travel to. They don't add up. There should be sixty, seventy, eighty years between each rebirth. But there isn't."

I think about each of my missions. 1876. 1927. 1961. I quickly figure out the years between each one. I was seventeen years old in all of them. Which means I was born in 1859. 1910. 1944.

"There are fifty-one years between my first two missions. And thirty-four between the last two. Those aren't the greatest lifespans, but they're something. And people live longer now. We'll have a long life, Blue. Long enough to find each other."

He shakes his head. "There are missions between those. There's one in 1944. Another in 1978. There's a pattern, going all the way back to the beginning. You haven't noticed it?"

Now that he mentions it, there is one soulmark, one time period, that gives me pause. When I was trying to find a specific soulmark in my garden, I tested out several to figure out how Porter had them organized. I descended there for only a few seconds, but it was the forties, I was sure of it. I hadn't thought a thing about it back then. I'd been too focused on getting to Blue. Finding the soulmark that would bring me directly to him, the one where we were in the same place at the same time. AIDA Headquarters in our most recent past life.

I was sitting in a chair, listening to a radio show. I remember hearing something about Hitler. The clothing I was wearing. The room I was in. It was the forties. I knew it at the time, but I haven't thought about it since.

"OK, so there were a few lives where we didn't live that long. There's no proof this one will be the same."

"Alex." The look in his eyes, the despair in his voice, the fact that he calls me Alex instead of Sousa, it all makes my stomach sink. "We weren't created to live long lives. We were created to have as many lives as possible, so we could be placed in as many time periods as possible. Fifty-seven points in time are better than three or four. Don't you see?"

I shake my head, not because I don't understand, but because it can't be true. And I don't want him to say the words, to make them real.

But he does.

"You and I, we've never seen our eighteenth birthday. We always die before, and we'll die this time just the same." He pulls me close. "I'm sorry. I thought you knew."

I exhale, letting out a huge breath, letting all the little truths I've clung to escape along with my blindness. And just like that breath, the Black exhales too, and we fade away, back to the stark, brilliant light of our realities.

CHAPTER 10

COUNTLESS AUTUMNS

The moment I land, sitting on Audrey's hospital bed, I pull my glasses off and hug her, my face buried in her neck. She holds me tightly, with so much love I can't bear it. It feels good to hold someone in the flesh, feel their real warmth, their real heart beating, not just the perception of it.

"It's going to be all right," Audrey says. "I promise." She rubs my back as my sobs come in waves. Her thin, fragile arms wrapped around me, and the fact that she feels like she has to comfort me, make me cry all the harder. I vowed to never let her see me come undone, but I was stronger back then. Before I knew about the expiration dates, hers and mine. Before I knew my parents would lose not one, but two of their daughters by the end of the year.

How are they going to survive that? How could anyone?

I'm infinitely connected to Blue. I know I'll see him again. There's no question. So as much as I want to find him, right now it pales in comparison to the need to spend every moment I can with my family before it's too late. Before I'm reborn, before I forget all about them, and my body becomes nothing more than a vessel to the past.

A mission. A paycheck for Levi and Micki.

If I'm honest with myself, I've never been a Wayfare at all. It's all been a lie. A disguise. A hideout. Me? I'm a Descender. Alex is the body I'm wearing for the moment, a body I might return to from the future someday. I might look upon my family's faces and no longer know them, no longer know what it's like to have this warm feeling in my heart for them.

I am not a Wayfare.

I am a number.

Nummer Fire.

Micki was right. I am only a tool. A weapon. Blue and I, our lives don't matter because we'll get another one. On and on until the end of time. I'll get another autumn. And another. And another.

But there are no autumns for Audrey. No more sitting on the front porch swing, handing out candy for Halloween, breathing in woodsmoke from the chimney, listening to leaves rustle like paper. Out of everyone, Audrey's the one who deserves more time. Her life matters—has always mattered—more than mine.

Why was I the one chosen for rebirth, when she would've benefited more? The world, the past, would've been better in her hands, not mine. She's optimistic in the face of death, telling me it's going to be all right, that she's prepared. When I look at my future, I see doom and gloom, I see darkness, but Audrey sees light.

In the midst of winter she gathers spring blooms.

And I love her for it. I love her more than anyone. She makes me better. Stronger. Before I met Porter, she helped me have purpose. She was the one who listened when I spoke about my visions. I told her they were nightmares. She was the one who held me close when I was scared, when I didn't know what was happening to me. When I thought I was going crazy.

Now I see things clearer. I should've been the one doing that for her. Making her better. Giving her strength. Giving her purpose. Maybe I didn't think I could. Maybe being a kid was my excuse. Maybe I relied too much on Mom to find a cure, when all along I could've been doing the same thing.

I've had countless autumns. Isn't it time I gave some back?

WARRIOR CELLS

I wake to a gentle shake of my shoulder. When I open my eyes, Mom is sitting beside Audrey's bed.

She's smiling. "I've been here for a while, watching you sleep. Reminds me of years ago, when you were both little nuggets." She smooths hair from my forehead. Her hands are cool, her fingers long and slender. Her glasses hang from a chain around her neck and rest against her white button-down shirt.

"What time is it?" I ask, sitting up slowly so I don't wake Audrey. It's still dark out.

"After midnight."

I rub my eyes. "Working late again?"

"Story of my life." Her eyes are tired, shadowed with dark circles. I don't think she's slept at all since Audrey was admitted. She's either been at work or here, rarely at home for the past two weeks.

"Hungry?" she says. "There's a twenty-four-hour Chinese place across the street. Fantastic dumplings."

I nod, and we slip out silently.

The restaurant is empty except for a waitress who seats us in a booth by the front windows. I can hear cooks in the back washing dishes and shouting over various kitchen noises. Mom orders tea and dumplings. She smiles warmly at our waitress, her hands folded in front of her. Light from red lanterns hanging above us mingles with her smooth chestnut hair, pulling out the red hues. Gentle music weaves between us from speakers in the ceiling, plinking strings and deep flutes and light wooden percussion. Mom looks at home in the lantern light, and I wonder how many times she's eaten here, alone or with her team, after long nights in DC, working at the AIDA West lab.

While we wait for our tea she glances around with a satisfied expression, like she's had many good memories here. I love seeing her out in the wild. Seeing another side of her, spending time with her.

After some time, she says, "It's been a while since we did something like this, hasn't it? Gone somewhere fun, just the two of us."

I shrug a little, because I don't want her to think it's a big deal.

She places her elbows on the table, her chin on her hands. "It's like I blinked and you were grown. I swear just yesterday you were tugging at my skirt, begging me to watch you do a cartwheel."

The waitress brings our tea, and Mom pours the deep amber liquid into two cups without handles, like tiny bowls. We cradle the cups in our palms and savor the warmth. Snow falls outside the windows, lightly blanketing the street, the lamps, the cars parked along the curb.

She watches me drink my tea, her head tilted to the left. "Now look at you. Almost a senior. Going off to visit cities on your own. Navigating life, shouldering all this on your own. I've been so wrapped up in my grief, my work. I haven't been there to help you through these past few years. And now you're grown. Ready to leave the nest, and I feel like I missed it. I should've done more things like this. I should've been there more."

"That would've meant taking time away from Audrey. That's the last thing I wanted you to do."

"But I've taken you for granted." She reaches out and tucks a loose strand of my hair behind my ear. "Always, in the back of my mind, I told myself I'd have more time. Time to spend with you after my work for Audrey was done. You weren't the sick one, so I pushed you to the back burner. I made you wait. And that wasn't fair."

How can she say that? It's never been about being fair to me. Fair doesn't factor in when your sister has cancer. It's like a universal law.

"I never felt like I was on the back burner. All my life you've been caring for others. I don't remember when it was just you, Dad, and me. Audrey's always been there, and you've been taking care of her. Then came Claire. Then Audrey got sick. Then Gran and Pops moved in. You had to ration your time. It's how it's always been, and I'm fine with it."

She shakes her head. "I should've done more mom things for you. I never volunteered at your classroom parties, never drove you to soccer practice, never welcomed you home after school."

I let out a laugh. "I never played soccer."

She laughs too, although her eyes are glistening with tears. "Well, maybe you would have if I were there to drive you."

There are a lot of things that might be different, had we made other choices. Maybe I've been too hard on myself, thinking it was all my fault, this Variant timeline, these circumstances. I've shouldered them all. But all of us make choices that change the course of time, tiny choices, every moment of every day. We all shape the future; whether we like it or not, we all create ripples that affect everyone else. Maybe my choices are part of a collective web. Maybe everyone feels like it's their fault. Maybe it's just part of being human.

Mom refills her tea and cups her little bowl with both hands. "You know, when I was pregnant with you, I used to lie in bed and dream about what kind of mother I'd be. I'd picture scenarios and how they might play out, how I'd discipline, how I'd provide for you, how I'd teach you things. I never pictured that I'd become this. The kind of mom who works all the time, rarely home, isn't plugged in with her kids. I was going to be like Gran, like the mom she was to me. She was always there. I never had to worry because she had my back. Twenty-four-seven, I could count on her. That's who I wanted to be."

"You think I feel neglected because you break your back, dedicating your life to saving people like Audrey? If I feel anything, I feel proud. You might not be like Gran, but that doesn't matter. You're a hero, Mom. And heroes can't be there for their families like normal people can. They have to sacrifice. We all get that. All of us."

A tear runs down her cheek, and she folds my hands into hers on the table. She sniffs. "I don't deserve you."

"I'm telling the truth."

I truly am. No lies this time. For once I opened my mouth and let truth spill out. And it felt good and redemptive down to the soul. I don't want to lie to my family anymore, not if I can help it. For the next few months, I want to be honest, and tell them how I feel. How privileged I am to know them.

When the dumplings come, Mom drops a few on a plate for me, using chopsticks like a pro. "I thought dumplings were appropriate. In China, they're eaten on New Year's to bring luck, like how we always have corned beef and cabbage. I thought we could use all the luck we can get right now."

"Cheers?" I say, forgoing the chopsticks and holding a dumpling up with my fingers. It couldn't hurt, hoping for a little luck.

We bump our dumplings together like wine glasses. "Cheers."

With the first bite, I make a wish, tossing my penny into Buckingham Fountain. I wish for a cure for Audrey, a life lived fully for her, and a happy ending for my family after I'm gone.

"Tell me about this cure you're working on for Audrey."

Between bites, Mom explains. "There's this relatively new treatment where we genetically modify a patient's cells, turning them into little warrior cells. The warrior cells attack the cancer cells, completely eradicating the cancer in the entire body. It's really quite remarkable. A few patients we've tested it on have been cured within a handful of weeks."

"You train their own bodies, their own cells, to fight back?"

"Precisely," she says smiling, chewing.

"Why can't you use the treatment on Audrey?"

"We've never been successful with late-stage cancer patients, only early-stage. On the late-stage patients, the warrior cells are too zealous—they attack other cells, too, not just the cancer cells. We need more clinical trials and testing. And that takes time and money."

Mom shakes her head and sighs. "The stupid part is, scientists have been studying this type of immunotherapy for decades. Back in the seventies, a team of scientists at AIDA had a ninety percent success rate with late-stage patients like Audrey. Ninety percent. That's huge."

"So what's the problem? Why can't you do what they did?"

"We have no idea how they did it. Their data was lost—*poof,* just like that—in a fire. The discoveries they made never made it into the history books, the medical research journals." She smiles at me in her sad-but-there's-no-need-to-fret kind of way. It's the same look Audrey gives me. She got it from Mom, but I never inherited it. I don't have enough hope in my veins to pull it off. "They didn't keep everything on hard drives back then, you know. It was all handwritten or typed on a typewriter, filed away in cabinets. That's what my team's been working on all these years. Recreating that lost data. Uncovering their secrets, what they did differently."

My skin tingles, and I sit up straighter. "And if you had those lost files? If they were sitting right in front of you?"

"Then we could get approval to conduct another trial, and we could start treatment on Audrey." She chews on another dumpling, staring out the window at the snow, her eyes far off. "I dream about it almost every night, actually, someone coming across the files in an attic somewhere. Some kind of unbelievably lucky fluke where the files were never in that fire. But I always wake up, and all I can do is get back to work."

"Maybe someone will find them," I say.

Her eyes slide back to mine. "That's why we're eating the dumplings, right? For extra luck."

We don't talk about Mom's work or the missing research for the rest of the night, even on our drive back home to Annapolis. I couldn't talk about it even if I wanted to. My hands are shaking too much. My heart is beating too fast. Because Mom doesn't need luck.

She needs me.

CHAPTER 11

COOL WITH BOGART

Sunday comes and goes, but I don't go to church with Gran, Pops, and Claire. The following week passes by, but I don't go to school. I can't concentrate on anything other than the lost data and how the hell I'm going to get it. I tell Mom and Dad I'm not ready to go back to school, that I want to spend as much time with Audrey as I can. They don't object. They call in for me, they drop me off at the hospital every day and drive me home every night. They give me money for the cafeteria and all the vending machine coffee I can drink. They know I may not get moments like this with my sister ever again, and right now, that's more important than a week sitting in classrooms, daydreaming about death, waiting with bated breath for my phone to ring so I can share my plan with Porter.

My plan to save Audrey.

I stopped by Porter's apartment twice, the space he rents on the top floor of Mrs. Yoder's little yellow Victorian house. There hasn't been one sign of life. He's not back yet, and I'm losing patience. It seems like forever since Micki saved me from the Descenders, since I helped plant them in the ground, since Blue told me I didn't have much time left. It felt so long ago because it was all death, death, death, and for the past week, I've been thinking about life. Nothing but life, and warrior cells, and helping Audrey get the armor and weapons she needs to fight back.

On Friday night, as I'm sitting with her at the hospital, watching *The Big Sleep* on my laptop and snacking on strawberry Fruit Roll-Ups, I get a text from Jensen. It's the fourth I've gotten this week, but I haven't replied to any of them. I haven't even read them. I don't know why. Maybe because I don't know what to say. Maybe I feel bad for not starting work on his car. Or maybe I think it'll be easier this way, if our friendship just sort of fades away. He's not like Blue. He wouldn't understand why I have to die.

We die, Sousa. It's what we do.

Oddly, these words of Blue's have always comforted me. Made death something I didn't have to fear.

Audrey glances at my phone. "Who is it?"

"Just Jensen."

"Just Jensen," she repeats, grinning.

My family has teased me about my crush on Jensen since before I can remember. It used to make me blush and fidget in my chair. Not anymore.

It feels like nothing bothers me anymore. Like I'm immune to it all.

I'm dying, Audrey. I speak the words silently in my head. Test them out where no one can hear.

Audrey unwraps another Fruit Roll-Up. "Has he asked you out yet?"

I snort, grabbing one for myself. "No way."

"Why not? I know he likes you."

"You're delirious. It must be your current cocktail of meds."

She gives me a *whatever, you know I'm right* look.

"He doesn't," I say. "I am *so* not his type. And even if he did like me, I wouldn't have time for that kind of thing right now anyway."

She arches a brow. "Jensen's the kind of guy you make time for, Allie."

I try to think of a way to explain why my plate is full without going into all the time travel, reincarnation, finding a cure for cancer before I die details, but it's useless.

Audrey frowns, wrapping the Fruit Roll-Up around her finger. "You can't use me as an excuse not to live your life, you know."

"I'm not, I swear." I wrap mine around my finger too. It's something we've always done together.

She gives me a disbelieving look.

"OK, so maybe you being stuck in here is part of it. But is that so bad? When I do start dating, it'll have to be with someone who likes hospital visits. He'll have to be cool with sitting here with me for hours, eating junk food."

"And cool with Bogart?"

"Definitely cool with Bogart."

She tears a bite of the fruit leather from her finger and nestles into her pillows. Lauren Bacall calls Humphrey Bogart a mess, and Audrey giggles. "You know, you've always reminded me of Bacall."

I tilt my head at the screen. "It's the shoulder pads, isn't it?"

Audrey laughs. "The nose. The lips. And you're both so…" She pauses, searching for the right word. "Blasé."

"Blasé?"

"Even when you're surrounded by all my cancer drama, you're the portrait of calm. The center of the storm. Nothing gets to you."

I laugh to myself, because a few days ago I broke down and cried all over her like a garden hose. And she's never seen me spaz out at school. But she's half right. I never had the luxury of being silly. Laughing freely, genuinely, like Audrey or Claire or Mom or Gran. They've always had this carefree way about them. Laughter came easy, from deep in their guts. I've always been bundled up to my neck, tied up tight, bound to the uncertainty and burden of my visions, my descending. Maybe in my next life I can be a better version of myself. Quick with a smile, a laugh. Maybe I'll ask Porter not to let me grow up so serious next time. Maybe give me a little more backbone, too, like Micki. I should be matter-of-fact when it comes to Gesh and his Subs. Not a confused little kid, getting blindsided, but someone with purpose and determination. Someone who knows what the hell is going on and how to deal with it.

"Hey."

Audrey and I look up, and the air in the room vanishes. Jensen's standing there in the doorway, in his slouched beanie and black jacket, a pizza box in his hands.

"Hey," I say, jumping up. "What are you doing here?"

Audrey pauses the movie and straightens her stocking cap.

"I texted you," he says. "Haven't you gotten my texts?"

"I..." I glance at my phone on the end table by Audrey's bed. "I did, but I haven't read them."

He frowns, and tips his head toward the door. "Can I talk to you for a sec?"

"Sure." I follow him out into the hall, rubbing my arms, hating how he looks right now, so hurt and rejected.

"You haven't been at school," he says, his frown making me ache all the way down to my toes. There are droplets of melted snow on his jacket.

"Yeah...things have been kind of crazy around here."

"I get that, I do. What I don't get is why you didn't tell me."

"About taking time off school?"

"About Audrey." He lowers his voice so Audrey can't hear. "You let me come over to your house last weekend and ask you to rebuild my car, and you never mentioned any of this. I stopped by your house after school today and your grandpa filled me in. Told me I could find you here. And then I saw your dad downstairs, and he said I could come up." His frown deepens. "I feel like a total jackass."

I touch his arm. "Please don't. I just didn't want you to have to worry about all this."

"But that's what friends do. They worry about this kind of stuff. They want to be filled in. They want their texts read."

I drop my hands to my side. I know he's right. Even if I'm not exactly sure how this friend stuff works, I know that much. I hadn't expected him to seek me out. I thought after a few ignored texts, he'd give up and move on.

"I'm sorry," I say. "This whole friendship thing is hard for me. I'm not very good at it."

The corner of his mouth hitches. "Hey, you can pull me out of the friend zone anytime, Wayfare. Just say the word."

I push his shoulder, and his smile blooms in full.

"Is that for us?" I ask, and he hands me the pizza box.

"It's my Sorry for Being a Jackass peace offering."

"I'll take it." Back in Audrey's room, I clear a spot on her dresser for the pizza and open the lid. Arugula, prosciutto, and fig from Matchbox. Pops must've told him it's our favorite pizza in DC.

I breathe it in and my mouth waters. "I can't believe you drove all the way out here. And stopped at Matchbox."

He shrugs, hands in his pockets. "I'm sure you're getting tired of hospital food," he says to Audrey.

"You're my hero," she says as I hand her a slice and a napkin.

Jensen backs toward the door, head down, honey-blond hair hiding his eyes. "I better head out. I didn't mean to interrupt your movie."

"Hey, Peters," I call out when he reaches the hall. "You cool with Bogart?"

Audrey looks at me, eyes wide, and I smile at her.

He ducks his head back in the room. "As in Humphrey?"

Audrey nods, grinning.

"I've seen *Casablanca*."

"Then you're in," Audrey says.

"Come on." I hold out a slice. "You provided the dinner. The least we can do is provide the show."

He smiles and joins us. I sit on the bed with Audrey, the pizza box at our feet, and Jensen takes the armchair in the corner.

"Oh, I never liked this scene," Audrey says, grabbing another slice and frowning at a nerdy-looking, buttoned-up bookstore clerk flirting with Bogart. He asks her if she has to wear her glasses. She says no and takes them off, and suddenly he's totally into her.

"See that?" Audrey says, pointing her floppy pizza slice at the screen. "She doesn't look any different without her glasses and yet he acts like it's this huge transformation. She was already sexy. She didn't need to take them off."

"Well," I say, stretching my legs out and sinking into Audrey's pillows beside her, "it wasn't sexy to be smart, independent, and own your own bookshop back then. You had to take your glasses off and let your hair down to get noticed by a dreamboat like Bogart."

Audrey makes an ugly sound in her throat.

"I like to think guys have evolved since then," Jensen says, chewing.

"I admire your faith in the male species," I say.

"Hey, I love it when you talk nerdy to me," he says, lifting a brow. "So, clearly, there's been some evolving going on."

Audrey grabs another slice and takes a huge bite. "You're just one of the rare good ones, Jensen. An anomaly."

He smiles, his ankle propped casually on his knee. We stuff ourselves while Audrey gives extensive commentary on the film and trivia about Bogie and Bacall. Jensen laughs along and lets us be ourselves, giggling and remarking on everything from Bacall's racy remarks to Humphrey's trademark nasally voice.

Audrey keeps glancing at me, and I know what she's doing. *Look*, she says with her eyes. *He's cool with Bogart.*

And for a moment, I forget everything, tucked away in this tiny pocket of the universe, without a care in the world except for the pizza disappearing too quickly. I forget it all and imagine what it would be like to live in this moment for the rest of my life.

But it ends too soon.

Near the end of the movie, the pizza long gone, Audrey grabs my hand. At first I think she's reacting to the fighting onscreen, but her eyes are wide and locked on mine, red blotches blooming across her neck, chest, and arms.

"Get the nurse," I tell Jensen, and he rushes out into the hall.

"You're going to be OK," I tell Audrey, holding fast to her hand. She nods, never taking her eyes from mine. Not even blinking. Her face is so pale, and she's trembling.

A team of nurses surrounds her bed, and I back away to give them room. They say she's developed an allergic reaction to her blood thinners. They say we have to wait outside. And I think my heart stops, because an allergic reaction at this stage could kill her.

Jensen leads me to the waiting room and when we arrive I can't remember how we got there. I was lost in thought as we traveled the halls, terrified that this might be the time I actually lose her, hating myself for not telling her how much I love her, for not shouting it before I left the room.

I make my way over to the wall of windows, moving numbly, like a ghost gliding across the floor. The city is lit up in the dark, a blanket of pinprick lights. Cars weave through the streets below, white and red blobs blurred by my tears. Snow swirls and sticks to the glass. But I don't see any of it. I only see her eyes. You can't imagine it unless you've seen it before, the light and life and fire in someone's eyes, unable to get out because their body keeps it caged.

Damn Porter. Why hasn't he contacted me yet? What if he never does? I could lose her. She could take her last breath before I lift one finger to save her.

Jensen's shoulder brushes against mine. He doesn't say a word, just takes my hand and holds it tight. In the tenderness of our joined palms, I can feel his heartbeat.

CHAPTER 12

ANSWERS

Jensen stayed with me until Dad arrived. Until the doctors let us know Audrey pulled through and was on a different medication, and I was given a second chance at saving her life. He stayed and made things bearable, showing me what real friendship was like.

Three days later, in my kitchen having breakfast with Gran, I finally get a text from Porter. It's from an unknown number. *I'm back*, is all it says.

Where r u?

He texts an address I've never seen before, which pushes me to my feet, leaving half my oatmeal unfinished. I tell Gran I'll be at the library, and she fusses around me, making sure I have a bottle of water and packing a few slices of banana bread so I don't get hungry. I hug her a little longer than usual, because I'm going to miss her relentless care for me. Her lemon verbena perfume mingling with the sugar and spices from whatever she baked that day. Her long gray hair pulled into a bun. Her cardigans with seasonal-themed stitching on the pockets. Today there's a snowflake glinting at me with shimmering thread.

I'm dying, Gran.

I make sure to tell her and Pops I love them before I go, look them in the eyes when I say it. Because I can't say it enough. Today might be the day I die. Blue said we never made it to our eighteenth birthday, which means any day between now and my birthday in August could be my last. I have to make them count. All of them.

I don't wear my parka or Chucks for my visit with Porter. I wear my black lace-up winter boots with thick socks, and the gray wool coat Gran got me for Christmas a few years back. I smooth my hair back into a long ponytail. I feel somber, so I want to look the part. I want Porter to know I'm not a kid anymore. I've grown up an awful lot in the past two weeks.

I take the Mustang, since Mom and Dad took the Civic to the hospital, and say a prayer that it won't break down on the way. The Mustang's been sputtering here and there, and bucking when I press the clutch or the gas. She's testy, angry for some reason. Or maybe that's me projecting my own state of mind on an inanimate object. Either way, I toss my toolbox in the trunk just in case.

The address belongs to a marina ten miles from my house. Some ritzy yacht club. I would've thought I was in the wrong place if Porter hadn't given me a code that opened the towering iron gates at the entrance.

I park the Mustang and follow Porter's directions down through the docks. Rows and rows of huge boats, bigger than my house, are docked here, the water bubbling and fluid beneath them despite the ice and snow everywhere else. I know enough about boats and marinas to know you pay top dollar for a spot like this in the winter. Most people have to store their boats on land when the Chesapeake ices over. Not these yacht owners. They can live on their boats year-round if they want. The marina takes care of everything they need.

When I find the slip number Porter specified, I stop, hands in coat pockets, and crane my neck to look up at the boat. It's beautiful. Sleek, shiny, hulking over me with two sprawling decks. The top is shrink-wrapped in clear plastic to keep the snow from piling up onboard.

I look around, expecting to see Porter waiting for me on the dock. Instead, I hear him call out to me from inside the shrink-wrapped boat. I look up and see him waving me around to the side, where a wooden ramp leads up to a door fashioned into the shrink-wrapped plastic wall. Porter opens the door and waves me inside, but I don't climb up. I stand below, on the dock, staring up at him silhouetted in the midmorning sunlight.

"This your boat?" I ask, because why not? Why wouldn't it be?

He has so many secrets I can't keep track anymore.

"Technically, it's yours." He's not wearing a coat, just his signature black polo and khakis, which means it's warmer inside the shrink-wrap than out here in the open.

"Oh, really? More of my treasure hunt spoils?"

He smiles, his eyes creasing at the edges. "You could say that."

"So we're pirates now?"

"I suppose we've always been pirates. With or without a boat, we're plunderers, aren't we? Scalawags?"

I don't return his smile. The wind kicks up and tosses my ponytail in front of my eyes.

His smile fades. I can tell he knows I didn't actually come to chat about boats. He rubs his pinky knuckle with his thumb. After a while, that quirk of his became sort of comforting to me. Right now it makes me feel cold and empty, and anger swells in me like the water beneath the docks.

He notices me staring at his hands, and he stops. Drops them at his sides.

"Micki said she kept the data records for my past lives," I say. "I'm going to need to see those records."

He shakes his head. "Alex, you don't know what—"

I step slowly forward up the ramp. "I know you're going to show them to me, because in the end you always give me the truth when I ask for it, brutally and honestly. Even if it hurts." I stop in front of him, look him in his watery, red-rimmed eyes.

"Alex…" His shoulders are slumped, defeat in his voice.

"You know the reason I'm here. You know why I want to see them."

He sighs and motions for me to come inside.

He leads me through another door and down some stairs into the huge living area below deck. Directly before me is a massive open space, natural light streaming in through rows of windows. Low, long, white leather sofas are surrounded by shiny mahogany workstations with computer monitors everywhere, some showing security footage outside the boat, some running diagnostic-looking programs, others powered down and waiting for use. An electric fireplace keeps the room toasty warm. To my left is a kitchen, sleek and modern, black and stainless, with every amenity you can imagine. Behind that are two hallways on either side, and I can see a bedroom down one of them, more sleek wood and a low platform bed with crisp white linens and a cowhide rug on the floor.

"Quite a step up from Mrs. Yoder's place," I say. We both stand in the living room, neither of us comfortable enough to sit down. "I'm sorry you couldn't get something nicer with the money from the Rembrandt. You know, because some of it went to my sister's Scotland trip. Turns out the trip's canceled, so if you wanted to trade up to a nicer boat, you could make that happen."

"Alex," he says again. This time he whispers it, like it pains him.

"Do you want to know why it's canceled?" I don't wait for him to reply. "She's in the hospital. Blood clot in her lungs. She can't travel now."

"Blood clots are fairly routine," he says, like he's scrambling to offer some hope or encouragement. "A little while on blood thinners and she should be right as rain. Scotland is beautiful in the fall. You could go then."

"She won't get a fall." I say it bitterly, because it feels like nothing he could say could give me hope. Not anymore. "And neither will I."

Porter winces, like I've cut him.

Tears glisten in his eyes, which makes my own well up. I don't want to cry. I've been crying too much lately. I want to be strong and grown-up about all of this. I want to be like Bacall. So I sniff and lower my chin. "The records, Porter."

ETERNAL YOUTH

Porter retrieves Micki from one of the back rooms and takes her aside, filling her in on why I'm here. I sit on one of the white leather couches, a mug of coffee in my hand, staring at the gleaming white marble coffee table in front of me. There are magazines stacked on one end. On the top is some scientific journal I've never heard of. I suppose the rest are the same. Light reading for the AIDA Club.

Micki slides a laptop in front of me, a spreadsheet displayed on the screen. "Dates of birth and death, as you requested." She clops away in her black wedges and black leather leggings.

I set my coffee down and scroll through all fifty-six entries. It doesn't take long to see the pattern Blue spoke about. Some lives are shorter, the records showing I died at age fifteen or sixteen, but for the most part, I'm seventeen. Over and over again. Never once turning eighteen. Some dates are missing, but most of them are there. Blue's data is listed side-by-side with mine. Sometimes his dates correspond with mine, sometimes they're off by a day or two, sometimes even a week's or a month's difference. But it's all right there, proof that Blue was right.

My arms are numb. My mouth is dry.

I down my coffee and hold the mug out to Micki. "Tea this time?" I say, not looking at her.

I can imagine her eyebrow arching sharply as she takes the mug. "I must say," she says, heading to the kitchen, "you're taking this better than I would."

"Yeah, well, I've had a few weeks of radio silence to think about it."

I hear Porter sigh through his nose, not in a sarcastic way, but remorseful. Like he feels bad for not getting in touch with me sooner, for not checking in on me and my family.

Good.

Micki fills the teakettle while I search the list for the life I lived in 1927 Chicago. Blue died not long after we met, murdered in the back of his deli delivery truck. It looks like I died a week later. The records don't show any other details. No names, no places, just dates, so I still have no idea who I was in that life in Chicago. I have a morbid thought about traveling the world and locating all my tombstones, resting flowers on my own graves.

Maybe then it wouldn't feel like my lives are just numbers on a spreadsheet.

"Am I stuck like this?" I look up at Porter, sitting on the couch across from me, his arms stretched across the back. "A never-ending cycle of eternal youth? Always dying and being reborn?" It's like some twisted cross between Peter Pan and Doctor Who.

Porter's frown deepens. He's been frowning since I arrived. "As far as we know. In your first life you died a week before your eighteenth birthday. Once we set the first reincarnation in progress, your age of death became a constant. Your soul kept resetting at approximately the same time in every life. There doesn't seem to be a way to stop the cycle. We didn't know it would happen, but there were many advantages to your shorter lifespans. More points in time means—"

"Yeah, I get it. More lives means more missions. My expiration dates are what make me so valuable." I match his frown. "You should've told me."

"No one should know when they're going to die."

"Audrey's dying." I meant to go on, but I have to stop and clear the lump in my throat. "My parents are going to lose two children by the end of the year. How do you expect them to survive that? You should've told me. I could've helped my family prepare."

"How?" Micki asks, clopping up to me in shiny black heels, handing me a mug of tea.

"I would've had time to think of something."

"All the time in the world can't prepare someone for a loss," Micki says, and she looks like she knows from experience. "There's nothing you could've done. Their mourning is inevitable, *was* inevitable the moment you were born."

"Maybe it's inevitable for me, but it doesn't have to be for Audrey."

Micki sits down beside Porter, elbows on her knees. They both watch me, brows furrowed, waiting for me to elaborate.

"If I'm going to die, I want my life to mean something."

Porter leans forward. "It does mean something."

"Kicking Gesh where it hurts, going on these missions—I'm proud of playing my part, I am. But we both know the time I have left isn't enough to bring him down. Not all the way. And I want to make my last few days really count."

Micki opens her mouth, and I expect her to say something snide, but she doesn't. "What did you have in mind?"

I look her right in her tiger eyes, unruffled, like Bacall looks at Bogie.

"I'm going to find a cure for Audrey."

CHAPTER 13

ANOTHER WAY

I pull a newspaper article out of my coat pocket—the one about the fire at the AIDA lab—and smooth it on the coffee table. "Here's what's going to happen. I'm going to talk, you're going to listen." Porter lifts his chin, like he's about to say something, but I stare him down. "I'm not doing any more missions."

Micki narrows her eyes at me, a skeptical purse to her lips. Porter rubs his pinky knuckle.

"What I mean is, I'm not doing any more missions for *you*. From now on the mission, the only mission, is finding a cure for my sister. I know it's out there. I just have to find it and get it to my mom before it's too late."

Porter leans forward to object.

"You owe me," I blurt out before he can say anything. Tears sting the corners of my eyes. "I've done everything you've ever asked of me. It's my time now, and you owe me."

He doesn't try to speak again. They both give me the floor. I explain my mom's research, the data that was lost in the fire. "I want to go back and save that data. Hide it so we can find it in the present, like we did with the Rembrandt."

Micki gets up, and I think she's going to walk out on me, but instead she fires up one of the computers at a workstation. "What time frame are we talking about?"

I scan the article I printed. "The fire started during a Christmas office party. Burned the entire AIDA research building to the ground. It was December 20th, 1978."

"You were seventeen years, six months, and ten days old. You won't be that exact age again for another month and three days."

My stomach sinks. I can only travel linearly, which means whatever age I am in Base Life, down to the millisecond, is the age I travel to in the past. Audrey may not have another month and three days left. "What happens if I go now? And retrieve the data a month before the fire?"

"You'd change history," says Porter. "Instead of the data being lost in a fire, it could be reported stolen. There could be an investigation. The impact could be too great."

"You have to go the night of the fire," Micki says, "and you have to be undetected. It's the story we have to protect. The story of the lost data—the belief behind what happened to it—can't be altered. That's the only way descending works."

"But Audrey could be gone by then. *I* could be gone by then."

"I'm sorry," Micki says, and she sounds like she means it.

"There is another way."

Micki and I look at Porter. He's digging circles around his knuckle, his eyes far off. "There are countless traditional Chinese remedies that have been used to treat diseases for ages. Gesh and I used to translate ancient texts back in the seventies, searching for lost herbal remedies, recipes to try. Some were useless, others worked on certain patients. One of our discoveries is currently used as a blood-thinning medication. Another for treating dementia."

I lean forward, elbows on knees, when he pauses. "What are you saying?"

"One of the texts mentioned a remedy that treated symptoms consistent with leukemia. Gesh and I believed that, if used in conjunction with chemo, the remedy could be the answer everyone's been looking for. The recipe wasn't included in the text; it's been lost over the centuries. But if you went back there, retrieved a vial, and buried it, then we could exhume it, test the compounds, and figure out the ingredients and measurements. I could recreate the drug, and we could have it tested for treatment."

"You want me to travel to ancient China?" It may not be recovering Mom's data, but it might be worth a shot in the meantime.

Micki taps away at her keyboard. "Not ancient. The Qing Dynasty, the year 1770."

I look to Porter. "And you think this recipe could help cure Audrey?"

"There is no guarantee; we'd have to run clinical trials, but I believe it's worth a try. It does come at a price, however."

"What price?"

"Gesh hasn't yet retrieved this drug for a reason. He's saving it."

"What the hell for? A rainy day?"

Porter speaks slowly, carefully, like the words boil inside him. "For when it suits his interests best."

"You mean when it's most lucrative for him," I say, disgusted. "Of course he'd hold a global cure hostage. The bastard."

Micki crosses her long dark legs. "I'm not so sure about this mission. He'll know it was us, if we go through with it." She trains her tiger eyes on me. "He'll know it was you, and you'd be compromising your sister's, and your family's, safety. Think about it. A miracle drug is discovered from the past, and one of the first ones to benefit is Audrey Wayfare? He'll look into your family. He'll find you. It could risk everything, all we've sacrificed to keep you safe."

"Then we open the drug up for everyone," I say. "Once it's tested and ready to go, we give it to all leukemia patients for free. Blanket the world with it so there are too many patients to track. And we make sure Audrey isn't the only one to get treated first. We treat a whole group of them in a clinical trial."

"That could work," Porter says, "but that's not the price I was referring to." He frowns gravely and folds his hands in his lap. No more rubbing circles on his knuckle. He meets my eyes. "There are benefits to this particular mission. You don't have to travel back to any specific date. You could leave tomorrow if you wanted. When we placed you in this time period, we weren't looking for any one treasure in particular. Any antiquities you could find and bury in a time capsule would be worth a considerable amount if we dug them up today. Qing Dynasty vases, bowls, other pottery. It's all worth thousands, millions even. But compared to that, the cure is priceless.

You wouldn't only be stealing Gesh's funding this time, you'd be stealing his ability to play god, to keep the cure out of reach for those who need it. Right now, the thrill of the hunt keeps him going. Finding you. Chasing you through time. Gesh loves a good hunt. Especially when he thinks he's one step ahead. But if you do this, you'll be declaring war. He'll retaliate. He'll call for blood. He'll turn his entire focus on you, all of his resources."

The back of my neck prickles. The hair on my arms stands on end. And maybe I'm selfish and a little too desperate, because I don't even consider the consequences Gesh's retaliation might have on Porter, Levi, and Micki after I'm long gone. I think back to Levi's words: *Don't worry about us. Make the right choice for you,* and say, "When do I leave?"

MY ONLY COMPANION

There's another level below the living area on Porter's boat. You have to go through a series of doors locked with high-level security to get down the stairs. Micki set up a mix of electronic and mechanical security, which makes me grin to myself. Having all electronic security makes you vulnerable. All you have to do is cut power. Same with using all manual locks. Enough muscle and you're in. But using both together is almost impenetrable. Not fully, but it makes the process harder. And no self-respecting thief has time for that.

Not that a common thief would have an interest in what lies behind the labyrinth of doors. The FBI, on the other hand...

It's a long, windowless room, almost an exact replica of one of the medical labs at AIDA. When I step inside it feels like I'm back there, at Headquarters, a lifetime ago. Stark white walls, tile floor, a bank of computers on one side, three reclinable chairs in the center, like the ones you find at a dentist's office. Bright lights, harsh and unnatural, overhead. Completely incongruous with the posh scene upstairs. This feels sterile, cold, and smells sharp, like stainless steel and rubbing alcohol.

I don't like it. It makes me remember the vile glint in Gesh's eyes and the wicked grin on his lips as he whispered heinous things in my ear. As he ran his hand up my leg.

I shiver and push the thought out of my mind. Gesh isn't here. Only Micki, and Levi, who's sitting at one of the computers. He swivels around in his chair and lifts an eyebrow at us. Just the sight of him makes me feel a bit calmer. His presence makes the room look less intimidating: this sleek, cool cat, lounging beneath surgical lamps instead of sunlight. His jeans are faded, his boots camel-colored, his button-down shirt perfectly slouched, his dark blond hair swept back. I swear, he could give up all the glamor of Sub hunting and start his own men's fashion feed on Instagram. Add Micki to the mix and they'd be internet style icons overnight. One smoking hot couple.

"Saddle up," Micki tells Levi, clopping in her wedges across the tile floor and grabbing the seat next to him. "We've got a mission. Take the middle one, Four." She nods at the dentist chairs.

I climb in and anxiety creeps under my skin, like I'm about to get a filling. It's reclined back almost all the way, and I close my eyes at the harshness of the lights. I hear Levi and Micki whispering as Micki explains the mission, and how we plan to leave in three days. Their voices, low and droning, lull me toward sleep. My mind wanders, trying to picture what China will be like in the 1700s, what I'll be up against.

What Gesh might do when I capture his flag.

"I'm sorry about your sister."

My eyes fly open. Levi and his frown are standing over me. "Thanks," I say.

"I think what you're doing is noble, but it's dangerous."

"Thanks," I say again, dryly this time. I reach around the chair for some kind of lever so I can sit up, but find nothing. So I lie there awkwardly under the lights and Levi's frown.

"It's further back in time than you've gone before," he says. "We wanted to work you up to that sort of distance. Three days isn't enough to learn the culture or the customs. One wrong word, one wrong move, and you could make an impact."

"I got it, Levi." I finally find the lever and pull it. The chair swings up, smacking against my back. If Levi were anyone else, he would've laughed. But laughing isn't in his DNA. He just stares at me like I'm a curiosity.

"As far as safety goes," Micki says, "it's a relatively harmless mission. You'll be starting out in Beijing, a homeless orphan living on the street. No one to miss you or report you missing when you go looking for the cure. There are convoys leaving daily filled with poor souls like yourself, heading out to remote villages, seeking healers. Peasants mainly, old and feeble. You shouldn't have to talk to any of them. The route is through a particularly gentle part of the country. Beautiful, too. The journey takes a few days, the convoys stop along the way, and you'll have to scrounge up your own shelter and food. Other than that, it's cake."

Levi folds his arms across his chest. "Except that you'll need money to pay the convoy and the healer. And if you're a homeless orphan, I'm guessing you won't have much handy."

Micki shrugs. "So she steals something to barter first. Easy enough." She grins at me, her sly, tiger smile. "And if you happen to steal anything else to bury along with the cure? A vase, perhaps? That would be the icing on the cake."

So that's why she's so eager to help me. The treasure. More money in the pot for her Sub-Hunting Fund. But I don't say a word. We'll need as much money as we can get to create the drug, run the clinical trials, and pass it out to whoever needs it.

"It'll be easy," Micki insists. "I'll be right there with you, guiding you the whole way."

"What do you mean you'll be with me?"

Her red lips spread wide. "We're doing things differently this time. Levi?"

Levi wheels a monitor over to my chair and unwinds a series of wires. "We've been working on a few things, like the ability to accompany you."

"Accompany me where? On my mission?" I don't like the

thought. I want—need—time alone, to regroup, to see Blue. With them there with me, I won't be able to relax. "I thought you guys were Subs. You can't descend, right?"

"We won't be descending," Micki says, "just ascending to Limbo. We can communicate with you from there, be your eyes and ears while you work, like Porter."

Porter's been a voice in my head since the first time I descended. He was there the first time I met Blue in 1927 Chicago and didn't want to leave the past behind. Porter shoved his voice into my head—it felt like frozen needles—and pushed my will out, trying to replace it with his own, but I managed to push back. I broke his connection with me. It ended up being such a silly, stupid, selfish thing to do. I altered history and had to go back and reset it, erasing my impact. Erasing my first date with Blue. My first kiss.

Now I know better. Now I know my connection to Base Life, to Porter, is a lifeline, keeping me from making an impact on history. That connection means the difference between ruining the entire mission and coming home a hero. One wrong move and I could miss my window for a touchdown. I could slip past Limbo and land right back in Base Life; I could age a few seconds and be unable to go back to the same time to do a touchdown, unable to erase the damage I've done.

Lives would be lost. History altered.

The world as we know it would end.

And I've already messed it up enough for one lifetime, let alone fifty-seven.

So I give Micki a single nod and say, "What's the process?"

"Remember the microchip in the Descender's brain?"

Oh god. They're going to implant something in my head. I press back in my seat, eyes wide, and she laughs.

"Don't get any morbid ideas. Remember when I said the chip manipulates the brain's natural vibrations? Makes it vibrate at a different frequency?"

I nod, white knuckles gripping the chair's armrests.

"All we're going to do is link your frequency with mine and

Levi's. We're going to slow our brains down into the theta realm so an OBE can occur."

"An OBE?"

Micki tightens her ponytail. "An out-of-body experience. You have them all the time when you ascend, but Levi and I never do. If we sync our frequencies with yours, altering our state of consciousness, you should be able to pull us with you. This way we're all in Limbo and we can all be on the mission with you in real time. We used to use this technique back in the day. Gesh called it 'tethering.'"

One by one, Levi sticks wires to my temples, my forehead, the back of my neck, brushing my hair away. His fingertips graze my skin, warm and soft. The screen Levi wheeled over beeps and blips, displaying a green jagged line like Audrey's heart rate monitor at the hospital.

"We're doing this right now?"

"Just doing a little test run."

It's quiet for a while as Levi finishes sticking wires across my chest and down my arms. Micki clicks away at her mouse. The sound echoes across the room.

"You tried to tell me, didn't you?" I say to Levi, my voice low.

He stops messing with the wires and gives me a questioning look.

"In the kitchen," I say, "when we talked at the safe house. You told me I could stop traveling, that I could live out my life how I wanted. That you guys would pick up later when I was reborn, and you'd train me in my next life. I didn't understand why you'd give me that option. Now I do. You knew I'd be reincarnated by the end of the year. You'd have a new weapon to sharpen and use for this war within a few months."

A cloud passes over his face. "It was never my intention to keep this from you. I wanted Porter to tell you. You just learned about your gift, and now you find out it's going to kill you. It's not fair to you."

I sniff and shake my head. Doesn't he know? Fair stopped applying to me long ago. The moment Gesh and Porter created me.

The moment Audrey got cancer.

Levi brushes another strand of hair from my forehead and resticks a wire that came loose. "I meant what I said. You're not alone in this."

He's wrong again. Even with them here, on my team, even with them in Limbo, crowding into my head, I'm still completely alone. Even with my family sitting next to me, their arms around my shoulders. Even tangled up in Blue's soul in Limbo, even tangled up with him in the past. None of it matters. Nothing is as it seems anymore. I'm alone wherever I go, whichever life I'm walking in.

The only companion I have now is the certainty of my untimely death.

That means I can't be stupid anymore. I can't walk blindly. I must open my eyes, chin lifted, fists raised, ready to fight for Audrey's chance. Because it's the only thing I have left that defines me. It's the only thing that runs through my veins and sustains my breath for another day.

The hope of life flowing through this doomed and damned vessel.

CHAPTER 14

THE TEST RUN

"Let's see what we've got."

Micki trades places with Levi, gliding her computer chair over to the screen monitoring me. The thin green line jumping across it is jagged and uneven, like the results of a lie detector test. Levi sits at the bank of computers, their screens running scrolling lists of data fed by the monitor.

"See that?" Micki says about the green line. "That means your brain's working. Congrats." She flips a few switches on the machine until there are three different-colored lines, one red, one green, one blue. "See this red one here? That's your excitement level. If you think of something exciting, it'll rise on the screen. This blue one tells me how bored you are."

The blue line is higher than the red. "Does that mean I'm bored?"

"Yes. And I'm extremely offended."

"But I'm not bored. I'm freaked out. Thoroughly."

"This is you freaked out?" she says, looking me up and down. "Good grief, Four. What do you look like when you're relaxed? Like a stroke victim?"

I give her the same look I've been giving her since the day I met her. She meets it with her usual tiger grin.

"The blue line isn't very high," she says. "It's just higher than the red, which means you're holding back, restraining yourself. If you think of something exciting, that red line will jump. Close your eyes and show me what ya got."

I close my eyes and lean my head back, settling into the chair. My mind drifts back to Blue, back to Chicago and our first date.

There are so many things I wish I would've done differently that night. When we were at Peg Leg, in the back room alone, sitting at the piano with the hazy orange lights filtering in through the grimy windows. I wish I had climbed into his lap, taken his face in my hands, and kissed him good and decent. I wish it had been passionate, his mouth on my neck, his hands on my back, his fingers unzipping the back of my dress...

"Damn." Micki says. "Skyrocket."

My eyes open. The red line skims the very top of the screen.

"Mind telling me what you were thinking about? Must've been delicious."

I shake my head, feeling my cheeks burn.

Micki leans forward and whispers, "Ohhhh, was it a memory about Levi?"

I didn't think Levi was paying attention to us, but when Micki says that, he glances over his shoulder. One quick glance, almost like sleight of hand, but I noticed. And I wonder if he noticed my red cheeks.

"What?" I say, feeling my face turn an even brighter shade of red. "Of course not."

Why would Micki bring up the past—the fact that Levi and I used to be together—when he's sitting three feet away? To embarrass me? To hurt him? Even though I'm not Ivy, not anymore, I still look like her, and it feels cruel to remind him.

Micki shrugs. "Meh. It was probably something nerdy like getting a new motherboard on Christmas morning. Or finding the right size screw in your box of random screws. You know, Things That Get Alex Hot."

I'm thankful for the subject change even if she is poking fun at me. "Yeah. Motherboards and boxes of screws. You got me pegged."

"Oh, now we're talking." Micki leans toward the monitor and taps a long red nail on the screen. "See that blip there?"

Along the green line, which has been scrolling lazily at the bottom of the screen, there's suddenly a huge spike that measures off the scale.

"What is it?"

"Your trademark. Your tell. That's how I know you're a Descender. That you have access to Limbo."

"You can tell that from my brainwaves?"

"Oh, yeah. Gesh discovered it ages ago. That's how he recruits his new Descenders. He has all his AIDA employees scanned with an EEG. It's procedure when you start working for the company. He finds those who have a strong connection to Limbo and pulls them into the fold. The stronger your connection to Limbo, the higher the spike in the frequency. Yours is off the chart. Pretty cool, huh?"

It's weird seeing this side of Micki again, resembling the feel-good scientist chaperone I thought she was in Chicago. Getting geeked about brainwaves. Especially after the crack about Levi.

Levi pushes his chair out and heads for the stairs. "Be back in a few."

Micki and I watch him go, me wondering if I made him feel uncomfortable, Micki's narrowed eyes diagnosing his motives, his actions.

When we hear the series of doors close and lock, she looks at me. "Do you have any memories of being with him? Any at all?"

An image of playing Polygon with Levi when we were kids flashes before me. Another image—of Levi watching Gesh torture me—flashes too. Those are the recollections linked to my Polygon stone. The memories that trigger my déjà vu. But I don't want to share those with Micki. They're private.

"Nothing," I say.

"He has tattoos. All over. Each one symbolizing his time with you. Did you know that?"

I shake my head and look everywhere, anywhere but at Micki. I don't want to think about Levi's tattoos, what they represent, or where they might be located. I'd rather think about the wattage of the overhead fluorescent lights or the speed of the processors powering the CPUs.

"You do know you used to sleep together, though, right? That you lived together at AIDA? That fine specimen of a man was your personal boy toy. You had him wrapped around your finger and dipped in chocolate. He did anything you asked. And I mean anything."

"Um," I say, squirming in my chair. "Too much info."

I'm so not in the mood to hear about my past self's sex life. Plus, it feels disrespectful to Levi. Not to mention that it makes me feel really freaking weird. And really freaking nauseous.

"Aw, did I burn your New Life virgin ears?" Micki pouts, a sarcastic puppy frown.

"I don't think we should talk about him like this."

"Suit yourself." She rolls her chair back over to the computers, typing and clicking. A huge laser printer in the corner whirs to life. "You'll start remembering things," she says after a while, her back to me. "The longer you live, the more you'll start to remember. At least, that's how it was for Ivy. She could remember all sorts of things about her past lives by the time she was your age. They were fragments, and I had to help her connect which ones matched which lives. I assume it'll happen to you, too." She swivels around to face me. "Little things at first. Sunlight. Melodies. Smells. They'll awaken something inside you. An image will flash. Then you'll remember deeper things. Like how you felt when he touched you. Kissed you."

I grip the armrests of the chair, trying to stay cool. "Would you stop?"

"I thought you'd want to be prepared. Those memories, they're going to feel real. And you may start having urges—"

"Oh god, please don't use that word. Why are adults always using that word?"

"What word? Urges?"

"Gah." I plug my ears.

She shrugs. "I'm just saying."

"Stop saying. And stop planting stuff in my head."

She raises a sharp eyebrow. "I'm planting stuff in your head now? How very sci-fi of me."

"Yes. You all are. Ideas and thoughts I wouldn't have on my own. Things I don't want to think about."

"Such as?"

"That Blue's a traitor, that he's working for Gesh and trying to find out who I am in Base Life. Now I can't stop thinking about that. What happens if I run into him in Beijing? I'm going to want to trust him, but now there's this seed of doubt I can't shake, and it's going to affect how I am around him."

It already has. But I don't want any of them to know I met with Blue in Limbo. That might be the only way I can see him from now on. I don't want to risk losing it.

"And now this," I say, "making me think things about Levi I don't want to think. Making me picture things. Gross things."

"I'm just giving you a heads up. If those memories resurface, things could get complicated. You could fall for him all over again, and that kind of age difference is sort of frowned upon these days."

"It's not 'sort of frowned upon.' It's illegal."

She raises her hands in surrender. "OK, OK. I'll drop it. I'm only trying to help. I know you don't like being kept in the dark."

I can't figure out if she's telling the truth or trying to trip me up somehow. She's right, though. I hate when Porter keeps things from me. Isn't that why I'm here right now? But the way she says it, like she enjoys watching me squirm like a mouse in an experiment, keeps me from trusting her completely. And now I'm going to feel weird around Blue *and* Levi, which might compromise my mission. Is that what she wants? For me to fail? What happens if I run into Blue in China? I wanted him to help me—be my partner, like he said he would. I wanted him to help save my sister. And I wanted to touch him, flesh on flesh this time, not like in Limbo. What am I going to do now, knowing Levi will be watching my every move?

On the death-and-world-destruction scale, making an ex uncomfortable doesn't register as important. At least, it shouldn't. So why do I already feel like an ass about it?

"Are you guys seeing each other or something?" I say to Micki. If she's going to dig into my personal life, I figure I can return the favor. "Is that why you're telling me all this?"

My question catches her completely off guard. She jerks, and her jaw drops. "Excuse me?"

"You and Levi. I'm not interested in him, OK? So you don't have to try to put me off. I'm already so, so far off."

The teasing glint is gone from her eyes. They're steely and sharp. "You think I'm telling you this because I'm some jealous girlfriend looking to sabotage things? You can't be that stupid."

"You've been working together for years, and you live here together on the boat, right? It's easy to assume you're a couple."

"He's my partner. He's like a brother to me. That's all."

"What, you're not into the frowny, broody, hipster type?"

She pins me with her eyes. "I'm not into the male type, period."

And now I'm back to fidgeting in my seat. "Oh."

"Yeah."

"I just figured…I mean…you said he was hot two minutes ago."

"I'm gay, Alex. I'm not blind. I know a good-looking guy when I see one. Doesn't mean I want to hold his hand and wear his promise ring."

Open mouth, insert foot. It's becoming such a regular occurrence for me it should be considered exercise. "I'm sorry. I've never actually had a gay friend before. I'm probably going to say a lot of stupid things."

"Wait, we're friends now?" She acts shocked. "I thought you didn't have any of those, let alone gay ones."

"I don't have many."

"I wonder why."

Touché.

"You know," she says, "You might want to consider making a few before your time's up. Porter, Levi, and I can't attend your funeral, you know. Too suspicious. Don't you want more than a handful of people there? More than a handful to miss you when you're gone?"

She doesn't know it, but I've thought about that very thing before. And she's right. I don't know of anyone from school who'd care enough to attend, except Jensen.

Maybe because I never cared enough about any of them.

Last year, when two seniors were killed in a car crash by a drunk driver, almost the entire school attended their funerals. I say almost because I stayed home. I was alone in my attic, converting Malena Anderson's factory car stereo into a touchscreen GPS system that synced with her smartphone. It seemed important at the time. Not so much anymore.

I've met lots of kids through my fix-it side gigs, but to them I'm the girl behind the counter frothing their lattes. I'm not someone they invite to a party after the big game, or call on the phone to complain about their parents.

I'm no one.

"You're right. I should make more of an effort to get along with people. Even you."

"God, Alex, that's so sweet of you." She turns back to the computers. "Now I totally feel like renting movies and eating ice cream in our jammies."

"I really am sorry. I thought you were being cruel before, about the Levi thing."

The tension in her shoulders loosens. She inspects her red nails and shrugs. "Well, maybe I was trying to poke at you, a little." She looks up. "I'm sorry too. What do you say we change the subject?"

"I'd say that's the best idea you've had all day."

She laughs, the kind of larger-than-life, confident laugh I heard in Chicago.

"So," I say, scratching around one of the pads taped to my wrist. "You weren't raised in Detroit, were you?"

"I was raised everywhere, honey." She wheels over to the printer in the corner and starts thumbing through a stack of papers feeding from the machine.

"And your parents? Were they really from Dubai?"

She stiffens. "I have no idea where my parents were from, and I don't care. They gave me up, handed me over to a psycho. I don't give a shit about them."

She bangs the stack of pages on the desk to make the edges even, harder than she needs to. The anger hovering above her shoulders makes me think she does care. We all care where we come from, we all want to know the answers, the missing puzzle pieces that define the beginning of our story. But not caring? It's a way for her to punish her parents, even if they're not around.

I'm a teenager. I know the technique well.

"What do you mean they handed you over?"

"Not all of Gesh's pawns were born and bred in captivity like you. Some of us were donated to The Cause for a payoff. Ever heard of human trafficking?"

"Your parents sold you?"

"Must've been a tidy amount," she says. "Enough to line their pockets and keep them quiet about it for the rest of their lives."

I shift in my seat, wishing I hadn't chosen this particular subject. I wanted to get to know her, not prick at old scars.

"Others," Micki continues, "like Levi's mother, were Gesh's devoted followers back in the sixties. They volunteered to have children for him, then handed them over."

Good Lord. Poor Levi. Poor Micki. I can't imagine growing up without the comfort and support of my family. To have no one but scientists raising you, your single purpose in life to serve and fight for The Cause. Destined to be a Sub or a Descender, based on the frequencies of your brain.

"What about me and Blue? Were we donated too?"

"Test tube babies. Surrogate mommies. You weren't donated for The Cause; you were created for it."

I'm quiet for a long time while she flips through the pages she printed, reading them over to herself. Levi returns with two steaming mugs and holds one out to me.

"No thanks," I say. "If I drink anything else I'll be camped out in the bathroom." I try to smile, but it comes out awkward. Lopsided.

The corners of his mouth don't even flicker at my stupid joke, and he doesn't pull the mug away. "It's for the test run to Limbo. It'll help you relax."

"Oh." I take the mug, feeling stupid, and try not to gag from the smell. I down the tea as fast as I can without breathing in, doing my best not to cringe from the aftertaste, which is even worse for some reason. It smells like bad breath and tastes like feet.

Levi sits in the chair beside me and drinks from the other mug. Micki rolls his sleeves up and sticks wires to his skin like he did to me. For the first time, I catch a glimpse of the tattoos Micki mentioned.

Soft, black tendrils of a vine wrapped around his forearms.

Ivy.

I look away. "So, what's the plan? I ascend to Limbo and see if I can pull Levi with me?"

Micki nods. "That's the plan."

Levi sips his tea, like he relishes the flavor. He looks so cool and peaceful, like he's having coffee at a corner café in France. Even in this windowless room, under stark, fluorescent lights. The way he moves, holds his mug, looks off into the distance, like he's contemplating the meaning of life at every moment. I'm suddenly nervous about being in Limbo alone with him. I like him. I want to trust him. He seems to care about me. But now I feel awkward, thanks to Micki. At the moment I'd rather hang out in Limbo with Tabitha than Levi.

"Here we go," Micki says, handing Levi and me each a pair of headphones.

We slip them on and recline in our chairs. Slightly throbbing sound waves hum in my ears, slithering into my head and making me feel disoriented. The tea and the droning sound waves work their magic. My heart beats slower, my thoughts fade into the background.

I don't know how long I lie there, listening. It feels like hours, but when I crack open my eyes, Micki is still standing between us, messing with the brain wave monitor.

She claps her hands together. "It's go time."

I don't need to reach for my Polygon stone; I have my déjà vu sitting in the seat next to me. I reach out for his hand. He takes it, and we're gone.

CHAPTER 15

SUPERHEROES

I don't know if it's the tea, the sound waves, the theta brain frequency, or Levi's presence, but this time when I enter Limbo, things are clearer, crisper. I hadn't noticed how muddled it was before, when I went in alone. It's like getting new glasses after wearing an old prescription for too long. The Black feels flexible now, moving in and out like a breath. It feels like I've been here a million times before. It's as familiar as the ceiling rafters in my bedroom.

Levi stands beside me in my garden, his hand still in mine. I expect him to gape around in awe, but he's cool as a cucumber. He lets go of my hand and moves through my soulmarks toward my fountain.

"I take it you've been here before," I say, following him, winding through the shafts of light.

"A few times." He sits on one of my benches, casually, like he's at the park feeding the pigeons.

"Aren't you tempted at all? By the soulmarks?"

"You mean am I tempted to travel back in time?"

I nod, stepping up to my fountain. Dipping my fingers in the warm water.

"I'm tempted in the same way any thinker or philosopher would be tempted. I'm tempted to know what it's like. To walk where my idols have walked. Maybe sit and have a chat with them. But on the other hand, I'm tempted the way the president is tempted to press the button on a nuclear war." I furrow my brow, so he elaborates. "What you do, Alex? Descending? It's one step away from mass destruction. So no. I'm not tempted. I'm not as confident as you."

I let out a dry laugh. "I'm not confident. And when you put it that way, it makes me feel like even more of an ass."

"Why's that?"

I wring my hands. "Because I enjoy it. I'm selfish. I'm like those gun enthusiasts who don't want to give up their guns. They know guns cause destruction, but they won't give them up because they like them too damn much. They like the feel of the steel in their hand. They like being in control. They like having the higher ground, feeling invincible, wielding something more powerful than themselves. They like it, and they won't give it up even if what they like is destroying the world. And because I like traveling so much, I obliterated an entire timeline. I've already caused mass destruction, and I'm ready to go back for seconds."

He frowns. "What makes you think that other timeline is any better? Without the Variant, without you destroying Gesh's life as he knew it, he would've gone full steam ahead, no obstacles. Because of you, he had to start all over. He's seventeen years behind in his grand plan, whatever it is. So all this? This is the best it could be, in my opinion. A world without boundaries for Gesh is a world I wouldn't want to live in."

"So what's stopping him from going back and creating another Variant? Changing all this? Erasing the impact I made on him?"

"How would he do that? He's not like you. He can't descend into his own body, because he doesn't have a soulmark. He's still alive. He'd have to descend into a body that died, one that has a soulmark in Limbo. And even if he did, how would he know what kind of impact to make? How would he know the Variant he created would turn out in his favor?"

"All he'd have to do is go back in time and make sure Ivy was never created. Then I wouldn't be here, and I wouldn't be screwing up his plans."

Levi shakes his head. "No, he wouldn't do that. He needs you for whatever he's planning just like he needed Ivy. It's our job to make sure we take him down before he gets his hands on you."

"You mean kill him." I don't say it like a question, because I already know the answer. I dip my hand in the fountain again, then lift it out, the memory of water pooling in my palm.

Levi nods, and we're quiet for a while, wrapped in the Black. My perception of him is exactly the same as in Base Life. He's wearing the same clothes, and every hair is perfectly in place. But I didn't notice his sleeves were down until he pushes them up, and I see the tattoos again.

I avert my eyes. The Black becomes a thick blanket of Awkward. I want to say something smooth, act like the tattoos don't bother me, break the ice so things aren't so weird between us, but it's too awkward to talk about the awkwardness.

"So," he says, hands clasped together, elbows on knees. "How's school going?"

I cringe a little, leaning my palm against the edge of the fountain. "Can you not ask me about school like that?" He looks so much like a concerned parent when he says it, and so far from the eighteen-year-old boy I saw half-naked at AIDA HQ two months ago.

And now I'm thinking about him being half-naked, and what tattoos I'd see wrapped across his chest and back, and wondering if my soul is flushing as red as I feel.

"Why not?"

"It makes you sound old, and I can't think about how old you are right now."

He makes a face, totally confused, then shakes his head. "I'm not even going to ask."

"Thanks. Don't."

"When were you planning on going back?"

My hand slips and plunges into the water. "How did you know I haven't gone back to school?"

"We keep an eye on these kinds of things. So? When?"

"I was thinking along the lines of never?" I wring the perception of water from my sleeve and flick droplets from my wrist.

"You have to go to school."

"Why? Why do I need school if I'm never going to graduate?" *I'm dying, Levi. Don't you know that?*

"Because life must go on. We have to keep up appearances. We can't risk doing anything suspicious. All the greatest superheroes had other identities. They had real, everyday lives to keep them grounded and their secrets safe. They had people to live and fight for in the real world. Superman had Lois Lane. Spider-Man had—"

"Mary Jane."

"I was going to say Gwen."

I fold my arms, both of which are completely dry now. I'm starting to get the hang of manipulating the perceptions. "Are you arguing for argument's sake?"

"I'm just saying. You need to be Alex too. You need to be more than Number Four."

"I'm trying to tell you, I can't. I don't know how. Not after all I've seen." I sit down next to him. "I don't know if I've ever known how. And Superman? Spider-Man? They're fictional. What do DC and Marvel know about being a real-life hero? It's not as easy as they make it out to be."

Levi makes a gruff sound in his throat, like a *harrumph* that isn't meant to be grumpy, which for Levi is the closest thing to a laugh I've heard. "If you're anything to judge by, then I think they've gotten a lot right."

I actually do laugh, for the both of us. "Like what? My ability to ruin everything on a daily basis? Or how I'm completely incompetent?"

"I was thinking more of how you never give up. You could be selfish, curled up in a ball, wailing about your impending death, waiting until it comes for you. Instead you're here, ready to do whatever it takes to save your sister. You work until the job is done, until what's broken is fixed. Now that's a Marvel-worthy hero. But you're right. You don't have an outlet. You can't take your glasses off and clock out. You're tortured. I can see that. It's not a game to you. It's your life, like it or not. And you choose to live on. That's a real hero."

"A hero who can stop going to school?"

His eyes narrow.

"Come on," I say, pleading. "I hate it there. I can't focus. And everything they teach feels worthless anyway, compared to what I know. I don't feel safe there. I feel like I'm prey, surrounded by predators."

"I hear you." He stares at the fountain, thinking for a while. "Let me do some digging and see what I can do. Until then, school?"

I heave a sigh through my nose. "School."

I let go of the Black, and we both disconnect from its grasp. We open our eyes to harsh overhead lights and Micki standing between us. She hasn't moved an inch since we left.

"All done?" she says. "I barely blinked."

"We're good to go," Levi says. He gives me a nod, like he believes we can do this thing, then lets his hand slip from mine.

MAKING AMENDS

It takes two days for me to make good on my promise to return to school. I head back the very day I'm scheduled to leave for China. I've read three books about the history and culture of the Qing Dynasty. Micki read half a dozen. She thinks we're ready, even though I'm not so sure. She assures me I'll learn what I need along the way, with her help. That's how they used to do it back at AIDA. And to ease the bundle of nerves in my gut, she suggested I make use of my day by going to school. It's either that or sit at home waiting until I can steal away to the library (a.k.a. Porter's boat), my knees bouncing, my stomach raw and tumbling.

I step through the double doors and stand there, feeling out of place in a completely new way.

School. My nemesis. House of my nemeses. I'm not sure how Levi's going to make it bearable.

The kids flow past me, coming and going, like I'm caught between opposite currents. They all look so young to me now, baby-faced and oblivious and hopeful, while I feel weathered and hunched. Old. Full of scorn and cynicism.

Time's running out. Maybe Micki's right. Maybe it's time to make amends.

During homeroom, before first period, I start a bucket list in one of my notebooks. First on the list?

1) Eat in the cafeteria. Sit with people. TALK TO THEM.

2)

And…that's all I can come up with for now. But this is good. One task to work on. No distractions. I can do this.

When my lunch period rolls around, I forgo the safety of my bag lunch and the computer lab and slip into the pizza line, wielding my very own tray of semi-edible fare for the first time in years.

"A truly remarkable sight." Jensen cuts into line beside me, sliding his tray next to mine on the ledge in front of us. He lifts his hands and frames me with his fingers, like he's shooting a movie. "In search of food, the elusive creature emerges from her den and tries her luck at the watering hole."

I shake my head, smiling, moving down the line. "Wow, Peters. I never knew you were such a huge Animal Planet fan."

"I'm a fan of all things nature. Birds. Bees. The like." He grabs two pudding cups and drops one on my tray.

"Pandas?" I say.

"How did you know? The panda is my spirit animal."

"Oh, good, because Gran has this great pattern for an embroidered panda cardigan. It would look amazing on you."

"Um, *yeah*, I know. It was on my Christmas list, but Santa totally stiffed me."

I laugh as I grab a carton of milk. So does he.

He leans in closer. "Come sit with me."

"At the jock table? Are you kidding?" I hand the cashier my lunch card.

Jensen squints his eyes in the direction of his friends. "We're skinny-ass basketball players, Wayfare. We don't really scream *jock*."

"Meatheads, then?"

"I believe the correct term is Athletic Types." We step out from the line and scan the room. "So where were you planning on sitting?"

"I was thinking Grady and Marco were my safest bet."

"The nerd table?"

I gesture to myself, especially my glasses. "I figure my natural camouflage will help me blend, yo."

He laughs, his honey-blond hair falling in front of his eyes.

"And hey," I say, nudging him with my elbow, "last I heard, Peters was cool with nerdy."

He claps me gently on the back. "Good luck, Wayfare. I'm pulling for ya."

He heads to his table and I look around for the only two kids I've spoken to on a semiregular basis in my Advanced CAD class. But I never make it over to them.

"Alex, oh, thank God you're back." Mrs. Latimer, head of the AV department, rushes up to me, two granola bars and a can of Coke in her hands. "We had an outage last week and now I've got a whole stack of DVD players that won't power on. Totally fried." She turns in the direction of the lab, then looks back at me when I don't join her, confused. "Aren't you coming?"

"Yeah," I say, letting out a sigh. "I'm coming."

I guess making amends will have to wait.

MR. SORENSON, CAN I USE THE BATHROOM?

By last period, I still haven't added a second item to the bucket list. Between Camilla Denison, one of Tabitha's friends, "accidentally" knocking my books off my desk in English, and Robbie Duncan, the douchebag Jensen got in a fight with a few months ago, snapping my bra strap in the hall, I wonder if having only a few people at my funeral is such a bad thing after all.

The Camilla thing isn't so bad. I'd like to tell her to grow up, to get a life, but whatever. It's the Robbie thing that really gets to me. First Gesh, running his hand up my thigh while his thug held me down, then Decoy Boy groping me in Grant Park, now this. All of them dickheads who think they can have whatever they want just by sticking their hands out.

The next time one of them reaches for me, I'm cutting his hand clean off.

With something dull and rusty.

I walk into my history class, scowling, expecting to see Vice-Principal Rodrigues standing in for Mr. Lipscomb like he was before winter break. Expecting him to tell me to smile once in a while, like he usually does.

Instead, I stop in my tracks.

Levi stands at the whiteboard where Vice-Principal Rodrigues should be. Dark gray slacks, mustard V-neck sweater. Half the class is already in their seats, whispering and giggling about the new teacher. Everyone is abuzz. There's an electric feel about the room.

Levi pretends not to notice me as he fills up the board with today's lesson notes in black dry-erase marker.

"Hey," I blurt out before I can stop myself.

He glances at me and nods politely. "Hello. I'm Mr. Sorenson. I'll be filling in for the rest of the year."

A manic giggle threatens to bubble in my throat. "You'll be filling in for the rest of the year. Here. In this class."

"Yes." He lowers his hand from the board. "And your name is?"

"Alex," I say, fighting the urge to roll my eyes at him. Must. Keep. Secret. Identity. Secret. "Alex Wayfare. I sit over there. In the middle."

"Well, Miss Wayfare, I suggest you take your seat, over there, in the middle, before the bell rings."

Surreal. Too surreal for Base Life. Couldn't he have given me some warning?

Jensen squeezes past me, smiling, and grabs his assigned seat in the back beside Tabitha. I slide into mine and trace the wood grain on the top of my desk with my pencil, leaving behind thick graphite marks. Mr. Lipscomb hated it when I did that.

But he isn't here.

Levi is.

I glance at Mr. Lipscomb's old desk. Levi has already moved in.

Stacked on it are leather-bound books by Nietzsche and Kierkegaard, moleskin notebooks, a cup of black pens, an agenda, and our history textbook, which, I want to tell him, belongs in the trash.

He'd agree with me.

Maybe having him as a teacher won't be such a bad thing. Maybe I'll actually learn something and get a passing grade. Maybe I won't feel so much like prey, but more like my big brother is here, looking out for me.

"Good afternoon," Levi says after the bell sounds. "I'm Mr. Sorenson." He marks his name across the whiteboard, writing in all caps like my dad does. Like an anal, perfectionist engineer. I realize this is the first time I've ever heard him use a last name, or seen his handwriting. Just like everything else about him, his handwriting is cool, and I kind of hate him for it.

"God, he's gorgeous," I hear Tabitha whisper behind me, off to my left. Camilla, who sits in front of her, giggles.

I want to turn around and say, *yeah, if you have a thing for thirty-six-year-olds*, but then I'd be talking to Tabitha, and I'd break my Not Talking to Tabitha streak.

"He looks like Charlie Hunnam," Camilla whispers back.

"Better than Charlie Hunnam. Like a Charlie Hunnam and Joshua Jackson sandwich."

God, whoever they are. I roll my eyes and try to ignore them.

"And his ass," Camilla says. "Fiiiiiine."

I can hear Tabitha press her lips together. "Mmmm. I might ask if I can move to the front row. Get a better view."

They both laugh, and I'm about to lose my lunch. They're talking about Levi. My Levi. I want to tell them to shut up, like he's mine or something, because he was mine once, a whole lifetime ago. Which is stupid. I know it's so stupid, but it's there nonetheless, a splinter of jealousy in my gut.

As for the rest of the class, looking up at Levi with wide eyes because he's the new, shiny thing, I want to stand up and say I knew him first, that he's my friend.

Sort of.

And that we hang out.

Sort of.

And I feel childish for all of it, and antsy, and wound up inside with a secret I can't tell anyone. It's different from my other secrets. This one is out in the open, standing in front of the class for the whole school to see, and I have to keep my mouth shut. Keep my distance. Endure what other kids say about him. Act like we've never met.

Thanks, Mr. Sorenson. Thank you. This makes school sooo much easier.

CHAPTER 16

WHAT WAS IT HEIDEGGER SAID?

After school, I catch up with Levi outside in the parking lot. Black fedora. Black scarf. Black double-breasted pea coat. Reeking of cool. Kids filter past him, weaving between parked cars, glancing at him and whispering behind cupped hands. As he opens the driver's door of a white-and-chrome vintage Mercedes coupe—yet another car I've most likely bankrolled—I say, "You made quite the impression today."

He stops, a black-gloved hand still on the door handle.

I hug my books to my chest and glance around, making sure no one's close enough to hear.

"I'm not here to make an impression," he says, keeping his voice down, his back to me. "I'm here to give you moral support. Make you feel at ease."

"Yeah, and I'm here for the food."

He tosses a canvas messenger bag onto the backseat and turns to face me. "You're doing that sarcasm thing again."

"Get used to it." I grin so he knows I'm teasing, and squint as the sun glints off a layer of fresh snow. "Come on, admit it. You enjoyed it. Up there spouting all that philosophy stuff. You were loving it."

"I'm good at playing a part, that's all. I've been doing it my whole life. I was acting. It's all part of the long con."

"Well, you're good at it. Almost fooled me. Especially that part about living a life with focused authenticity. Who was it who said it? Heidegger? That we should choose our own path, not the one prescribed for us?" I direct my squinting at him. "A bit misleading, don't you think, especially for me?"

"Is this how it's going to be? You're going to criticize my lessons every day after class?" He folds his arms and squints his eyes, but there isn't any venom behind it. I can tell by his tone that he's amused. If he were normal, he'd be grinning back at me.

Robbie Duncan walks by with his friends, gaping like an idiot at Levi and me. "Ooooo, Alex. Already in trouble with the new teacher? Or did you want to check him out up close? Maybe let him give you a *ride* like Peters?" He cackles like a hyena, and so do his friends.

I raise my middle finger in his direction. A salute to his douchebagness.

Levi frowns, and I think he's going to scold me. Instead he says, "I'd like to punch that kid in the face, but I feel like that would be frowned upon."

"I don't care. I'll help hold him down."

Levi pulls his keys from his coat pocket, his eyes sparkling a bit when he looks at me. "It was nice meeting you, Miss Wayfare. See you tomorrow."

Yeah, or tonight for our China mission. Whatever, Mr. Sorenson.

As Levi pulls out of his parking space, Jensen appears at my side. "So, new teacher," he says. "Making a better impression than you did on Mr. Lipscomb?"

"What are you talking about?" I turn to look at him. "I always make a good impression. Mr. Lipscomb loved me."

Jensen laughs and whips his hair from his eyes. "This new guy's pretty popular with the ladies. Honestly? I don't see it. Do you think he's hot?"

"Hot? He's a teacher. I don't think the two words go together."

"Way to avoid the question, Wayfare."

I shrug. "He's all right, I guess. Better than Lipscomb, at least."

"Ha, yeah, way better than Lipscomb." Jensen glances at three yellow school buses lined up in front of the school, and shifts his duffle bag on his shoulder. "I gotta jet. Game tonight."

I clap him on the back like he did to me in the cafeteria. "Good luck, Peters. I'm pulling for ya."

He walks backwards toward the buses. "You tuning in?"

"I'll try." Truth is, Pops always listens to the local game broadcasts streaming online. Sometimes I join him, but not tonight. Tonight, I'll be on the other side of the world.

Jensen smiles at the hope I've given him, then jogs away. I turn away too, and flip my hood up. Not because of the cold, but because of the tears in my eyes.

I'm dying, Jensen.

God, I'm going to miss that boy.

THROUGH THESE EYES

"Did you know about the Levi thing?" I ask Porter when I get to the yacht later that night. I drop my backpack at my feet and fall onto one of the white leather sofas.

Porter looks up from lighting a pipe in the kitchen, and waves his match until the flame goes out. Tendrils of smoke curl toward the ceiling. "About him being your teacher?" He puffs on the bit, pulling the smoke into his lungs. "I thought you'd think it was a good idea."

"Porter, it's the worst idea. The absolute worst idea in the history of ideas."

"Because?"

"Because he's cool."

"He's cool?"

"He's cool, and already super popular, and all the girls think he's gorgeous and talk about his ass and how he's a sandwich, and I'm Wayspaz the Fix-It Freak, and I don't want him seeing me like that."

Porter sits down beside me, both arms stretched out across the back of the couch, clenching the pipe between his teeth. "Like what?"

"Like how all the other kids see me."

A freaky nerd. The girl who hides out in the computer lab at lunch because she has no friends and has seizures during class and pukes on cute boys.

Porter lays an age-spotted hand on my shoulder. He holds his pipe with the other. The smoke envelops us, woodsy and deep. I've grown to like his particular brand of tobacco. It's comforting, like one of Gran's afghans. "Levi has an enormous amount of respect for you. No amount of teasing at your school is going to sway him of that."

I know Porter's right. I know Levi isn't susceptible to high school rumor mills and popularity contests, but I can't help feeling uneasy. Like I'm under a microscope now, worrying that his respect for me will slip a few notches each day. Just like I fear him being there with me on this mission, watching my every move.

"Can we change the subject?" I reach into my bag and pull out a new book about Beijing that I got from the library. "What will Beijing look like in 1770? I can't find any drawings or paintings, only recent photographs. What will I be up against? And what was my name?"

"It will be much more sparse than the modern photos you've seen. More trees, more hills within the city. Canals. Bridges. More wooden buildings and homes than stone. I'm not sure where you'll be when you land, but you'll most likely be sleeping on the streets. You'll be dressed as a boy, and you won't have much money, if any."

"Why will I be dressed as a boy?"

"It was easier, I suppose. Safer for an orphan girl at that time. Your name was Lo Jie. Micki says you worked for a man called Wei. He trained at the Shaolin temple when he was young, but fell out of favor with the abbot and left as a young man. After that he built up a crime syndicate in Beijing, outsourcing orphans like you to do his dirty work for him, sending them out on missions."

"Great. I'm a thief." The thought is disappointing, but I suppose it's not much different from what I do here, with Porter. We run an underground crime syndicate, don't we?

"Don't look so disappointed. Being a thief will work to your advantage. If you need money, you'll need to steal something to sell.

Your muscle memory and training should make that easy for you."

"You're saying that after I land, I have to scope out the city, find something to steal, steal it, and sell it without getting caught, all before I can take the trip to see the healer? How will I have enough time for all of that? The Black always kicks me out. Sends me back to Limbo. The longest I've ever stayed in the past is a day and a half."

"Not this time. We'll be with you, connected to your soulmark. The more souls that are combined, the more energy you have, the more power you have over the Black."

"Is that why I always stay longer when I'm with Blue?"

Porter nods. "Your combined energy helps you remain in the past. This time, our energy should be so strong that you'll be able to decide when you come and go. Possibly even strong enough to break a soulblock."

"Are you serious?" I say, remembering the suffocating, drowning feeling of a soulblock, when Gesh or his Descenders tried to trap me in the past.

Porter nods. Exhales smoke. "Should be. But let's hope it doesn't come to that."

I take a deep breath and ask what I've been meaning to ask for a while. "What happens if I run into Blue? What if he wants to be my partner, help me with my mission?" Like he said he wanted when we met in the Black.

"I was going to talk to you about that. Micki says he also worked for Wei. It's likely you will run into him there. If so, I would use extreme caution. Don't divulge anything, not one thing, about your life here as Alex Wayfare."

Despite Porter's warning, I can't help but smile at the possibility of seeing Blue again, but I don't let Porter see it. "The thing is, I've already divulged a secret to him, in Chicago, before I knew the rules. I told him I was from Annapolis. That my name was Alex. If he were working for Gesh, wouldn't he have used that against me already? To bring Gesh to my front door?" I shake my head. "I trust him, Porter. More than I trust Micki. And I know him better than

Levi. I don't believe he's working for Gesh. I can't believe it."

Because that would mean I've been wrong about him. Blind. Stupid.

Porter is quiet, contemplative. He puffs on his pipe, and after a long while says, "Well then, I say trust your gut."

I give him a look, because I don't believe the sudden change in his tune. "I don't think Levi and Micki will approve of that advice."

"No, but I trust you, Alex. I have no reason not to. You've been a fine pupil. You have good instincts. You're ready for this. And you're right, you know Tre better than we do. Maybe we are missing something. We know Gesh has the ability to track you, we just aren't sure how. The most logical hypothesis is that he's using Tre to spy on you, but it's possible he may be using a different method. I have a few theories; I just need some time to test them out. Until then, all I know is that I believe you can do this mission. I believe if anyone can save your sister, you can." He leans forward, his pale blue, watery eyes on mine. "I believe in *you*."

It takes me a moment to respond. "Thank you. That means a lot."

"We're coming to the end of this thing, you and I. I thought it was about time you knew how much I admire you. Always have."

He squeezes my shoulder, then smiles, sad and reminiscent, and leans back, smoke clouding his face. I flip through the pages of the book on my lap, trying not to smear them with tears.

As much as my trust in Porter has wavered, I'm going to miss him. I know that once I'm reborn, he'll raise me up, and I'll get to know him all over again. But not as Alex. As someone totally different. I'm going to miss him as I see him now.

Through these eyes.

FOR AUDREY

In the room below, I settle myself in the center dentist chair. Levi and Micki rest on either side of me. Porter hooks us to the same machine while we sip the runner's-feet-flavored tea.

I scrunch my nose after downing mine in two gulps. "Dare I ask what gives this such a lovely aftertaste?"

Porter takes my mug away. "That would be the sedative."

"So, you've been drugging me. Fabulous."

Micki makes a face similar to mine as she swallows. "Best not to ask which drug."

I draw in a few deep breaths, steadying my nerves.

Levi notices. "You'll do great. We'll be with you the whole time."

My smile is a small, sad thing, and I wonder why I smile at all. What I really want to do is confess that I'm scared out of my mind. I'm so afraid I'll fail. I'm not sure it makes me feel any better knowing they'll be with me.

I want to say all of that, but instead I just smile.

I smile, and I don't know what the hell for.

Until Levi reaches for my hand, and Micki reaches for the other.

"You're not going to fail," Micki says, like she can read my mind. Like she's already connected to my soulmark.

"I'm not prepared. I should've studied more. Maybe we should wait a few more days."

"Audrey may not have a few more days," she says. "And I did my research. *I'm* prepared. This is what I was trained for. To be your guide so you don't have to shoulder it all on your own. I'll walk you through, every step of the way. Porter will bring the muscle and keep you safe. Levi will keep you focused. We're all in this together. We want to save your sister as much as you do."

Her tiger eyes are soft and sincere, but there's a hesitation in my heart. Always a hesitation.

"For Audrey," Porter says with a nod.

"For Audrey," say Micki and Levi.

I want to say it too, but I can't form the words. I'm too emotional from it all. Every fiber of my body is conflicted, twisted up between suspicion and belief, between hope and defeat. God, I want to trust these people at my side. I want to believe them when they say we'll triumph. I want to, but I won't, not until I cross the finish line. Not until I come home a hero.

Porter hands us our headphones. I slip mine on, letting the humming sound waves lull me into a stupor. I feel heavy, my eyes unable to open. My soul wriggles, restless, ready to ascend. The Black spins a web around me.

Porter rests a hand on my shoulder. "Here we go."

And just like slipping into a dream, we slip into Limbo, into my garden. The soulmark that leads to China sways and dances before us, its light reflecting across our faces. We all reach out at the same time.

Here we go, capturing the flag.

For Audrey.

CHAPTER 17

TUNNEL TO CHINA

When I landed, images, colors, and sounds emerged from the light, but I couldn't get a clear picture of my surrounding like usual. Everything was blurry, streaked, and I couldn't catch my breath.

What's wrong? Why can't I focus? I asked Porter, our minds linked through my soulmark, but before he could answer, I figured it out. I was running, full tilt, racing through the streets of Beijing.

I put on the brakes. Pulled myself to a stop. Gulped deep breaths, hands on my knees. Sweat beaded and rolled down my spine. I had to get accustomed to my host body before I went any further. I had to know where I was, who I was, and what I was dealing with.

My shoes were lightweight, made of soft material, the tips pointed upwards. My pants were black, flowing and soft, gathered at my ankles and tucked into socks. My gray jacket was fastened at my neck and collarbone with strips of fabric, like laces, and it had loose sleeves so long they hid my fists. It was midday, blisteringly hot, but my clothes were surprisingly cool, breathable and comfortable even though they were ragged and threadbare. Two daggers were slung at my hips like pistols. The handles felt familiar, well worn with use. I ran my hands over my head—a tight cap, and a long black braid that snaked down my back.

All males wore their hair this way. Micki's voice sounded inside my head, and unlike the first time Porter communicated with me this way in Chicago, I welcomed her information. *A shaved forehead to show allegiance to the Qing rule, and a long braid down the back.*

I pulled off my cap, black with gold trim, wanting to run my fingers across my shaved forehead, to feel fingertips against scalp, like Audrey does every day. But I had a full head of hair. Not one strand cut.

Keep that cap on, Micki warned. *It's part of your disguise. As long as you wear it, you should be able to pass as a boy.*

I resituated it, tucking any loose strands beneath the rim, and glanced around. A narrow stone alley stretched out before me, sunlight bathing the path. Brick walls reached high above on either side. As I looked around, I noticed something heavy slung across my back, a pack held tight by a purple fabric strap tied across my chest. Unfurling it revealed a thick porcelain vase, bright yellows, reds, and oranges flashing in the sun. Intricate lotus carvings and delicate paintings of dragons and koi fish.

Are you seeing this? I asked Micki.

Jackpot, she said. *What's on the medallion?*

I turned the vase over in my palms. Two carp danced and wound together in waves of blue and jade.

Didn't I tell you this was going to be cake? Micki says. *Your past self already did the thieving for you. A vase like that just sold at Sotheby's for over eighty million.*

Relief flooded my veins. This would save me days of preparation.

What's that inside the vase? Micki asked.

Wrapped in red silk was a tiny bowl, the deepest vermilion, rimmed in gold, with yellow flowers and white scallops painted along the face.

Perfect, said Micki. *Hock the bowl—it's red porcelain, not as valuable, but it should buy you passage to the healer. Bury the eighty mill for us in Base Life.*

"Jie, what are you doing?"

A young man ran toward me, shouting my name. "Jie. Hurry." He wore the same kind of clothes as I did, the same cap, only slightly different in design and color, and had a long braid down his back as well.

As quick as a whip, I wrapped the bowl and vase and tied them snugly against my back. My reflexes were so fast, my movements fluid and nimble. I felt light but strong. Stronger than I'd ever felt.

As the boy approached, my body tensed, my fists clenched. He seemed to know me, but my instinct to protect the stolen goods took precedence. They were my ticket to see the healer, to fund the cure for Audrey, and I wouldn't let anyone take them from me. My stance shifted wide into a deep squat, my feet planted firmly on the stone pavement, my fists held above my thighs, my daggers within reach, preparing for an attack. The horse stance. I knew what it was called. It was automatic. I felt a rush of power flow through my arms to my palms.

I was ready to fight. And more importantly, I had the ability.

Holy shit, I said to my team. *I know kung fu?*

I could feel Micki's laughter in my head, tinkling almost. *Damn straight you do.*

"Jie," the boy shouted again when he reached me, panting. "They are coming."

My host body's memory translated the Chinese language for me without hesitation. It was one of the perks of descending. I could take the fluency of the language back with me to Base Life as a residual, having learned an entire language in less than a millisecond like I had with Danish. But as amazing as that was, it paled in comparison to what stood before me. The energy in my palms evaporated and I relaxed my stance.

This was no ordinary boy.

"Blue?" The nickname slipped out before I could stop myself.

No, no, Micki warned. Her laughter was gone now. *His name is Tao Jin. Don't call him Blue.*

Damn. Only a few minutes into the mission and I'd already made my first mistake. Calling him Blue would cause suspicion if he didn't remember me, if he was only Tao Jin, a stranger to me in this life. I could make an impact on him.

But he flashed me a grin, and suddenly my Blue was there, in the flesh, standing before me. There was his cheery, mischievous smile and intense, unabashed gaze. There were his hands, the hands I'd memorized, smudged with dirt, but shaped the same way. His nose was a bit thinner, his skin deeper in color, his eyes rounder and darker, almost black. I thought his eyes would be the same shade of blue-green in every lifetime, but here he was, proving that theory wrong. It didn't matter, though. It was him. His stance, his gait, his broad shoulders, everything was the same, but so very different too, his features stolen and worn like a glove in every time period. But it didn't matter which one he wore. He was always beautiful to me. Achingly so.

"Blue?" he said, smiling from ear to ear, his eyes dancing. "Don't let anyone else hear you call me that, Sousa."

Be careful what you say to him. It was Levi this time. I could feel his suspicion, his frown, filtering down into my soul from Limbo. I didn't let it affect me, though. I let Levi stay cozied up inside my head, along with Micki and Porter. They could be as suspicious as they wanted, but I knew Blue would be an asset. Having his help would only make this mission easier.

The cure was in sight. I felt it, tasted it. Saw Audrey up and dancing again. I was going to save her life. I was shivering with the possibility.

A shout from behind me made Blue's eyes flit over my shoulder. "You'll have to fill me in on why we're in China later. They're here. Are you ready to fight? Or do you want to run?"

I whirled around. Three men in black uniforms and red caps poured into the alley and charged us, weapons held high. Spears. Swords. They shouted for us to stop. Called us thieves.

As much confidence as I had in my past-life body and her skill with the daggers, I was too chicken to test it out right then. And I was desperate to protect the eighty million on my back, so I said, "Run."

MY TEAM'S BETTER

We ran like we did through the back alleys in Chicago. I didn't slow down; I let my body lead me where it wanted to go.

The alley opened up into a sprawling plaza packed with villagers.

It was some kind of festival, or a street market, with booths and tents packed in tight rows, the din of the crowd so loud I couldn't hear myself think. I thought I would lose sight of Blue, but I never did. We snaked and scurried through the crowd as deftly and swiftly as mice, as though connected by an unseen thread.

We ducked beneath a camel lumbering along, loaded down with wooden trunks and woven bags. We slipped past merchants selling silks, colorful pinwheels and umbrellas, delicate birdcages, and wooden wind chimes. We skidded around a portly man selling a rich-smelling stew, which bubbled and steamed from an equally portly pot. We leaped over creaking wooden wheelbarrows laden with burlap bags of rice. Villagers balancing carrying poles across their shoulders, with hanging baskets of leafy vegetables, stumbled to stay out of our way.

We passed archery demonstrations, children performing acrobatics, and a woman painting faces. The sights, the smells, the sounds overwhelmed my senses. Sweat stung my eyes. But I let my muscle memory guide me, let my body do what it was trained to do. This body was used to all the senses, even though they were all new to me. I had to give Lo Jie the reins, and not let my Americanness get in the way.

As we moved farther from the market, the noise died and the crowds thinned. The streets wound around buildings, some with wooden walls, some with brick, and all with tiles on the roofs. We paused behind a statue of a Shi Shi lion, peering around to see if we'd lost the guards.

We hadn't.

They were on our tails, charging down the street. They weren't even winded.

"We're not going to make it," said Blue.

"Then we fight." Lo Jie wouldn't let me chicken out this time. She was prepared to defend the stolen goods on her back.

I stepped out into the street to meet the guards, and squatted into the horse stance again, this time with my daggers in my fists. I breathed in through my nose, focusing all my energy into my palms.

Be careful, Porter said. *You must fight clean. Fighting is not out of the ordinary for your past life, but remember, you cannot kill anyone.*

I nodded, just once, even though Porter wasn't there to see me. I understood. The guards charged at me in a flurry, and I met them head on, giving in to Lo Jie's instincts. I couldn't let my fear get in the way. If they captured me, I'd have to redo the mission. So I let Lo Jie do her thing.

I spun, I kicked, I blocked, I sliced my daggers through the air. My blades tasted sunlight. We were a blur of black and gray, of fists and steel. I paid no attention to their weapons like I would have expected. Instead, I focused on their elbows. I could tell exactly where their hits would land or what moves they were about to use by the direction and lift of their elbows. I counteracted each time, without thinking. It was like driving the Mustang. Once I had it mastered, the movements came naturally.

A kick to the neck. A spin in the air. A chop to the side of the head. A twist of the arm. A heel to the back of the knee. My body leaping into the air. Two feet planted squarely in the lower back. I was mighty. I was winning. Three against one. Until I realized Blue wasn't fighting with me. He was nowhere to be seen.

Had he left me to fight these men on my own?

I faltered, only slowed down for a fraction of a second, but it was enough for one of them to crack a blow to my ribs with the long wooden handle of his spear.

Down I went, twisting so I landed on my side instead of crushing the pack on my back. The man with the spear stood over me, wearing a small smirk behind a thin mustache so long it reached his collarbones. I nicknamed him Mustachio.

On Mustachio's left was a short man with a round belly and his front teeth missing. I named him Toothless. The third was built like an oak tree, stocky, thick, tall. His shaved head glistened with sweat and made him look like a bouncer standing outside a club, so that's what I named him. Bouncer yanked me to my feet, held my arms behind my back, and twisted my daggers from my hands.

Mustachio looked me up and down with a sneer. "You have

much skill. You have been trained well in the Seven Star Fist. But you are no match for the Royal Guard."

Showed how much they knew. I wasn't done yet.

Pushing back against the solid tree trunk that was Bouncer and using him as leverage, I swung my feet into the air, striking a kick to Mustachio's jaw. He stumbled to the ground, clutching his chin. I twisted free from Bouncer, turning to face him.

He came at me with a yell, wielding my daggers, but I deflected every hit, as though I stood behind an invisible shield. Our arms waved like windmills, chopping and churning, until I found a chink in his armor, a hole in his defense. His arms couldn't move as fast as mine—his massive biceps restricted his range of motion, but my skinny arms flew like hummingbird wings. When his elbows were spread wide, exposing his chest, I pulled my energy from my gut and pushed it into my hands. With a mighty shout, I struck his chest with my palms. I felt the energy leave me and explode into him. He flew backwards, hit the ground, and didn't get back up. My daggers went skittering across the stone pavement.

The faint swish of a blade grazed the back of my neck, the soft tendrils of hair behind my ear, and I spun to face Toothless. He swung at me with his sword, slicing and swooping and jabbing as I pivoted and contorted my body. I had no weapon to deflect the blade, I couldn't reach my daggers, and I grew weary of bending and ducking and spinning out of the way. I had to get in close, between his hands and his shoulders, where the blade couldn't reach me, but he was too quick. He kept his body protected, kept me at arm's length under a barrage of flashing steel. I was wearing thin. Too tired from running, too tired from fighting.

He swung at me, aiming to cut me in half, and I used all the remaining strength I had to curl backwards into a flip. I arced through the air. The sword swept beneath my shoes, but by the time I landed on my feet his blade was back, sweeping up from my thigh to my ribs, the point slicing through my pants and jacket.

My hands fumbled at my torn clothes, then the tip of his blade tapped the bottom of my chin.

"You have been trained well, that is certain," said Toothless between shallow breaths. "But not well enough. Your partner deserted you. You did not have a chance against me and my team, a young child fighting alone."

"That may be," I said, my gaze flicking over his shoulder. A silent shadow crept behind him, stepping between the dazed Mustachio and Bouncer on soft feet. "You do have a great team," I continued, "The only thing is..."

Toothless furrowed his brow, waiting for me to finish.

Blue lifted a wide stone bowl above Toothless's head. *Crash.* Down it came onto his skull, shattering to pieces. Toothless's eyes rolled back, and he crumpled to the ground with the other two, his sword clattering at my feet.

Blue and I stood over the three of them as they lay there, moaning in pain, and I grinned to myself. "The only thing is, my team's better."

CHAPTER 18

THE WESTERN GATE

"Sorry I was late," Blue said as we hurried away, leaving the guards where they lay. "I'm not as skilled, and I needed to find a weapon. I knew you could handle them."

I secured my daggers at my hip, smiling at him, but honestly, I felt let down. Embarrassed. Maybe he wasn't as skilled as me in this past life, but I wished he hadn't disappeared like that. It only made him look suspicious to Micki, Levi, and Porter.

But Blue didn't know they were watching. He didn't know he was being evaluated. And we won, didn't we?

You need to get to the western city gate, Micki said, interrupting my thoughts. *The convoys leave from there. Have Tre lead you if you can't remember the way.*

I touched Blue's hand. "We need to get to the western gate."

He nodded, and we turned down a street on our right. "Are you going to tell me what we're doing in China now, Sousa?"

"We're going on a road trip."

He smiled, and we ran faster. We weaved through a poorer side of town, overgrown with twisted trees and weeds. It felt like a jungle, it was so thick. The streets were dirt. There were women washing clothes in barrels of water, children with smudged faces chasing each other and laughing, and old men with even older-looking beards sitting on porch steps smoking long pipes. The air was filled with a combination of scents, some delicious like stews bubbling over fires, some sweet and fresh like the tunnel of honeysuckle vines we ducked under, and others sharp and pungent. They quite literally smelled like shit.

Yep. That's exactly what you smell, Micki said. *No plumbing, you know. But they had fascinating uses for excrement back then. They used to cook it with human hair to use as fertilizer. Sometimes they'd distill it like wine and spray it on their crops. Brilliant, no?*

I scrunched my nose at the thought.

Still enjoying time travel? she asked. *When the time comes, you'll have to find a comfy log in the woods to do your business.*

Focus, Micki. I tried to sound stern. She was distracting me.

Yes, ma'am.

We reached the gate drenched in sweat, the sun high in the sky. Just outside the city wall, there was a line of horse-drawn wagons waiting in a queue. Blue nodded at a fat man sitting behind a table under a tent, fanning himself as beads of sweat poured down his red, blotchy face. An old woman using a crooked cane handed him a fistful of bronze coins, and he waved her toward one of the wagons.

Micki whispered the name of the healer, and I approached the man behind the table. "I'd like passage to see Shang Guan Jian."

The fat man thrust out his hand, never once looking at me, waiting for me to fill it with some sort of payment. He coughed and hacked into his other hand while I carefully unwound my pack. I presented him with the bowl. He took it, turned it over in his hands, coughing all over it, then nodded and waved Blue and me to the first wagon in line. I bowed my head in thanks.

We were on our way.

LO JIE

"I love this," Blue said, sitting beside me. The wagon bounced and swayed, and we leaned against each other for support. "Being here with you, alone, not a care in the world."

I had cares, plenty of them, but I knew what he meant. I settled against him and watched the countryside move past at a snail's pace.

The first leg of our trip wound through a wide, rocky valley with tree-covered mountains reaching high above us on either side. We passed through little groves of spruce and pine and oak and maple, their leaves and branches rustling now and then in a barely-there breeze. Ferns and lily-of-the-valley dotted the path. Squirrels and chipmunks scurried among them, while woodpeckers and swallows swooped overhead. I had expected China to look exciting and new, quite a bit more tropical, but beneath these peaks I could almost believe I was back on the White Mountain Trail in New Hampshire, vacationing with the family when I was eleven.

You're thinking of Southern China, said Micki. *Bamboo, pandas, rice paddies. The North is completely different. It's a lot like where you come from.*

Even though it was similar, and somewhat familiar, it was still breathtaking. There were so many greens there couldn't possibly be a name for each one. And even though the types of trees were the same as back home, they were older. They had a wild and ancient air about them, steeped in silence.

Like they held centuries of secrets.

I closed my eyes and let the sun warm my face. The wagon rocked. "I should do this every winter," I said to Blue, not missing slush in my shoes or bitter wind or chapped lips. "Descend someplace warm to thaw my bones."

"You make it sound like vacation, but this isn't a vacation for you, is it?"

Watch what you say, Levi said before I could reply.

I knew Blue's question was a little prodding—he wanted to know why I'd brought him to China—but did Levi really think I would spill all my secrets? Tell Blue everything? Didn't Levi trust me at all?

After a few hours in the wagon, the road lazily rising up one of the mountainsides, our driver pulled his horses to a stop. The path ahead was steep. Those of us who could walk were instructed to follow behind the wagon to lessen the burden on the horses.

Blue and I didn't mind. It was a slow walk as we stepped our way through rocks and roots, up, up, into the treetops. We didn't speak; we were content to walk side by side, listening to the birds in the trees and the thoughts in our heads.

Micki could joke about the less appealing aspects of descending, but they didn't bother me. I liked time travel. I liked taking a stroll through the past. The differences were what made it so appealing. It was quieter. Calmer. Things moved slower, with more purpose. There were fewer distractions. You could focus on one thing at a time. The breeze in your hair. The sun on the back of your neck. Your footfalls on soft earth. There were no strip malls. No endless concrete developments. No billboards, no advertising, no gridlock, no noise. Just quiet breathing, and the ever-present notion that you are a very small thing in a very big world.

I didn't want to give it up. Even if it was one step away from mass destruction, like Levi said. I wanted to keep descending like I wanted to keep kissing Blue. It wasn't logical, it wasn't sane, but it was fact.

I hunched my pack and resituated the worn, threadbare strap across my chest, patting the vase to make sure it was in one piece. I fingered the hilts of my daggers, remembering what it felt like to use them.

Would I bring kung fu back with me to Base Life?

Each time I slipped into one of my past-life bodies I carried a little piece of them back with me to the present day, like souvenirs. Once I brought back better vision; once, courage in the face of danger, and maybe even a thirst for it. In one of my past lives I was considered the best female sharpshooter west of the Mississippi. Shooter Delaney wasn't just any train robber, she was one of the best in a sea of men and knew how to hold her own. Her fearlessness walked with me now as I climbed through the forest. Old me, the old Alex, would've jumped at every snap of a twig, would've sprained her neck from looking over her shoulder in this unknown wilderness. But not in Lo Jie's body.

In her body, I was confident, headstrong. *I need no one.* That was the refrain that kept rolling inside my head. I couldn't figure out if it was my own thought or if it was Lo Jie's shining through like sun through paper screens. At times, I've felt the struggles of my host body, and I've had to overcome them. Sometimes those instincts and muscle memories were helpful, like on this mission when I had to speak Chinese, or if I needed directions to a place only my past self would know. If I let those instincts take over I could blend in and fool everyone into thinking I wasn't an imposter. Descending only worked when no one was suspicious.

At other times, my host body's instincts were difficult to control. Like the one I felt now, an overwhelming sense of independence. It wasn't my own emotion—I needed my family, I needed a warm, loving household to come home to. But Jie was strong and self-reliant. She knew how to navigate her world alone. She could tell the time of day by the way the sun felt on her shoulders. How intense it was, what direction it came from. Not an exact time, mind you, but exact times didn't matter much back then.

I could feel the stillness of Jie's mind. Not less intelligent—she was as sharp as the daggers at my hips, but she only had one focus at a time. One single goal, like keeping the stolen vase safe. There were no pressing engagements worrying her, no notifications on her phone pinging every two seconds. Her mind was clear of clutter, her thoughts arranged like perfect garden rows, everything in its place, ready to be plucked when needed.

She had muscles I never knew existed. Her body was hard and firm and lean. Her hands were callused, her skin brown from the sun, her lips dry from thirst. Her brow was set with fierce determination.

And I liked her.

I liked who I'd been.

I liked that I could climb a mountain without feeling winded. As the hours stretched on, thick heat clung to my back. Sweat rolled down my chest. I hummed "Wayfaring Stranger" to pass the time, a song Dad used to sing to us before bed.

I am a poor wayfaring stranger
Traveling through this world of woe.

Our path lifted us up and out of the poplar and pine, opening into a wide farm field, with rows and rows of vegetables and fruits planted along the sloping terrain. It was just like the song said: *I know my way is rough and steep, but golden fields lie out before me.*

My stomach growled, so Blue and I left our convoy behind

for a while to wander through the rows. We split open snow peas and popped the sweet seeds in our mouths. We ate handfuls of goji berries straight from the bush. Horseflies buzzed, and we swatted them away with our caps. Dragonflies danced lazily above rows of string beans. As we filled our pockets with peas and beans and berries, not enough to be missed, it reminded me of picking vegetables on Gran and Pops's old farm in Virginia. Audrey and I were the only ones who liked okra fresh from the stalk. We'd sit in the sunbaked dirt, our knees burned red, our feet black from wading in creek mud. We'd reach high, snapping off the little green pods, and snack on them until we were full. And the tomatoes. Oh, how I missed them. Gran and Pops grew cherry tomatoes so savory you could make a meal of them. They made you want to sink to your knees, thankful to the southern Virginia sun for giving them such flavor. Tomatoes didn't taste the same in Maryland.

I missed those days with Audrey, filled with sunshine and grass and dirt between our toes. I liked sharing it with Blue, but it wasn't the same. I wanted my sister with me.

As dusk fell, we reached the top of a ridge. There, situated at the very edge, like it might topple down into the ravine below at any minute, was an inn. The wagon came to a stop in front of it and we were instructed to secure ourselves a meal and a room for the night.

"I don't have any money," I said to Blue, feeling a little panicked. "We'll have to sleep outside." I didn't have a bedroll. I didn't have any food except the few bits left in my pockets. I'd been in such a hurry to leave Beijing that I hadn't thought about those kinds of things.

Blue pulled a handful of coins from his pocket. "You don't, but I do."

He flashed a smile and my panic dissolved, and I stood on tiptoes to kiss him on the cheek, quick and sweet.

Don't do that, Porter said. *You're supposed to be a boy, remember?*

I backed away from Blue so fast I almost tripped. Blue had to snag me by the elbow to steady me. Thankfully, it didn't seem like anyone saw us.

Not that we think there's anything wrong with that, Micki added, *but your fellow travelers might think otherwise. So, maybe nix the PDA?*

This was going exactly as I feared. It was like having my parents along on a date. Only I wasn't on a date. I was on a mission. And I needed to start acting like it. I needed to get a grip.

"You OK, Sousa?" Blue placed a hand on my arm, gave it a gentle squeeze.

"Fine," I lied, forcing a smile. "Can you handle the room situation? I need a minute."

While he went inside, my feet led me off the road to the edge of the ridge, in the shadow of the inn, looking out across the valley. The wind swept up and tangled loose strands of my black hair in my face. I hugged my arms to my chest. There were tree-draped mountains cutting across the earth as far as the eye could see. Green at first, lit by golden setting sun, then steadily fading into blue as they met the horizon. The Great Wall snaked across one of the ranges in the distance, looking like a strip of white lace trim on an emerald dress.

Behind the inn, off to my right, was a rocky outcropping made of smooth boulders, weathered by decades of wind and storm. I set my mind to climb it and meditate at the top as the sun set. Not that I'd ever meditated before, but Lo Jie had, and she led me to the top, one soft footfall at a time. On the topmost stone, I lowered myself onto a wide, flat spot. I sat cross-legged, my hands resting in my lap, and closed my eyes. Breathed in the air.

And let my mind go.

BETRAYAL

Much later, when I opened my eyes, night had fallen across the mountains. My meditation had been so deep I hadn't noticed the air growing cooler or the night sounds awakening across the ridge. The flickering of cooking fires outside the inn painted the surrounding trees red and gold. Stars had spilled across the sky, a mess of scattered diamonds settling themselves into the black.

So this was why Jie's mind was so clear, so focused. She tended to it, cared for it, kept it healthy and strong. She didn't string herself out on stress and caffeine. She paused, left the here and now, just like I did when I slipped away to Limbo. Only this was different. This wasn't escaping life. This was another part of living. It was like breathing, like fueling one's body with foods straight from the earth. It was maintenance. Respecting the body, respecting the mind.

And I could get used to it.

"May I join you?" Behind me, Blue climbed the rocks as quiet as breath.

"Of course."

He sat beside me and wrapped his arms around his knees.

"Do you think the stars stare back at us?" I asked, wanting to use more of the Chinese language. I loved the way it felt to form the words and cup the vowels and consonants on my tongue, holding them to the roof of my mouth rather than against the back of my teeth like in English. The rise and fall of inflections, the intricacy of the tones. It felt like picking up an instrument and knowing how to play every note in perfect tune without a day of practice.

"Oh, I think they watch us with rapt attention," Blue said. "Especially during the day, when we ignore them, when our eyes can't see past the blue. It's quite the partnership, you know. We put on a show for each other. We're both spectacles."

As he spoke, I stretched out on my back, hands clasped behind my head, admiring his profile. The slope of his nose. The curve of his lips. The set of his jaw. Then I turned my gaze to the endless stars above us, and the constellations I knew by name. They were all there, shining the same as they do over two hundred years in the future. They traveled with me, my companions on this journey. Orion was driving, Cassiopeia was riding shotgun, and I was in the backseat singing "Stardust" and "Orion is Arising" and "Catch a Falling Star".

"You know how some people think they're worthless?" I said to Blue, feeling thoughtful and philosophical for the first time in a long while. "Not interesting enough, not beautiful enough, not smart enough? I think the stars must feel the same way. They go about their lives never knowing how breathtaking they are, how we rely on them to guide the way, or how many songs and sonnets have been written about them."

Blue continued to smile, a small, contented thing, as he listened. His hand found my knee, rested there. "Thank you for pulling me out of the dark, Sousa."

I sat up and kissed his cheek. Nestled my nose behind his earlobe, rested my chin on his shoulder. He smelled like dust and sweat and woodsmoke and earth. Distant firelight flickered against his warm skin. My fingers traced his forearm, the perfect muscles there. Slowly, almost as slow and lazy as a dream, our hands began to search each other, and we grew warmer still, kissing slowly, with purpose, savoring every moment.

I'd forgotten how wonderful it was to kiss him. How wonderful he tasted. How wonderful his skin felt beneath my fingertips, his body pressed and contoured against mine, my back cradled firmly in his arms. And I couldn't help it, I wanted all of him, as much as I could get this far outside reality, this far outside ourselves.

What are you doing? Porter said, his voice elbowing between Blue and me.

I swatted his words away. I couldn't let my team spoil this moment, so I closed the door on them, blocking them from my mind, pushing them out like I did to Porter back in 1927. They didn't even put up a fight. Maybe because I caught them off guard, they weren't expecting my sudden betrayal.

I hadn't expected it either.

I had expected to be focused on my mission. To be levelheaded. But that was before I was faced with an entire evening, stretching on and on, alone with Blue. There wasn't a thing I could do about finding the cure until morning light, and I couldn't think of a better way to make use of my extra time. It was selfish, like most decisions I make concerning Blue.

Selfish, selfish.

And yet...

"Let's go to your room," I whispered, breathless, as his lips found my neck.

CHAPTER 19

GOOD IS RELATIVE

Alone in Blue's room, alone in my head, we could do whatever we wanted, be whoever we wanted.

We crashed onto his bed, kissing, his hands on my hips. I tossed my cap across the room and tugged my braid loose, letting my long hair fall around us. We untied our jackets and dropped them to the floor. My daggers followed. His hand slid up my back, to the nape of my neck, and he clutched my hair in his fingers. I gripped his undershirt in my fists. And it should've been perfect, but it wasn't.

Even though I shut everyone out, we weren't completely alone. My selfishness followed us into the room. It stood in the corner, morphing into the shape of shame and guilt. It begged for my attention, for me to stop and consider the damage I might do by blocking out my team. They were my lifeline, weren't they? My backup so I didn't fail?

That hulking shadow in the corner was stern, frowning, and I could imagine how angry Porter would be with me when I reconnected with him. He'd yelled at me before. Been beyond pissed at me. Before I left on this mission, he told me he trusted my instincts.

How would he trust me now?

Blue tucked his hand up the back of my undershirt, his fingers skimming my bare skin, and I wanted to arch toward him and give him the permission he was waiting for, but the heat between us faltered. The flame guttered, then snuffed out. And suddenly, I was cold.

"I can't do this." I climbed off of him.

He sat up, concerned. "Sousa, if you're not ready…"

"It's not that." I scrambled for an excuse that wouldn't reveal anything about my team, and I came up with one so glaring, so obvious that I felt stupid for forgetting about it in the heat of the moment. "We're not supposed to use these bodies like this, are we? It's against the rules."

Not to mention extremely disrespectful. What if Lo Jie didn't want to do this kind of thing? I was using her body like a puppet to get what I wanted, just like Gesh.

And it made me feel sick.

Blue shook his head, scrubbed his hands over his face. "You're right. I'm sorry. I wasn't even thinking about that." He didn't press me to keep going, didn't push me, just backed down right away, agreeing with me. "When I get around you, my head goes all fuzzy."

"Come here." I wrapped an arm around him, knowing exactly what he meant. "Why are you so good?"

"Remember what I said in Chicago, Sousa? Good is relative."

I should've gone to my room, but I didn't. I didn't want to be alone, and I didn't want to face Porter just yet. I was too ashamed. A coward.

Blue and I curled beside each other, letting ourselves give in to sleep.

A STRANGER

I don't know how long we slept before I awoke. Blue thrashed in his sleep, whimpering, crying out.

"Blue?" I shook his shoulder. "What is it?"

He woke with a start, a sharp breath. His eyes darted around the room, round and frightened. "Where am I? Where have you taken me?" He spoke in English, his voice rough like sandpaper.

I touched his arm. "You're in China. You're on a mission with me, remember?"

"Don't touch me." He snatched his arm away. He scowled at

me like he had in 1876, when we were train robbers, when he was Heath, when he didn't remember who I was.

I lifted my hands, palms out, letting him know I didn't mean any harm.

"Where is he?" Blue demanded.

"Who?"

He leaned forward, his eyes almost maniacal, and he whispered, "The one who uses chains." He rubbed his wrists. "The one who pricks my veins and spills my blood and cuts me open."

The hair on the back of my neck stood on end. I didn't like seeing Blue like this. It scared me. "I don't know what you're talking about."

His eyes narrowed. "Who are you?"

Before I could answer, his body shuddered and collapsed. And then he was asleep again, fitfully so. For what seemed like an hour he thrashed, cried out, shook. I wanted to relieve him of his torment, but I didn't know how, other than to send us both back to Base Life. End the mission. And I wasn't going to do that. Not without the cure for Audrey.

What did that say about me? My willingness to let Blue suffer so I could save my sister?

I held him fast and still, and whispered truths into his ear. "You're safe," I said. "You're strong. You can beat this, whatever it is. I'll find you. You'll be reborn."

He began to repeat me, twitching, his eyes still closed. "Reborn, reborn, reborn, again, again, trapped, trapped, chained, chained."

"Blue?" I reached for his shoulder, but my touch was like a hot coal to him.

He sat up, eyes wide again, and backed away from me to the far corner of the bed. "Don't touch me. Don't touch, don't touch. Don't hurt me."

"I'm not, I wouldn't—"

"Fire, burning, flesh, ash…" Blue wrapped his arms around his knees and rocked back and forth, his eyes locked on something unseen in the corner. "Ash, fire, burning, fire, fire, fire, blood, teeth."

On and on he went, ranting, and I couldn't keep going without Porter's help. I reconnected, and my team toppled into my mind like they were leaning against the door I'd closed, eavesdropping.

What's going on? Porter demanded.

I don't know, I said, panicked. *He's having some sort of attack.*

They were furious, all of them, their anger filling my head like thick flames, but Porter didn't scold me yet. He focused on the task at hand.

Could be his memories seeping through from his time at AIDA, Porter said after listening to Blue.

When we were tortured. When Gesh cut us open and rummaged inside our brains.

What do I do?

Nothing. Let it run its course.

Blue's eyes snapped to mine. He stopped rocking. "Tell me your name."

"What?" I whispered.

He cocked his head to the side, and something terrifying glinted there, deep and dark. "Your *name*." He dragged the word out, and fear slithered around my heart. That's what Gesh's Descender had asked me in 1876, right before he painted a limestone bluff with my blood.

I glanced at my daggers lying on the floor.

"He'll stick it in your eye, you know," Blue said. "He'll stick it in your eye if you're useless for The Cause."

His words felt like poison in my gut. "Who will stick what?"

"It's like an ice pick." Blue pressed a finger into the inner corner of his eye. "Pop!" His eyes danced with fire, and he laughed.

He's talking about a lobotomy, said Porter.

Why the hell is he talking about a lobotomy?

Gesh used to perform them.

Shit, Porter. What's happening to him?

And then suddenly, the fire in Blue's eyes faded, slowly, slowly, until he was rocking again, hugging his knees. He looked smaller, folded in on himself like a wounded child.

It felt like a lifetime, sitting at the end of that bed, watching Blue turn into a cornered, caged animal, then into something fierce and delusional, and then back again, his fear as palpable as the sweat beading across his skin.

But as quickly as it began, it ended.

"Sousa?" The madness in his eyes was gone. His muscles loosened, his arms dropped to his sides. "What are you doing awake?" He crawled over to me and pulled me close, like I was the one needing comfort.

Maybe I was. Now.

He had no idea what had happened. Had no memory of it. I couldn't form words. I let him hold me for a while, but I no longer felt the warmth from before. I was frigid, tense, waiting for it to happen again. For that light to snuff, for Blue to disappear.

At one time I thought of him as the only constant in my life. The one true thing. But Blue wasn't constant. He was the most shifting, changing piece in the entire puzzle. Maybe I never really knew him at all.

Maybe Porter, Levi, and Micki were right. And now I had to go to them, cap in hand, asking for forgiveness.

Porter didn't lay into me until I gathered my things and went to my own room. Until I closed the door and sank against it.

What the hell happened? he boomed. *Why were we disconnected?*

His anger shook within me, and it was all I could do to keep the tears inside. *I'm sorry. I just needed some time alone.*

You did it on purpose? Have I taught you nothing? Any number of things could've happened to you. What if you were soulblocked? We wouldn't be there to help you. You had us worried sick.

I'm sorry. I messed up. I didn't waste my breath justifying myself. There was no defense, only guilt.

Silence. From all of them. Levi the most. It was like he wasn't even there.

Where's Levi?

He disconnected.

Porter didn't have to say why. I knew. Everyone knew. We didn't have to talk about my blindness, my weakness when it came to Blue. Nothing they could say would convince me to knuckle down and fight for this mission. I had to convince myself. I had to stop being such an ass.

Because it wasn't about me and Blue anymore.

Maybe it never was.

MY COPING MECHANISM

The next morning, after a breakfast of steamed pork buns and porridge alone in my room, we boarded the wagon with the other passengers and set out on the second leg of the trip. I sat beside Blue, and our conversation was short and light, if there was any conversation at all. I felt cold and stupid and weird around him now. It wasn't fair to him. He had no idea why I had turned silent and prickly, but he didn't try to pull answers out of me. He let me brood and frown and stare out across the mountains as we rocked and bounced along the top of the ridge. We were at the top of the world, but I felt like I'd fallen to its depths.

At midday the convoy stopped at the shores of a small lake, and Blue and I rested our aching bones beneath the shade of larches and willows. The branches danced and swayed over us. Like my soulmarks, their movements were hypnotic.

As I lay there, I hugged the vase to my side. I knew it wasn't the smartest thing to do, journeying so far with eighty million strapped to my back. I probably should've stashed it somewhere by now, but I couldn't bring myself to part with it. Not until I had the cure and I knew the mission was a success.

Our driver, Zhen, waded into the lake and tossed a net for fish. His bald head glistened in the sun, and his long salt-and-pepper braid dipped in the water as he stooped to work the net. After a while I wandered over to the two old ladies who shared our journey. One sliced sweet potatoes beside the fire and warmed wine in a pot over the flames while the other prepared a stew for the fish. I asked if I could help, and they nodded, smiling.

They put me in charge of boiling rice, which was smart, given my extreme lack of cooking skills. They called me a good boy, a nice boy, and I wondered if I'd crossed some kind of gender barrier, helping with the cooking.

You should be fine, Micki said. *There are definite gender constraints under Confucianism, but on a journey like this everyone is expected to lend a hand.*

The tall, wiry one who used a cane was called Ning. She had very few teeth and long gray hair twisted in a knot. She smiled with her entire face, which was covered in lines, deep creases spiderwebbed across her cheeks and forehead. Mei was smaller and rounder, with white hair covered by a white shawl tied under her chin. She had the same pronounced wrinkles, and after only a few minutes with the both of them I knew the lines had been cultivated from years of belly laughing and squinting in sunlight. They pointed out their husbands, Honqi and Quon, who were scaling Zhen's fish. They were both thin, wispy men, with sinuous muscles and sun-weathered skin. They wore conical hats and scraggly beards.

Blue helped fillet the fish. He laughed along with the other men and seemed to enjoy himself, despite the tension between us. It was nice watching him smile again, hearing his laugh, but I knew it wouldn't last. It could disappear in a split second. And I found I was expecting it, tense, like waiting for a balloon to pop.

Tre, Nick, John, Heath, Tao Jin—they were all suits he wore, chosen from a rack. I knew his face, his hands, his smile, his voice, but I didn't know *him*. Not in the way I once thought I had. And I felt like a fool.

Such a stupid, stupid fool.

Had it all been a fantasy, this portrait of Blue I'd painted in my head? It was like I used him as a warped coping mechanism. He distracted me from real life, from my visions that spiraled out of control, from a dying sister and grieving family, from bullies who forced me into hiding, from the popular boy I didn't think I deserved.

Blue was a way to deal with it all. More escape. More ignorance.

And an ego boost, feeling like someone finally wanted me.

Only he didn't know me. Not at all.

If Lo Jie's independence and self-discipline taught me anything, it was that life was sacrifice. It was work. Only cowards tried to escape it. The strong didn't sit around waiting for life to hand them what they wanted, complaining about their lot—no, they respected themselves enough to work hard and fight for what they deserved.

Death was near. It was time to put away the fantasies and learn to live with myself, with what I'd been given. Truthfully, my life wasn't as bad as I'd imagined. I wasn't alone like Lo Jie; I wasn't sleeping on the streets, wondering when I'd get my next meal. My life was hard, and monumentally screwed up, but wasn't everyone's? I had people around me in Base Life who loved me, protected me. They were steadfast. My foundation of stone. So why was I chasing something so unreliable in the past?

The passengers gathered around the fire, spooning fish stew and sweet potatoes over rice. They told stories about their ancestors and how the hero Pangu created the heavens and earth. Wind was his breath, thunder was his voice, his left eye the sun, his right the moon. I grew heavy and content, listening to the cadence of the language. We drank warm wine and bit into sweet plums and cherries, wiping the juice from our chins. Our lips were stained red from it. Our bellies were full from it. And in the afternoon, we traveled down the other side of the mountain, each of us satisfied, legs stretched out in the wagon, eyes closed, snoozing the rest of the day away.

We'd be at Shang Guan Jian's farm before sundown. If everything went my way, I'd have the cure buried with the vase by morning light.

It was within reach.

If I didn't screw it up.

CHAPTER 20

TRUST

At the bottom of the mountain the path grew too steep, and once again, we were asked to walk behind the wagon.

Blue finally spoke as we picked our way through rocks, sliding on loose dirt. "You've been distant today. Did I do something wrong?"

I was quiet for a while, focusing on my footfalls, looking for the right words. My faith in him had faltered. It was as shifting and unstable as the gravel beneath our feet, but I wasn't sure how to tell him, or how to sift through all the questions circling in my head. At last I said, "How much can you remember, Blue? How much, really? You don't have to spare my feelings. You can tell me everything, unless it hurts too much to talk about."

"What do you mean? Why would it hurt?"

"You were talking in your sleep last night."

His eyes darkened. "What did I say?"

"You were terrified. You kept telling me not to hurt you and talking about fire and chains and an ice pick in your eye. I think you were remembering our time at AIDA, when Gesh tortured us."

His jaw clenched. "I don't remember saying any of that."

"Do you remember our life at AIDA? Do you remember the terrible things he did to us? Does it plague you? Is that why you have nightmares?"

"No." His voice was flat. "I don't remember any of it."

I stopped walking. "I don't believe you."

He stopped too, and looked at me, hard. "You think I'm lying to you? After all we've been through, you don't trust me?"

"I'm worried about you, that's all. I want to try to help, if I can."

"This isn't helping. This is prying."

"So now I'm prying? I thought you wanted me to help you remember. I thought you wanted me to find you."

He shook his head at me, disappointed. "You're not trying to find me. You're trying to sort out if you can trust me with this mission of yours. It's clearly more important than us, whatever it is."

"It is important. I wouldn't be here if it wasn't."

"Yeah, and I've been helping you. I've journeyed all this way for you, and you still haven't told me why or where we're going. I've trusted you all this time. Isn't that worth something?"

"It isn't up to me. There are others who—"

Porter's voice snaked into my head. *Don't mention others.*

"What others?" Blue asked, narrowing his eyes. "Others back in Base Life? Are you working with someone?"

Shut it down, Porter said. *Not another word.*

I bit my lip so words wouldn't tumble out at my feet.

Blue frowned, glanced away. "Maybe I was stupid to trust you."

It was like a kick in the gut, hearing him say that. "Please don't be like that."

"Like what? Sensible?" His eyes were fiery. Dark. Like they were last night in his room. "How can you ask me to trust you when you won't trust me in return? If this thing is one-sided, then you're just using me."

"I'm not, I swear." I stepped toward him but he didn't welcome my approach. "I like having your help, I'm not ashamed to admit that. But I like spending time with you, too, whatever we're doing. You have no idea how frustrating it is not sharing things with you. And I want to trust you, I do. I just don't trust who might be using you."

"Using me?"

"In Base Life."

"No one's using me, Alex."

"How would you know? If you can't remember?"

He sighed. Clenched his teeth. His fists. "I just know." Anger rolled off him as he stalked away down the mountain. Leaving me standing there alone, regret burning my stomach.

Focus on the cure, Porter said. *Your sister.*

Porter was right. If I were allowed to explain things to Blue, maybe he'd understand my mission and how important it was. But that wasn't possible. Maybe later, in our next life, I could make amends.

At least, that's what I told myself.

Audrey had to come first. I had to save her one and only life. I had a race to finish. And if that meant leaving Blue behind in order to win, then so be it.

CAPTURE THE FLAG

Shang Guan Jian's farm was nestled among a sweeping expanse of little green hills, hidden between the mountains. Cows and sheep roamed the grounds freely, nibbling the grass. His hut sat in the sun on one of the hills, almost completely obscured by flowering shrubs and vines. We found Jian tending to his garden, wearing a simple dark coat and pants, tied at the waist with a thin rope, a conical hat perched on his head. A thin gray mustache curved down to meet a long goatee, wispy and wiry. His skin was brown and sagged with deep lines, smeared with sweat and dirt, but when he smiled his whole face lit up, and you couldn't help smiling in return.

He took us into his hut, one by one, and each person came out with an amber bottle clutched in their hands, hope in their eyes. I waited until last, leaning against the wagon, arms crossed, trying to keep my anxiety in check. To my surprise, Blue went in after Ning, and remained inside for quite a while. He emerged empty-handed and joined the other passengers, never once glancing in my direction. When it was my turn, I slipped inside with shaking hands, my nerves betraying me.

Jian's house was dark and cool. Bunches of dried grasses and flowers hung from the ceiling. Jian was so short he could probably walk through the hut without ducking, but I had to stoop to find my way to the back, where he waited.

He stood behind a long wooden table covered with fist-sized piles of wrinkled roots, dried berries, leaves, and mushrooms, shaved bark, seeds of every size and shape, and dozens of tiny bowls with different-colored powders. There were intricate wooden boxes with compartments filled with different types of tea leaves. There was a mortar and pestle. And behind him, rows and rows of glass jars filled with the same kinds of ingredients.

Jian stood quietly, his weathered hands folded before him, waiting for me to explain why I'd come. I told him I had a sister, young, and listed her symptoms, the ones Porter read in the ancient Chinese text, the ones Audrey suffered from every day. I had only mentioned three or four when he thrust an amber bottle into my hands.

It couldn't be that easy. He had to know all of her symptoms. He couldn't possibly know exactly what I needed. Not yet.

I hurried on. "She bruises easily, and bleeds without clotting."

He nodded more vigorously and pushed the bottle at me.

Take it, Porter said. *He knows what you mean.*

I took it. Tucked it inside the vase and rewrapped my pack across my chest. I placed my fist to my palm and bowed to Jian. He smiled, then motioned for the door. I turned to go, but realized I hadn't paid him.

"I owe you money," I said, glancing at my daggers. I wondered if he'd take them as payment.

He shook his head. "Your brother paid for you."

Blue.

I closed my eyes, guilt washing over me. Even though we'd argued, he still covered for me. I hoped Micki and Porter were paying attention. Those weren't the actions of a traitor.

Outside, I found Zhen milling around the wagon, tending to his horses, but Blue and the others were nowhere to be seen. "Tao Jin?" I asked Zhen, and he nodded toward the trees beyond Jian's farm fields. I headed for them, thinking the forest might provide the perfect hiding place for the cure.

The shade was welcome. Beneath the silver birches and oaks, I smelled something fresh, felt a cool breeze on my face, heard water gurgling and churning.

A new goal crept its way to the forefront of Lo Jie's mind.

Thirst.

The forest floor sloped downward, and at the bottom of the bank there was an area of smooth, flat, white rock the size of a football field, with a crooked line of gushing water flowing through it. I stepped down the bank, my feet sinking into soft soil and leaves left over from winter. The other members of my convoy were there, wandering about the creek bed, stretching their legs and backs. Honqi and Quon were fishing with wooden poles in a deep pool off the bank. Ning and Mei were squatting by the creek, washing their jackets by rubbing the fabric against the smooth stones.

I didn't see Blue.

If he needed time to himself, I wanted to give it to him, just like he gave to me. I didn't want to push him away or force him to talk when he wasn't ready.

I knelt at the edge of the water for a drink and splashed the dust from my face. After I drank my fill and the ripples settled, I saw Lo Jie's reflection for the first time. Her face was oval, her lips full and pink, her cheekbones high and sharp, her dark eyes fierce. She was a natural beauty, wild and willowy. I didn't see much of myself in her, except for her button nose and square chin. Out of all the bodies I'd been in, she was the most different from me, both in appearance and personality. Maybe that's why I liked being in her shoes so much.

I walked along the smooth rock, stepping over driftwood and scrubby weeds, following the water downstream and out of sight. I wound around a few bends until I was completely alone in the vast China wilderness. The gentle, soft soil bank on my left grew steadily steeper into a jagged, rocky bluff. There were crags and crevices, high above the flood line, that would make a perfect resting place for the remedy for centuries to come. Cask Carter had taught me how to hide loot back in 1876. He stashed his train-robbing spoils all across the Midwest where only bats and birds might find them.

I let Lo Jie pick her way up the side of the bluff, using her lean strength and nimble body to pull myself to a thin ledge near the top. The wind swirled around me, tugging loose strands of hair from my braid. I rested the vase and the remedy, still wrapped securely in the cloth pack, in a crevice shaped like a crescent moon. I tucked it beneath a blanket of moss and twigs, then stood on the ledge, chin up, chest out, closed my eyes, breathed in, and felt a rush of freedom sweep through me as strong as the wind.

You did it, Porter said. The pride in his voice made my chest swell. *You captured the flag. You won.*

Part of me wanted to ascend to Limbo right then and there, but I had to return Jie's body to Beijing so I wouldn't make an impact. I had two more nights before I could close this mission, and I didn't know how I was going to last that long. I was so anxious to get back to Audrey. To set her free from her cage.

As I breathed in and out, I went through the movements of the Seven Star Fist, slowly, letting Jie lull me into a meditative state, calming my anxiety. Every move was so detailed; every one of my muscles engaged with purpose. Squatting, bending, breathing, stretching my leg up to touch my cheek, it all worked together to focus my body and free my mind. The moves reminded me of practicing yoga with Mom and Gran on Sunday afternoons. The bow stance was like the warrior pose, which had always been my favorite. I felt so strong in that pose, like anything could come at me.

Now I felt it even more so.

I once heard someone describe kung fu as meditation in motion. Now I understood what that meant. It was control and freedom and relaxation all in one. And once Audrey was healthy again, I'd teach her everything Jie knew. Maybe it would be something we could do together, something for her to hold onto when I'm gone, something for her to remember me by.

· · ·

SURROUNDED

When the sun skimmed the treetops, gold and glittering, I finally climbed down from the bluff and headed back to Jian's. I must not have been gone as long as I thought because all of my journeymates were exactly as I had left them by the water's edge. Honqi and Quon were still fishing on the other side of creek. I crouched beside Ning and Mei, who were still washing their garments, to give my own jacket a rinse.

As I pulled off my jacket, I glanced around again for Blue. I was worried about him. I felt awful about our argument, and somewhat responsible for his tortured existence. He was plagued with nightmares, had endless memories from past lives coming and going without warning, and a girl he thought he could trust dragging him across time at her every whim. It made me feel sick to think about. It made me angry that I couldn't do a damn thing about it, not in this life.

But maybe in the next.

Micki and Porter had been surprisingly silent the entire afternoon. They had let me meditate and they didn't try to talk me out of my concern for Blue. It was refreshing. I enjoyed my little patch of alone time at the water's edge, soaking my jacket and rubbing it against stone.

"Am I doing this right?" I asked Ning.

She didn't respond.

I glanced at her and Mei. They stared straight ahead, slack-jawed, jerking their jackets back and forth against the rocks like they'd forgotten how to use their hands.

"Ning?" The word came out as little more than a whisper. Something was so very wrong with the whole scene. My body knew it before my brain did; my mouth was bone dry.

Ning turned her head my way, cocked to the side, but she left her gaze behind, still staring down at her hands. Then her eyes snapped to mine, her movements disjointed and frightening. It was like watching an alien trapped in a human's body, unsure how to use its new vessel.

That's when I scrambled backwards to my feet, my heart thudding in my throat.

Descender, I hissed to Porter.

Get out of there, now!

I tried to lift my soul to Limbo, arcing upward, but it was too late. I was already under a soulblock.

CHAPTER 21

TRAPPED

Break through, break through! Porter shouted, but my shock was too great. It rooted me to the ground, cementing my focus on the Descender rising to her feet before me, twisting Ning's lips into a cruel snarl.

I had no idea how they found me—my mind whirled with questions, but I didn't have time to think it through. With a swift hand, Ning swung her cane at me. I bent backwards, the cane grazing my chest as it flew past.

Don't fight, just get out of there.

Easy for him to say—he wasn't the one blocking blows from a cane with his forearms. If I couldn't concentrate to help Porter break the soulblock then I had to fight my way free and run, run until the soulblock was out of range. And if I wanted to save this mission, I had to do it without killing anyone.

That meant keeping my daggers at my hips. I didn't want to take any chances.

The next time Ning raised her cane above me, I grabbed her arm, twisted it around to her back, and locked her shoulder. Then I twisted harder, dropping her to the ground. She collapsed, clutching her arm, wailing out in pain.

That's enough, Porter said. *Now run.*

I turned to race back toward the farm, but that's when Mei awoke from her zombie-like state and charged me.

Two Descenders.

The moves burst out of me, my arms waving, my feet shuffling forward and back, side to side, as I deflected her jabs and punches.

My forearms were iron bars. My hands were shields. All of my meditation moves were there, fluid, natural, as automatic as breathing. I threw a kick into her chest. Down she went, smacking her head on the smooth rock under our feet, and I knelt over her to see if she was OK. She was still breathing, but she'd have a nasty headache.

I started for the creek, hoping to leap across and disappear into the forest beyond, but Quon and Honqi lifted their fishing poles with a roar and came at me, splashing across the stepped falls. They charged at me like madmen. I turned again toward the farm, but Jian and Zhen raced down the bank, each armed with a shepherd's whip.

Six Descenders. How was that possible?

I tried to ascend again, but it didn't work. The soulblock was too strong.

There are too many, I told Porter. *I can't break through.*

Quon and Honqi reached me first, their pants dripping with water. They spun and sliced their poles through the air, and I jumped and kicked my way through the barrage. Quon swept his pole down and around, and I threw myself back against the earth, missing the blow, then sprang up in the same movement. I drove a kick into the softness of his belly, and as he stumbled backwards I twisted the pole out of his fingers. Using it like a pole vault, I struck it into the ground, lifted myself into the air, and threw my feet into Honqi's chest. He flew backwards and onto the rock. Standing over him, I dropped my knee onto his thigh, power driving down as I channeled my chi through my knee. He reached for his leg, crying out in pain, and I turned back to finish the rest.

Alex, you have to concentrate. You have to get out of there.

Porter didn't realize what he was asking of me. How impossible it was. My brain was full of fight; there was no room for anything else. I was too busy battling them, one by one, sometimes several at a time. Whips whizzing past my ears, my body bending and flexing and turning. There was no time to concentrate, no time to meld my energy with my team's and break through the soulblock.

Instead, I fought with all my might, until they were all writhing on the ground.

"You're good."

I turned around, and Ning stood behind me. She spoke in English, her voice dry and flat. "They said you would be, but you're just a little girl. How good can you really be?"

My eyes narrowed. I wanted to make her pay for that remark. I lowered into a deep squat and smacked the pole against the ground with a yell that said, *come at me, bro.*

She did, cane held high.

She jabbed and I smacked. I stabbed and she sliced. I swept the pole at her feet, but she jumped. I sliced at her neck, but she bent backwards. She sliced back at mine, and I leaned to the side, expecting to feel the swish of air on my skin.

Instead, I felt the crack of wood across my collarbone. Saw a flash of light, heard the bone break. I dropped to my knees and fell to my side, clutching the injury, eyes squeezed shut.

It wasn't a gunshot, but it hurt like one.

The Descender stood over me, hunched in Ning's withered body, her sweet face marred by the Descender's scowl.

"Why don't you just kill me?" I said, wishing I had the tiniest bit of strength left over to beat the Descender senseless.

A slight smile flickered at the corner of Ning's mouth. "I didn't come to kill you, *Nummer Fire.* I came to deliver a message."

I clenched my teeth. "Then deliver it."

Something sinister flickered in Ning's eyes as she stared at me, watching my blood draw red lines between my fingers. Then, as quick as a snake strike, she reached for one of my daggers, pulled it out, and plunged it into my belly.

Blood pooled in the crook of my stomach. The mission was lost, and Gesh's message was loud and clear.

I can't win.

It was like a punch in the gut at first, deep and dull, bringing tears to my eyes, but then it burned, burned so badly I wanted to give up everything right then and there. Let death take me. But I couldn't. If I died in the past, under a soulblock, my soul would ascend straight to Afterlife. My body back in Base Life would be empty, cold, and lifeless in the dentist chair. My family would have to bury me, and I couldn't do that to them right now, not with Audrey still in the hospital.

Not without a proper goodbye.

With her message delivered, Ning's eyes rolled back into her head. I felt the Descenders rise to Limbo, and the snap of their soulblock, freeing me. Before Ning regained consciousness, before I could see the shock and bewilderment on her face, I sprang to Limbo, fleeing the scene. I had to do a touchdown before everything carved itself into stone.

THE TRAITOR

"What happened?" Porter says when we land back on the boat after the touchdown. "Why didn't you break the soulblock?" He's pointing the blame at me, but I'm not at fault. Not this time.

"There were six of them," I say, catching my breath, pressing a hand to my stomach, relieved to find no sign of blood. "The soulblock was too strong."

Micki shakes her head. "This wasn't part of the plan."

Yeah, no shit.

I scowl at her. "Seems to me it went exactly as planned."

She stops pulling wires from her skin and sits up in her chair. "Excuse me?"

I square my shoulders and narrow my eyes, like Bacall. "How long have you been in Gesh's pocket? Since the day you left AIDA? Or did he get to you recently?"

She looks at me like I've grown a second nose. "What the hell are you insinuating?"

"There's no way Gesh could've tracked me to that exact moment and place in time. He'd have to know intimate details of my mission, details no one outside this room could've known. The exact day I'd leave, the exact age I'd be when I descended, which convoy I'd take out of Beijing, and who I'd be traveling with. Porter said Gesh needs weeks, months, sometimes years to find specific soulmarks in Limbo. Someone tipped him off. You kept pointing the finger at Blue, insisting he was the traitor. That should've been my first clue. But Blue didn't know any of the specifics until he was there with me. He couldn't have known beforehand, which means Gesh couldn't have ambushed me without *your* help."

Micki's claws come out. "You've got some nerve."

"Tell me I'm wrong."

"You ungrateful little…" She trails off, but my eyes match hers, dagger for dagger.

"Go ahead. Say it."

Her nostrils flare, but she doesn't explode. She doesn't say one word to me. She stalks over to Porter, leans in and says, "I tried to make it work," then leaves without a glance back, slamming the door.

"Micki," Porter calls out, but she doesn't return. He groans and rakes his hands across his short white hair. "What do you think you're doing?" he says to me. "She works for *us*."

"Then tell me how Gesh knew. Tell me how it's possible, how Blue could've possibly tipped him off in real time, during the mission. How Gesh had time to find each one of those soulmarks: Zhen, Quon, Honqi, Jian, Mei, Ning. Explain it to me, and I'll go apologize to her right now."

The muscles in Porter's jaw work as he thinks, scrambling to come up with something, anything to prove Micki's innocence.

"That's what I thought," I say, crossing my arms.

"Levi?" Porter says, nodding in Micki's direction. Levi goes after her, most likely to smooth things over. They should be trying to smooth things over with me. I'm the one who was betrayed. Stabbed and left for dead.

Porter rubs the bridge of his nose. "If Micki were working for Gesh, she would've handed me over to him long ago."

"Maybe it's me he wants, not you."

"Then don't you think she would've handed you over by now, too? Instead of working with you? Helping you?"

I shrug. "Maybe she wanted to watch them hurt me. Maybe

this is just another way for Gesh to torture me, I don't know. But I do know she doesn't like me, so it makes sense that she's the one working against me."

"She doesn't have to like you to be loyal. She believes in your ability. She knows what you can do. That's enough for her. We are your team, Alex. We're on your side."

"No, *you're* my team. You alone. And we need to get back to work. I need to go back to China."

"Back?"

"Right now. Take another convoy to another healer. Gesh won't see it coming. He won't be prepared like he was this time."

"You can't go back. Now that he knows you're after that cure, he'll keep that timeline secure. He'll station Descenders there. He'll have soulblocks all across Beijing. It'll be a minefield."

"Then we do what I wanted all along. We go back to 1978 to retrieve the case study files."

Porter shakes his head. "I don't know…"

My body shivers with frustration, anger, as I try to scramble over the obstacles thrown in my way. "I don't need your permission. I'll do it alone if I have to. It's the only chance I've got left, if Audrey holds out long enough."

"That's not what I meant. The seventies mission is dangerous. You don't know the details yet."

I give him a look. "I've done dangerous before."

He shakes his head. "Not this dangerous."

"Porter, I've been shot, stabbed, and almost strangled to death. What could possibly be worse than what I've already gone through?"

Porter's pale, watery eyes meet mine, and he frowns. "The Mafia."

CHAPTER 22

PREPARATIONS

For the next week, I'm like a caged animal, pacing back and forth in my pen, foaming at the mouth, ready to get back out there. I don't care how dangerous my next mission is. I'll walk through fire to get Audrey what she needs.

Which is exactly what I'll be doing.

As I left Porter's, he gave me a thin file on my past life in 1978. I've gone over every inch. In the life before I was Ivy at AIDA, I was Janet McKenzie, one of the many daughters of a New York City mobster. An internet search on James "Jimmy" McKenzie brings up thousands of results about his misdeeds and one very chilling mug shot. Sagging, glaring eyes, and a vicious expression that makes goosebumps bloom across my arms. He was the type of guy who chopped up ex-girlfriends and tossed their pieces across their mothers' front yards. He was the type of guy who locked little kids in refrigerators to coerce their parents into paying their debts. Porter was right when he said the mission is dangerous. I'll be heading straight into the lion's den, right into the middle of a mob family without the proper training. The family's instinct is distrust. The slightest suspicious look or remark could get a knife to my throat.

So I've got to do my research. Alone this time. Without Micki.

The only problem is, there isn't much. Not on Janet anyway. She's this obscure kid, only mentioned now and then along with Jimmy's other children, and usually described as crazy. There's a copy of a letter from one of her siblings recounting a night when they found her wandering down their street stark naked. I frown, feeling bad for her. Living in a family like hers would definitely make someone go insane.

She died when she was seventeen, obviously, but no one knows how or why, and there's no exact date. The history records have forgotten all about her. And that makes the goosebumps rise too.

Is Jimmy the kind of guy who murders his own daughter, then covers it up?

There are a few scribbles in Micki's handwriting on sticky notes inside the file. After reading a couple, it looks like she was working on Janet's cause of death, trying to complete the records.

When had Micki made the notes? Before I met her? Or did she start working on them after I told her about my plans to retrieve the lost data? Would she tell Gesh what I was trying to do? Had she already? Would his Descenders be waiting for me?

One of the notes catches my eye. Three words: *Ypsilanti State Hospital.*

A memory flashes through my mind. It was no ordinary hospital; it was an asylum, plain and simple. I remember walking the halls, the long corridors stretching out as far as I could see. Me, shuffling along in slippers, a nurse guiding me to my room. Moving slowly, so slowly a spider could spin a web from my shoulder to the ceiling. My mind blank, my emotions dulled.

It isn't a welcome memory.

Micki said I would start remembering my past lives. I guess she was right.

On Saturday morning, I'm pulled away from more Janet McKenzie research by a knock on the front door. It's Jensen, grinning like a loon. I completely forgot I promised we'd work on his car today. His shaggy hair is tucked under his beanie. His black jacket hangs open over a faded flannel shirt and fitted white henley. I shake my head as we head to the garage, wondering if he knows how perfect he always looks.

Knowing him, he does.

• • •

ERASING THE LINES

"Try it now," I say, peering around the hood of Jensen's Corolla.

He turns the ignition, and the car rumbles to life. His eyes light up through the grimy windshield. "You did it."

"Yeah, but we're not done yet." There's a wheezing sound coming from the fuel injectors, and the belts are whining more than Claire when she doesn't get her way. "There's still a lot of work to do before she's ready to race."

He cuts the engine and climbs out of the driver's seat to join me under the hood. I flatten myself across the engine and the mess of tubes and connectors, reaching down to the timing belt. My fingers run along its frayed length. "This needs replacing. It's too brittle to last much longer. Can you hand me that socket wrench over there?"

He slides between me and the workbench, his hand grazing the side of my hip as he squeezes past. It's the third time he's touched me like that this afternoon, and it's starting to weird me out. Earlier, when he handed me a pair of pliers, his fingers brushed mine in a way that seemed intentional. Especially when he could've just dropped them in my hand. Then later, we bumped into each other as we both rounded the front fender at the same time. I raised my arms so I wouldn't get grease on his shirt and squeezed by on my tiptoes. He, on the other hand, placed both hands on my waist and "helped" guide me past. I didn't think friends touched each other like that, but I'm not exactly well versed in the friendship realm. He probably doesn't mean anything by it. He probably touches all the girls like that. But even so, each time it happens, I become hyperaware of him, hypersensitive to his touch, and lose my concentration. I can still feel that spot on my hip like he seared a mark on my skin.

"How long will it take to replace it?" He hands me the wrench, then leans back against the workbench, resting his elbows on it.

"Not long." I loosen the alternator bolts to I can get to the timing belt pulleys. "We can do it Saturday, no prob. Should only take a few minutes."

When he doesn't say anything for a while, I glance over my

shoulder and totally catch him staring at my butt. He snaps his eyes to the garage ceiling and rubs the back of his neck like nothing happened, but I know what I saw. I stand up so fast, so surprised to catch anyone, let alone Jensen, checking out my Base Life body, that I smack my head against the hood, drop the wrench, and spit out one very long, very bad word.

Jensen leaps to my side. "You OK?"

I press my hand to the top of my head, feeling a bump forming, biting my lip.

Jensen snares me around the waist. "Let me look at it," he says, trying to pull my hand down.

I don't want him to look at it. I don't want to drop my hand, because pressing it against the pain is the only thing keeping me from stringing another long line of profanities together. And I don't want him to stand so close or have his arm around my waist. It's too dangerous.

I wriggle out of his grasp and put some distance between us. "I'm fine. It's nothing."

"What happened? What spooked you?"

"You did. You were checking me out." Maybe it's the pain, I don't know, but something inside doesn't want to filter everything I say anymore.

"So? I check you out all the time." He gives me this wry smile and steps closer, but I back away and bump into the workbench. "What's the big deal, Wayfare? We're both hot. It's only natural to want to enjoy the view now and then."

I can't decipher if he's really saying what I think he's saying, or if I've knocked my head so hard I'm hallucinating. "Did you just say I was hot?"

"You make it sound like that's news."

"It is news. I'm not...I mean...no one ever..."

"You can't be serious."

I stare at him, my head swimming, my eyes watering from the pain. Is *he* being serious? No guy, not ever, has told me I was hot, or beautiful, or attractive in any way, shape, or form while in my Base

Life body. And as completely pathetic as it sounds, I've wanted to feel the tiniest bit desirable for such a long time. In my own skin. As Alex, not as Susan or Shooter or Lo Jie. And here's Jensen, one of the hottest guys at South View High School, saying *I'm* hot. He must be teasing.

"I've been checking you out for years. You're telling me you just now noticed?"

"I…"

He reaches for me. "Let me look at it."

I step up to him, frowning, making sure he sees I'm frowning, and drop my hand. I don't like the way he flirts with me when he knows I have a boyfriend, and I really don't like the way I enjoy it. I can't slip up and let him think I'm into it. Into him. The way he moves and touches me, with all his confident moxie, like no girl on earth would refuse him. I frown even harder, my expression reaching scowl territory.

"Smashed up pretty good there, Wayfare. You need ice."

He guides me to the house and into the kitchen, opening doors for me along the way. Gray winter light seeps in through the windows, and soft, grainy shadows sit in the corners of the room. All is quiet as he snags an ice pack from the freezer and hands it to me. I sit on one of the barstools at the kitchen island, ice pack pressed to my head, frowning down at a crusted splatter of spaghetti sauce on the counter from the night before.

"Did Gran run to the store?" Jensen asks, looking around.

I shrug. "I guess."

"So we're alone?"

My breath hitches in my chest. The smack on my head must've knocked me into an alternate reality, one where everything Jensen says makes my stomach do a backflip. Or maybe I've descended back in time, before I met Blue, when Jensen was the only boy I ever thought about. "I guess," I say again.

He leans against the counter beside me, his arm brushing against mine. "How long do you think she'll be?"

I shrug again. "Ten, fifteen minutes?"

"Plenty of time to do the dirty."

My eyes snap to his. "What?"

"Dishes." He laughs and heads toward a stack on the counter. He fills one side of the sink with sudsy water.

"Oh." My shoulders slump. I totally thought he was going to make a move. The move I could feel coming, inching closer each day. The move I didn't know I wanted him to make until right that instant, when disappointment filled my chest.

Turns out he just wanted to do something nice for Gran.

What the hell is wrong with me? I toss the ice pack back in the freezer and join him at the sink, working grease from my hands under a stream of warm water. I don't need ice. I need pain. I need a throbbing headache. Anything to distract me from my few moments alone with Jensen.

He scrubs at a plate, and I grab the spray nozzle, press the trigger, and shoot it full-blast in my side of the sink. My frustration eases slightly.

Jensen hands me the squeaky-clean plate, I spray off the suds, then I place it in the dish rack to dry. Again and again, he passes me a dish and I blast it with water. Killing the bubbles. Dulling the thrill that dared bloom inside me a moment ago.

I'm a horrible person.

Blue deserves better.

And maybe I'll be better the next time around. In my next life. I'll write a letter, give it to Porter for safekeeping. I'll remind my future self to find Blue and apologize to him for all the hell I've put him through.

"I can pick up a new timing belt after school tomorrow," Jensen says.

I nod and blast more suds. Warm mist sticks to my cheeks. My forearms. The kitchen windowpane.

"What time should I get here next Saturday?" he asks.

"Whenever." *Blast, blast, blast.*

"Ten?"

"Sure." *Blast, blast.*

"Anything else I should pick up?" He hands me a bowl this time.

"A new fuel injector wouldn't hurt, but I'll try cleaning this one first. Sometimes they just get gunky. That would save you about sixty bucks." I spray the bowl and balance it behind the plates.

"Yeah, cool. That sounds good."

There's all this awkward silence between us, and I hate it, and I hate myself, and I'm frowning so hard at the dishes I could probably scare the dirt and grime straight down the drain.

When I turn back toward him to grab the next dish, he leans down and touches his mouth to mine. Softly. Barely. Lightning quick. Just like that.

Everything stops. My breath, my heartbeat, my whirring mind, my throbbing head.

My pent-up frustration dissolves on his lips.

He gives me this sheepish look, like he's worried I might be upset. But when I don't scold him or push him away, or do that frown-scowling thing, he leans in again. He kisses me softly, gentle and sweet, but then, before I know it, I'm caught up in his arms.

And it's good. Oh, is it good. Better than I ever imagined.

His hands are soapy and wet, and the water soaks through the back of my shirt, but I don't care.

It isn't perfect and effortless and fluid like it is with Blue. It's awkward, and our mouths don't move in rhythm. It feels childish, almost, like two kids trying it out for the first time. But that doesn't mean I want it to end. It feels like jumping from a tire swing into the water, like finally having the courage to let go, fall through the air, and trust yourself enough to go under.

My first real kiss in my own skin.

He stole it, but I'd never dream of asking him to give it back. It belongs to him now, and that's fine by me.

On the surface, I'd kept the lines of our friendship clearly drawn. But down deep, way down in the shadowy places of my heart, behind doors I've been too afraid to open, the lines are smudged. And even though I pretend, even though I hope, there are no constants when it comes to Blue. Just the ebb and flow of variables, rubbing against the constant that is Jensen. Blue is a sea of unruly waves, choppy one moment, still as glass the next. Jensen is a stone, weathered, maybe, but always solid, firm, there. The same. It's one thing that keeps me grounded. One thing that keeps me from losing my ever-loving mind. And each time Blue changes direction, he wears away the truth, smearing those thick black lines until there is only gray.

Do I pull out a Sharpie and re-ink the lines? Or do I wrap myself in gray?

My thoughts tip and turn, warring over whether I should stop kissing Jensen. Maybe it should be an easy decision. Maybe it would be for anyone else. Technically, I'm still with Blue, at least until I get a chance to talk to him, explain why I'm giving up, why I need to move on right now, and that maybe we can pick back up in the next life. That's why my body is tense, my hands curled into fists as my lips melt into Jensen's, half of me wanting, half of me angry.

Angry at both of us.

My body makes the decision for me. I'm still holding the spray nozzle. My angry fist closes around the trigger, and Jensen and I are blasted apart by a stream of water. He jumps back, completely soaked, jaw dropped, hands out, looking at me like I shot him.

"What was that for?" He swipes water from his face, laughing, thinking I meant it as a joke, or maybe an accident.

But honestly, I think it was the only way my subconscious could stop what was happening.

"I have a boyfriend." I say it firm, lay it right out there.

His playful expression clouds over. "Come on, Wayfare."

"Come on what?"

"We're not at school. You don't have to keep pretending about the boyfriend thing."

At first it takes a minute to realize what he just said. Then I feel sick, like when Audrey and I used to ride the Tilt-a-Whirl at the county fair. My stomach churns, my hands shake, and I'm tempted to spray him again. "You think I'm making him up?"

"Aren't you?"

I've never felt truly mortified until this very moment. I thought Jensen was my friend, but this feels like something Tabitha would do. This feels like the worst kind of high school humiliation, like his friendship and flirting was simply setting up the pins so he could knock them down.

"I think you need to leave." I move toward the kitchen door.

"If you have a boyfriend, then where is he? Why isn't he here instead of me? If he's so real, why doesn't your family know about him?"

I stop and spin around. "How do you know my family doesn't know about him?"

"I asked Audrey."

And the hits just keep on coming. "You talked to Audrey about me? Behind my back?"

"At the hospital, when you were in the bathroom, I just asked her if you had a boyfriend. She said no. I thought you told her everything. I just figured—"

"You figured what? That I couldn't possibly get a boyfriend? Because I'm Wayspaz the Fix-It Freak?"

His brow furrows. "That's not at all what I'm saying."

I grab his coat from the rack by the door and shove it against his chest. "You really need to leave."

He looks hurt and pitiful, water dripping from his hair onto his forehead, but I'm too angry to care. As he leaves, the door closes on yet another perceived friendship, yet another betrayal. First Micki, now Jensen. I sink to the floor, sobbing into my hands.

Growing close to people—it's just not worth it.

They all let you down in the end.

CHAPTER 23

VULTURES

I force myself back to school on Monday for an English test, but it ends up being a waste, because I fail it.

I stalk through the halls, my anger a long, thick robe trailing behind me. It hunches my shoulders. Sags my skin. Makes me scowl at everyone, even Irene, the sweet old janitor who brings me homemade cranberry-orange muffins when I'm in the AV lab, and chats with me about her grandkids and her horses.

I'm angry at Jensen, for waiting to make a move after I was already taken, for humiliating me. I'm angry at Blue, for being this elusive ghost, haunting me, making me doubt this thing we had, whatever it was. I'm angry that I had to leave before we could reconcile. Instead, the last words we shared were spoken in anger. I'm angry at Micki, for leading me right into the lion's den, for knocking my sister's cure right out of my hands. But mostly, I'm angry at myself. And I want to give up, end my existence and move on to the next, but I have to hang on a little while longer, until I exhaust every option for Audrey.

During lunch, I hunch over the stack of fried DVD players Mrs. Latimer left for me, grumbling to myself like a little old witch over her potion pot.

"It isn't worth it, you know, spending your days in a rage."

I look up and Levi is standing at the AV counter. I have no idea how long he's been there.

"Did you come here to talk me out of my anger?" I say, stripping a wire with a little more force than needed. "Remind me again to live my life to the fullest? Be happy?"

"No. Even though that's what I want for you. I came to say I understand. For most of my life, I lived with that rage. It was all I knew, and it almost destroyed me, until I learned to channel it and aim it where it belonged."

"Micki's a traitor, Levi."

"Even if you were right, which I don't think you are, Gesh would still be the one to blame. Not her."

"I'm happy to blame both of them, thank you very much." My sister is dying. Doesn't he understand that? And it's Micki's fault I don't have a cure in my hands right now. How can he stand here and defend her?

"I've worked with her for a long time. She's loyal to us. Always has been. If she had defected, I would've noticed."

I drop a few dots of solder on the wire and cement it in place. "You accused me of having a blind spot when it comes to Blue. I think you have a blind spot when it comes to her."

He frowns, places his hands flat on the counter. "I hate seeing you like this. I wish there were something I could do."

I look at him, dead on. "You could believe me."

We're interrupted by a group of kids passing through the AV room into the computer lab for next period. Robbie Duncan is among them. When he notices Levi and me talking, he laces his hands behind his head and thrusts his pelvis, moaning.

I scowl at him, wishing the heat of my glare could melt his skin off.

"You better go," I say to Levi. "The vultures are circling."

ASSHOLE DICK FACE

Hidden within my fog of fury, it totally slips my mind that there's a college fair in the gym today. My entire pre-calc class is excused to attend, and everyone is fired up and excited to skip class and grab brochures from their dream universities.

The gym is packed. The murmuring voices drone in my ears. I

wander through the booths, honing my scowling skills, thinking how college is a waste of time for a time-traveling girl with a time bomb strapped to her chest.

At the end of one of the aisles, Tabitha sits at a booth with her other drama club members. They're holding a raffle to raise money for their spring production of *Mamma Mia*. I wouldn't care, except Robbie walks up to her booth and says, "Wow, Tab, is that Resting Bitch Face, or are you just happy to see me?"

She scowls at him with almost as much venom as I did earlier, and folds her pink-manicured hands on the table. "I'd rather have Resting Bitch Face than Asshole Dick Face."

I can't help but laugh out loud. Maybe Tabitha isn't all bad.

But my laugh makes Robbie turn his juvenile dickery on me. "Hey, Wayspaz. I heard a rumor today. Want to know what it is?"

I roll my eyes and keep walking, because whatever he has to say to me is so not worth my time. He doesn't notice my disdain. Either that or he doesn't care.

He falls into step beside me. "Everyone says you've been spending a lot of time with Mr. Sorenson. Alone."

I ignore him, but there's a group of kids in my way, lined up at the George Washington University booth, and I have to stop.

Robbie steps in front of me. "Know what we all think? We think you're banging a teacher during the week, and Peters on the weekends."

I don't even flinch. Nothing he could say would shock me. Nothing any of them could say would knock me off my axis. Not anymore. I turn back around toward Tabitha's booth, but he steps in front of me again, grabs my arm. "Hey, I'm talking to you."

I look down at his hand, fury bubbling beneath my skin. "Get your hands off me and leave me alone." How dare he touch me again, like it's his God-given right? How dare he think I'm required to listen simply because he's speaking to me?

"God, Wayspaz," he says, his voice booming a little too loud. "I just came over here to talk to you, and you're being a total *bitch* to me."

Tabitha looks up from her booth, and I swear there's a hint of disgust in her expression, aimed at Robbie, not me. Which is weird, because I would've pegged her as one of his cohorts, maybe laughing because she thinks I deserve to be verbally berated.

But I'm the one who lets out a laugh. Like that word is supposed to hurt me? He picked the wrong girl to try to wound. I've been to hell and back, and Robbie Duncan calling me a bitch doesn't even register on my pain radar.

Not even close.

I yank my arm away and move to squeeze between him and Tabitha's booth, my fists curled, but he grabs me again. Lifts me off the floor. I struggle with him, but his chubby, freckled arms are wrapped around my elbows, and I can't get the right leverage.

"Stop it, Robbie," I hear Tabitha say, standing up.

"What the hell does Peters see in you?" Robbie says, holding me tighter. Then he lowers one arm, his hand groping at my butt. "Oh, now I see." He laughs, squeezing my butt, my thigh, helping himself to anything he likes.

That's when the rage finally lets loose. He can say whatever he wants. Words have no power over me. But the moment he touches me like that, it brings back all the memories with Gesh and Decoy Boy, and I snap. It only takes a fraction of a second for Lo Jie's instincts to kick in. In a blur, I take advantage of his lowered arm and twist out of his grasp. I spin around, pull all the energy from my gut and slam the heel of my palm into his stupid, slack-jawed face.

He hits the floor. People all around us gasp. The gym goes still, quiet. Everyone watches.

Tabitha rushes to my side. "Are you OK?"

She asks me, not Robbie, who's now twisting on the floor, hands cupped over his nose as blood leaks out between his fingers.

"I'm OK," I say, shaking from the adrenaline rush leaving my system.

"You should disappear," she says. "Like, now."

"Why? I defended myself."

Tabitha frowns. "Mrs. Gafferty won't see it that way. Trust me."

Before I get a chance to take Tabitha up on her advice, Mrs. Gafferty, the principal, shouts my name across the gym. She marches toward me, the only one moving in a crowd of jaw-dropped statues. "My office. Now."

Mrs. Gafferty makes me sit outside her office for over an hour while she talks to Robbie in the nurse's office and interviews a few more students who were witnesses. She's saving me for last, hoping I'll calm down, but I won't. My legs are jittery and jumping, my fists white-knuckled, my mind stewing.

The worst part is, she called Dad. And when he arrives, he doesn't look disappointed; he looks worried about me, all loving and concerned, and his expression makes me want to cry and curl up in his arms. "Alex, what happened? They said you got in a fight?"

He's so confused. He can't understand this side of me, the side that gets in fights at school, the side that gets suspended. Maybe he wonders if he even knows me anymore.

The truth is, he doesn't.

"I don't want to talk about it," I say, staring at my fists clenched in my lap.

He sits down beside me. "I know this thing with Audrey is difficult for you right now, but—"

"I don't want to talk about it," I say again, louder.

Dad sits back in his chair, surprised. I never raise my voice at him like that. But I'm so raw, so angry, I can't maintain a facade. Not even for him.

Mrs. Gafferty's door opens, and Tabitha walks out. She glances at me, but I can't read her expression. Mrs. Gafferty calls us in and closes the door. She motions to two chairs in front of her mammoth cherrywood desk.

I give my account of the incident, and Mrs. Gafferty lets me speak without interrupting, but she's stoic. Dad, on the other hand, looks mortified. He's sitting at the edge of his seat, looking at Mrs. Gafferty in a trusting, let's-fix-this-together way, because Dad is exactly like me. He doesn't like leaving things broken. He wants to repair everything in his path.

When Mrs. Gafferty finally speaks, I'm not surprised by what she says. Dad thinks we can all work together to come to a good conclusion, but Mrs. Gafferty is tired of me making waves in her school. Suspension wasn't enough a few months ago. Now she's going to call for my head.

"I don't need to tell you that you're facing expulsion this time, Alex." That's what she says. *It's your fault and you're going down, kiddo.*

Dad holds out a hand. "Now wait a minute. I don't think expulsion is the right decision when Alex was defending herself."

"Defending herself?" Mrs. Gafferty's eyebrows climb her forehead. "She broke another student's nose, Mr. Wayfare. Maybe you don't understand the gravity of the situation here. Your daughter committed a violent act on school grounds."

"The situation," I say, scooting forward, "is that he assaulted me, and I defended myself. I told him to leave me alone, and he didn't."

Mrs. Gafferty shakes her head. "Only one witness says she heard you tell him to leave you alone. And even if that was the case, you had to know that would only provoke him further."

I can't help letting my jaw drop. "Telling him to leave me alone is *provoking* him? Are you asking me to just grin and bear it next time?"

"I'm saying sometimes it's best not to make a scene. You're not only facing expulsion here, Alex, you could be facing a lawsuit from Robbie's father."

That makes me pause, and I finally feel an ounce of remorse for what I did, but only because I hadn't thought about how it might affect my family.

"Robbie was only teasing you. Joking with you. He probably has a crush on you, for goodness' sake." She delivers this in a you're-as-dumb-as-a-doorknob tone, like I'm oblivious about guys liking me, and if only I knew his actions were crush-driven, then everything would be OK. I'd sigh with relief. *Ooohhhhh*, he likes me! Hallelujah! A boy actually likes me! Here, have a free ticket to my body!

The expression on my face doesn't hide my horror and disbelief. But she ignores it and keeps going. "It's what kids do," she says. "And you reacted completely out of proportion."

Obviously she's never been kidnapped in Grant Park by a Descender who raked his hands all over her chest. Obviously she's never had her bra strap snapped in the hall or her butt groped by Asshole Dick Face Robbie. And obviously she's never been held down on a desk while Gesh stuck his hand between her thighs. Looked at her like she was his possession, to do with as he pleased.

Dad leans forward, his fists about to break the arms off his chair. I've been so steeped in anger that I haven't noticed Dad's body language. How furious he is too, how much he's been holding back this whole time. "With all due respect, Mrs. Gafferty," he says, steam rolling off of him in waves, "I disagree. That boy sexually assaulted my daughter. If I had been there to witness it, he'd have more than one broken bone, I can tell you that much."

Mrs. Gafferty's eyes widen. "Mr. Wayfare—"

"If you punish Alex for defending herself, and you let this boy off the hook, the message you're sending to the students on your campus, to your girls, is that it's perfectly acceptable for them to lay their hands on another human being in violence. That's exactly what that boy did to my daughter. He laid his hands on her with full intent to hurt her. To subdue her and assert his strength over her. That is damaging on a thousand different levels. I'm not saying what Alex did was the right choice, but I do believe it was damn well warranted. The way I see it, Robbie Duncan is at fault here. He initiated this incident, so punish him. Set the standard here. A precedent. Be the hero for all the girls on your campus."

She presses her lips into a thin line. "I'm not interested in being a hero. I'm interested in making sure those at fault receive the proper punishment."

Dad nods and stands like the conversation is over. "I'm glad to hear it. You can give me a call when you've decided how to punish this boy."

"Sit down, Mr. Wayfare. We're not finished here."

"I believe we are." He waves a hand at me. "Let's go, Alex." And we walk out. Just like that.

And I follow after him, not caring whether or not Mrs. Gafferty decides to be a hero, because Dad already is. He protected me, stood up for me, when no one else would. For the first time all day, the rage subsides, and I feel relief.

And exhaustion.

We both slide into the Mustang, where the squeak of the seats and the smell of the vinyl wrap me in comfort. I press my forehead against the passenger-door window. My breath fogs the icy pane.

"I thought we were done with this," Dad says, turning the ignition, firing up the engine. "With these visits to the principal."

I want to say I'm sorry, that I didn't mean for it to happen, to involve him in yet another school issue, but I just sit there, staring at my hands, winding and unwinding a loose thread from my parka sleeve around my finger.

"Did you really break his nose?"

God. Yes. In two places, apparently. But no words come out. *It won't ever happen again.* I could say it with honesty. I'll be dead soon enough.

Dad's quiet for a long time. I'm afraid to glance at him, fearing I'll find disappointment clouding his kind gray eyes, but when I finally get the courage to peek at him, he's not looking at me. His eyes are straight ahead, one of his fists raised in my direction.

"Fist bump," he says with the proudest of smiles.

I choke out a laugh through the tightness in my throat. I tap his knuckles with mine.

"Promise me, Bean. If anyone ever touches you like that again without your consent, makes you feel threatened, and they don't take no for an answer, you break as many bones as it takes, you hear me?"

I sniff, blinking back tears. "I promise."

CHAPTER 24

HOW TO SURVIVE

That night during dinner with Gran, Pops, Claire, and Dad, there's a knock on our door. Gran answers it, and leads the unexpected guest into the dining room.

It's Levi, looking apologetic, balancing a stack of books and folders in his arms.

I stand up too quickly, knocking my fork to the floor, surprised to see him here, in my home, with my family. A collision of worlds.

Dad stands up too.

"Dad, this is Mr. Sorenson, my history teacher."

Dad wipes his hands with a napkin and shakes Levi's hand. "Nice to meet you, Mr. Sorenson. What can we do for you?"

"I'm sorry to interrupt your dinner, Mr. Wayfare. I wanted to stop by and talk to you and Alex about what happened today, if that's OK."

My eyes widen at Levi, and I wish he were still connected to my soulmark so he could read my thoughts. *What the hell are you doing here?*

Dad ushers us into the living room, and we all sit, staring at each other awkwardly.

"Mr. Wayfare, I want to start out by saying I completely agree with you about the incident this afternoon. I don't believe Alex should be held at fault. I've only been at South View for a short time, but in that time I've come to know your daughter as an honest, hard-working student, with drive and passion that is, I believe, vital to her future community. Expelling her would be a mistake."

Dad looks impressed. "Thank you, Mr. Sorenson. I appreciate

that. I'm sure Alex does too."

"And so, I hope you don't mind, but I've taken it upon myself to devise an alternative plan for Alex's last semester." He hefts the stack of books onto the coffee table. "I recommend Alex study at home, under my tutelage, where she can be close to her family during this unfortunate and difficult time. I've already gotten approval from Mrs. Gafferty. I just need the nod from you both."

Dad grins at me. I grin at Levi.

So maybe he finally did do something to make school bearable for me. And maybe there are still some people I can trust, who have my back. My heart swells in my chest, and I nod and thank him even though I want to tackle-hug him. I totally would if Dad weren't there.

Dad coerces Levi to stay for dinner, which is customary in our household. If you step through the front door, day or night, you'll be wrangled into dinner one way or another, whether you like it or not.

Whether you eat meat or not.

"You're a vegetarian?" I ask Levi when he gently refuses Gran's pot roast.

"Vegan, actually."

I take stock of the dinner table. Mashed potatoes with milk and butter, glazed carrots bathed in even more butter, and tossed salad.

"Eat up," I say, nudging the salad bowl across the table toward him with a grin.

He does. And we talk long into the evening, him, Dad, and me, about everything. School, politics, even AIDA. And Levi knows exactly what to say to impress Dad.

And I love him for it. I really do. He's wrapping me up in another lie, but it's a lie that keeps my family safe, helps lessen their load, helps keep me sane. Makes Dad feel comfortable letting Levi and me chat out on the back porch, alone, hot mugs of coffee in our gloved hands, our foggy breath mingling with the steam. The sky is clear, cold, and dark blue, the stars twinkling, the moon lighting up the forest beyond our backyard like a spotlight.

We're quiet for a long time, sipping our coffee, until at last Levi speaks. "It's not that I don't believe you about Micki. It's that I don't *want* to believe it. She's been my partner all this time. I trust her like you trust Tre. Can you understand how this might feel for me? Thinking she might be a traitor?"

I sigh and look down at my hands. "Of course I do. I just don't know what to do with all this anger. With all this failure. I don't know how to aim it in the right direction, like you said I should."

"You haven't failed. Not yet. You've still got 1978."

My throat feels tight. "Audrey may not make it until then. What am I supposed to do if I can't save her? How is my family supposed to survive losing both of us?"

Levi's eyes are far off. He swallows. Frowns. Then tells me exactly what I need to hear, what I've needed to hear for years now.

"It's unbearable at first, losing someone you love; I won't lie to you. You can't function. You're numb, but you're angry, too. So angry at everything. At the unfairness of it all. And you let yourself go because nothing matters anymore. You wander, lost, because that's all you can do. Forget about eating and showering. None of it matters, least of all your own well-being. Because you feel guilty taking care of yourself. You're still alive to brush your teeth and get dressed and head out the door. They aren't. And you can't smile or laugh or find any enjoyment in anything because they can't do those things. And if they can't, then you can't. But then..." He trails off, takes a deep breath. "It gets better. Slowly, after a handful of years go by. You start to forget. Their voice. Their smile. Their scent. It all fades, and you're left with glimpses. Snatches of light. You're left with all the good memories. And you eventually let yourself enjoy things again. Little things, like a walk along the shore, or the first time you smell woodsmoke in the air and you know fall is around the corner. You start to thaw, and little bits of color appear, like crocuses in the snow. And after a few more years, you're suddenly OK. You're better. You let yourself live again, because you died with them, you know, and you had to be reborn." He finally looks at me, his eyes sincere. "That's how they'll survive, Alex. That's how they'll get through it. It will take time, but they will get through it."

This time, I do hug him. I don't care if he's just telling me what I want to hear, playing me, like he plays everyone. It feels real, because he should know. He watched Ivy die in his arms, and I don't think he's let himself smile since. I know I won't see the crocuses in the snow, and I won't have enough time to heal before my time comes, but knowing my family might gives me the hope I need.

We say goodnight to Levi well past ten, after Gran and Pops and Claire have gone to bed. He leaves me with homework and says he'll be back at the end of the week to see how I'm doing. I flop down on the couch and stare at the stack of materials he brought over: folders and folders of Xeroxed worksheets and study guides.

And then it hits me. How I'm going to save Audrey after all.

TRUST IS RISK

The next morning, after I drop Claire off at school, I swing by the marina to talk to Porter. As I pull into a parking space, I spot Levi walking to his car.

"You look like hell," I say, climbing out of the Mustang.

"Thanks." He walks my way, and I can see bags under his eyes.

"Did you sleep?"

"Not a bit. We were working on a lead all night."

"What kind of lead?"

"Porter thinks he knows how Gesh tracked you in China. But we need to do a test run with you to make sure."

"You mean a way that doesn't involve Micki?" I frown. "So you still believe she's on our side."

Levi's frown matches mine. "We trust her, Alex. As much as we trust you. We want to prove her innocence."

I push my glasses up and meet his eyes. "Like I wanted to do for Blue?"

Levi swallows, unsure of what to say. He glances at his watch. "I'm sorry, I've got to get to class. I'm already late. But I'll see you tonight?"

He jogs to his car, and I watch him go, wondering about that little thing called trust. What the hell is it, exactly? And why does it make us do such stupid things? I head to the boat, wondering what I would say or do if I was wrong about Micki. If I was wrong about everything.

Porter must have seen me coming on the cameras, because he's standing at the top of the ramp, holding the door in the shrink-wrapped wall open for me.

"Good morning," he says. "What are you doing here so early?"

"I have a plan."

"And that is?"

I follow him into the living room but I don't sit down. I can't. I'm too anxious. "We do the 1978 mission."

"Wasn't that already the plan?" He digs around in one of the kitchen cabinets and pulls out a box of tea bags.

"No, the plan was to wait a few weeks. Not anymore. I want to go tonight."

He pours steaming water from a kettle into a mug. "We've been over this. We have to go back the night of the fire. Stealing the files any sooner would create an impact."

"Only if we *steal* the files."

He stops what he's doing, tea bag hovering over his mug. "Go on."

"I'm not planning on stealing them. I'm planning on making a copy."

He stares at me, silent, still.

"They had copy machines back then, right?" I say. "We break in after hours, copy the data, take the copy, and leave the original. No one will ever know we were there."

He lets out a laugh. Drops the tea bag into the water. "You're a genius, Alex Wayfare. Do you know that?"

I grin. "You're just now realizing this?"

He laughs again. "It's definitely worth a try."

"We slip in, slip out. No impact. If we mess up, we redo the mission."

He eyes me, brow raised. "You keep saying *we*."

"Because I think you should come with me."

"I'm always with you."

"No, I think you should descend with me. Into another body. Be my partner the way Blue used to be. I need your expert Cancer Researcher eyes to go through the files and copy exactly what Mom needs. I know it takes a while to find the right body, someone who won't be missed for a few days, someone in the same vicinity as the mission, but if anyone can do it, you can."

"Alex, remember what I told you at the *Ristorante*?"

I remember now. He said he has a handful of soulmarks in reserve, like a garage full of classic cars, each one stationed in different time periods. It's how he traveled back in time before we first met and left a note at Johnson's Auto Garage. The note that led me to him. The note that changed my life.

"Does that mean we can go tonight?"

I expect him to say no, that we should prepare first, but instead he says, "I won't ask you to wait any longer. I'll meet you in your garden. It'll give me a chance to test out my tracking theory."

I throw my arms around him, and he hugs me in return. He smells like black tea and cigars, and I realize I've missed hugging him. I haven't let myself lately. My faith has been too unsteady. But I realize something in that moment, as I squeeze him tight.

Trust is risk. That's what it is. That's what it's all about.

It's never steady, not really. I used to think my trust was a guarantee, that my faith in someone meant everything would work out for the best. And if it didn't, then I was a fool for letting myself trust. I used to think Blue was good, always good. That I could believe in him. Now I know that's not true. He screws up, just like me. There are no guarantees. I've let Porter down countless times, and he still trusts me, despite it all. It's because he *chooses* to trust me, to take a chance on me, take the risk. Like we're family.

"I'll help you retrieve those files, Alex, if it's the last thing I do."

I want to say it's more likely the last thing *I'll* do, but I just say thank you. Thank you, thank you, thank you, a million times.

• • •

TIME FOR TRUTH

I spend the rest of the day with Audrey. We watch *To Have and Have Not* with Bogie and Bacall, and the nurses bring us more lemon Jell-O than we can possibly finish, but we don't mind taking up the challenge. When Hoagy Carmichael hits the screen, crooning and playing the piano, my heart sinks, and I long for the days when I still believed in Blue, when he was my fantasy. And maybe it's the nostalgia, or the regret, or the shadow of death standing just outside the door, but something makes me want to be honest with Audrey.

I don't get up the courage until she's half asleep, nestled beside me on her pillow. I lean down and whisper in her ear. "I'm going to tell you some truth right now. Do you want to hear it?"

"Mmmm," she says, eyes closed, a small smile on her face.

Here we go.

"I'm a time traveler. I travel to far-off lands, places, and times you can only dream of. With a snap of a finger, a gasp, a blink, I am there. I've skinny-dipped in the sixties, robbed a steam train in the 1800s, run from gangsters during Prohibition, climbed the mountains outside Beijing. I don't know how many reincarnations I have left. I don't know my first parents, my first family. All I know is that I'm an orphan of the stars, born to countless families with countless sisters and brothers and lovers and friends. Countless enemies, I suppose, as well. I've toured Dante's castle in Limbo. I can speak Chinese and Danish. I've stolen treasures worth millions, turned them over in my hands. I've been shot twice. I broke a boy's nose at school. I know kung fu. I'm dying. I don't know how to trust. I'm angry, and I'm bitter, and you are the only bright spot in all of it."

I look down at her, and her eyes are still closed. "Mmmm," she says.

"I'm going to save you." I wrap my arms around her. "You'll see."

• • •

GO TIME

"Ready?" Porter asks, standing across from me in my garden, my 1978 soulmark dancing between us.

I nod.

"It'll be a Tuesday," he says. "It's winter. Your father just pulled off an airline heist, one of the largest payoffs in his history as a gangster. He's going to be on edge, suspicious of everyone and everything, afraid someone will tip off the feds. Within the next few weeks, he'll systematically kill off all those involved in the heist to silence them, then take their portions. He's ruthless, Alex. Cutthroat. So keep your head down. Don't make waves. Sneak out, find a car, and meet me on the University of Michigan campus in Ann Arbor. That's where the AIDA research lab is located. I'll be in a body called Sam. Any questions?"

"Won't my gangster dad be suspicious of me disappearing for a few days?"

"You've got a history of mental illness and wandering off, remember? If you have to, play that card. Play dumb. If you think it's too hard to slip out, just ascend, and we'll wait a few days. Try again."

I reach for my soulmark.

"Good luck," Porter says.

The white light envelops me, and like a magnet, I'm pulled back in time, my soul settling into my past-life body for one last shot.

I have to make it count.

CHAPTER 25

ON THE ROAD

The blinding light faded into darkness, little by little, until all I saw were flecks of white swirling in front of me. I was hurtling through them, like I was flying through space, speeding through stardust.

Then it all came into focus at once. I was behind the wheel of a car, driving down a deserted highway, carving my way through softly falling snow. I slowed down and pulled over to the side of the road to catch my bearings.

I was alone. It was a little after five o'clock. And I couldn't believe my stupid luck. I wouldn't have to face Jimmy McKenzie or find a way to sneak out of his house. Janet had done all the legwork for me, same as Lo Jie stealing the vase. If I had left a day earlier or later, I might not have been so lucky. There were no obstacles between me and the cure. It was a clear shot, arrow straight, and I shivered inside with excitement.

I pulled the visor down and flipped up the mirror. I wanted to meet Janet. Her face was longer, leaner, her eyes sunken and tired. She had more freckles, but her hair was the same dusky blond color, with maybe a slight reddish tint, cut into a pageboy style that made her face look even longer. She was thin, almost skeletally so, like she was sick. She was a complete one-eighty from Lo Jie. Janet's mind was a whirl, her eyes darting, heart racing. Like a mouse on the run from a prowling cat.

What was she running from?

As I ran my fingertips across my face, my freckles, I noticed a shadow that snaked across my cheekbone. I turned on the dome light and looked closer. A bruise, purples mingling with greens and blues, bloomed across my left eyelid and up the side of my nose.

She wasn't running from something. She was running from some*one*.

Maybe her own murdering father.

The thought made me glance in the rearview mirror. I needed to get back on the road in case she was followed.

The car was a '74 Gran Torino. Burnt orange with chrome, black dash, black steering wheel, black bench seats. Cassette tapes were scattered on the seat next to me. There was a map on top of them, folded to display Pennsylvania.

She'd made it all the way from New York City to Pennsylvania before I took over. I'd have to go through Ohio to reach Michigan. I wasn't sure how long that would take, so I pulled back onto the highway and got going.

I took note of where I landed, what mile marker, so I could return Janet's body back to the same location at the end of the mission. I couldn't leave her in Michigan after I hid the files. She'd have no idea how she got there, and that kind of shock could make an impact. Returning her back where she came from—even if it was a few days later—would be confusing for her, but not enough to change her original course. Porter told me it happens all the time. People claim they've lost hours or days of their lives and can't recount the events. When that happens? We know a Descender was involved. It's not enough to change the course of the future. Only big impacts can do that—destroying something, killing someone, letting someone fall in love with you. Those are the big ones, the waves that cause catastrophic ripples across time.

Like me kissing Blue and tangling his heart with mine.

For the next five hours, I bobbed my head to Creedence Clearwater Revival and Simon and Garfunkel and the Steve Miller Band. I sang along to the songs I knew, the ones Dad grew up with, the ones he played while we worked on the Mustang.

I pulled over at a truck stop for dinner (potato chips in a can, red cream soda in a glass bottle, and a candy bar called Chocolite), burnt coffee, and a bathroom break. By the time I reached the

Michigan state line past Toledo, I knew that car inside and out. It might've looked like a muscle car, but it didn't drive like one. It was an automatic, which was a shame. It floated on the road like a boat and pulled to the left, but it got me where I needed to go.

A little after eleven o'clock, and after a few wrong turns through the university campus, I found AIDA's research building and parked on a side street. If Micki were there with me, she could direct me where to go. Without that kind of intel, I was driving blind, but that was OK with me. I'd rather it be just me and Porter, like when we first started.

I stepped out, dusted the snow from my bellbottom jeans, and hugged my denim coat to my chest, the shearling collar guarding against the cold. I leaned against the front fender of the car, breathing in the December air. There were simple white lights strung across the Greek architecture buildings. There were wreaths hung on street lamps with red bows. It was kind of nice reliving the Christmas spirit all over again. Back in Base Life, it was almost February.

The campus was empty and silent, save a few cars winding their way through. While I waited for Porter to show, I ran through possible cover stories in case I had to explain myself to anyone. But the first person I met was Porter.

"Hello, Alex."

I turned around, and there he was, wearing a young man's body, maybe a few years older than myself. He was tall and broad with deep, dark skin, a flashing smile, and…wait for it…an afro. Porter in a black turtleneck and a honey-brown leather jacket. Porter in corduroy bellbottoms and glossy snakeskin boots.

Oh, I was in heaven. Looking him up and down, I let out a whistle. "Damn."

"What?"

"You're fine, Porter, my man."

"I'm…fine?"

"This body you're in. It's attractive. If only I knew this guy way back when, know what I'm saying?"

"Alex," he says in his most dignified, authoritative voice.

"These bodies deserve respect. We're borrowing them without their consent and making them do things they wouldn't otherwise. We've discussed this."

"Are you saying you don't want me to stare at your butt?"

"Please do not stare at my butt."

I laughed for the first time in ages. A real, honest-to-goodness belly laugh. God, I loved teasing Porter. It made all the death and demise bearable for one tiny moment.

We sneaked around the building, crunching through the snow, hiding in the shadows, looking for a tilt-out window left ajar. We spotted only one, on the second floor. In the hazy glow of the street lamps, we could tell it was popped just an inch or so. There was a ledge, so Porter laced his fingers together and hoisted me up. Luckily, we were both tall, and I reached it without much effort.

I shimmied along the ledge to the window and pulled on it, expecting it to give way freely, but it was stuck. Which is probably why it was left ajar in the first place. I tugged on it, my fingers going numb with cold, my nose and cheeks icy and burning. Then headlights swept over me and I froze, flattened against the side of the building.

Like that would help.

A maintenance truck parked in front of the main entrance below me, off to the left. A chubby man with a thick mustache and a mullet climbed out and rolled a janitor's cart inside. Porter had disappeared. I prayed the janitor wouldn't see my footprints leading up to the windows. He left the front doors propped open as he made several trips carrying his tools inside, singing along to his portable radio.

I swore under my breath. If we'd waited a few more minutes, we could've sneaked in behind him. Instead, I was stuck on a ledge in the dead of winter, yanking on a window that wouldn't budge. Porter, my trusty ladder, was nowhere to be seen.

When the janitor finally closed the entrance doors, I wrenched on the window so hard one of my feet slipped off the ledge, and I clung to the frame with my fingertips, pulling on it with all my body weight.

That's when it swung loose with a mighty groan. Hoisting my foot up, I scrambled to climb up. Then I slid inside, crash-landing on a desk. Papers and pencil cups went flying.

"*Shhhhh*," I said to the pens as they scattered across the floor.

"What are you doing?"

I almost jumped out of my skin, thinking the janitor had found me. Lo Jie's fighting instincts kicked in, and I whirled around, ready to strike. But it was only Porter, standing in the hallway, his afro silhouetted in the open doorframe.

"How'd you get in?" I hissed.

"Snuck in behind the janitor. And look"—he held up a set of keys—"I swiped his keys off his cart while he was in the bathroom."

Of course. Of course it was that simple for Porter. He was too patient, too calculating, to climb up the side of a building and dive through a window.

After we cleaned the mess I'd made, we found the right lab, and Porter tried the keys until the deadbolt gave way with a *thunk*.

"I'll gather the data," he said. "You look for a copy machine."

The lab was made up of two rooms, one large area with a dozen tables where the actual experimenting took place, and another, smaller, office-like space with filing cabinets, a little kitchenette, and two desks overflowing with papers, books, and folders.

Porter turned on a desk lamp. In the far corner stood a fat copy machine, the lid lifted high like a salute. By the time I got to it, Porter already had a handful of papers for me to scan. I flipped a switch on the machine, and when it whirred to life, my stomach did a backflip.

But then it made a whining sound, high-pitched at first, then lower, until the lights on the machine flickered and faded altogether.

"What happened?" Porter asked, piling another stack on top of the other. "Did you blow a fuse?"

I flipped it off, then turned it back on. It did the same thing as before. Fired up, then wheezed and died. "It's drawing juice, just not enough to stay on. I think the power supply is failing."

"Then we need to find another machine, and fast."

"No time," I said, my eyes already darting around the room. "If I go traipsing around the whole building, trying key after key on that ring, I'll run into the janitor. We're safer if we stay in one spot. Besides, I can totally fix it."

Porter raised his thick black eyebrows. "You can?"

"You doubt me, Saturday Night Fever? Watch and learn." In the kitchenette stood a massive four-pot Bunn coffee maker. I slid it away from the wall and ripped its power cord from the socket. Scientists needed their coffee, I knew that well. Dad had one of the same machines in his engineering lab. I could use the coffee maker's power supply to give the copy machine a little CPR.

As I tried to pry the electrical panel off the back of the coffee maker with a letter opener, Porter handed me a Swiss army knife. "Thought this might come in handy. Found it in Sam's glovebox."

I leaned over and kissed him on the cheek. "Tall, dark, handsome, *and* a quick thinker? Talk about swoon."

Porter rolled his eyes and went back to thumbing through drawers and drawers of files.

I cut the coffee maker power cord and brought it over to the copy machine. Even modern machines need a strong surge of power when they turn on. After that, the copying draws very little juice. As long as I could get the machine over that initial hump, it would be smooth sailing.

"How do you know about *Saturday Night Fever?*" Porter asked, tossing a few more pages on my pile. "I thought you didn't watch movies."

Using the scissors on the Swiss army knife, I stripped the coating on the power cords, revealing bare wires. "It's one of Mom's favorites. I've seen it a gazillion times."

I twisted the wires of both power cords together, then connected them to the copy machine. I plugged each cord into a separate wall socket and hit the switch.

The desk light dimmed and the coffee maker's power brick popped, sending a thin trail of smoke rising to the ceiling. But the copy machine whirred to life and sat humming happily, waiting for me to feed it the first page.

It took less than ten minutes.

Porter's eyes were wide. "Remind me never to get on your bad side."

I winked at him, and started copying like a madwoman. With Porter there with me, I felt invincible. I wondered if that's what it felt like to be partners with Blue. Back when we worked together and understood each other. I wondered if that's what it was like to truly lean on someone else, putting not just your life in their hands, but the lives of those you loved.

It took us less than an hour to find what we needed, copy everything, put the pages back where they came from, and rewire the coffee maker and copy machine. I felt bad about frying the coffee maker cord. The scientists would have to go without coffee for a day or two, but it was a small price to pay to save countless lives in the future.

Back downstairs, we hung the janitor's keys back on his cart, then sneaked out the front doors and past the maintenance truck. The janitor was digging around inside it, his back to us, no doubt looking for the keys he thought he had misplaced.

We were back to my car by midnight, the files tucked safely inside Porter's jacket.

He smiled warmly at me, a look of pride on his face. "You did it."

"We did it."

"I'll take these to my safe deposit box in Cincinnati. You take care of yourself, you hear?"

I nodded. "See you on the flip side, Sam."

It was all up to Porter now. All I could do was pray that he made it to Cincinnati. I wouldn't know whether we succeeded, truly succeeded, until I was back in Base Life, and the files were in Mom's hands.

CHAPTER 26

TANGLED UP IN BLUE

On the way back to the Michigan state line, Bob Dylan serenaded me through swirling snow, past flashing lights and construction warning signs, and off the main road onto a detour through the woods. He sang about a girl he once knew, and how he was all tangled up in blue.

I knew what he meant.

All the driving gave me plenty of time to think. I thought about Blue. About Jensen. About Micki. About everything being so complicated. So messed up.

I missed Micki, which surprised me. I had liked having her there to guide me through China. I missed trying to figure her out, her tiger eyes, her high heels. I missed the friendship that could have been. We were just finding our groove when I pushed her away. I accused her without proof; I ignored Porter and Levi when they said they believed in her.

Was I wrong? Like I was wrong about Blue?

And I missed Jensen. I tried to convince myself that he was a jerk, that all his kindness had been a ruse, but I knew deep down that wasn't true. I knew he felt bad about kissing me, about accusing me of lying about Blue. But I was so embarrassed that I couldn't deal with the situation. And I was so angry, because I wanted to kiss him again.

More than again.

What did that say about me? What did that mean?

Blue and I had been through hell and back together. We'd journeyed across continents and battled foes. We were soulmates, weren't we? Our stories were sewn together at the seams, transcending time.

So why did I hate myself for pushing Jensen away, for losing my only chance with him? Why did I wish for a little bit of time with him before I died?

Watching the light in Blue's eyes go out as he looked at me that night at the inn was a prick in the softest part of my soul. I knew things would never be the same between us. And as morbid as it sounded, I actually looked forward to death, being reborn, because it would release me from Blue's hold. I'd feel lighter if my mind weren't twisted around thoughts of him, weighing heavy with guilt. I wished I'd never met him. I wished my mind was my own, and not tangled up, knotted up in Blue.

I didn't realize how soon those knots would unravel, how quickly I'd be set free from my guilt.

I didn't realize the lights up ahead, blocking the road, belonged to a sleek black Cadillac. I didn't realize, until I slowed to a stop, squinting through the snow, that a man stood in front of that car, with gray hair and vicious eyes, a revolver in his hands glinting in my headlights.

"Get out of the car, Janet," the man said.

It was Jimmy McKenzie. I recognized his face from his mug shot online.

I threw the Gran Torino in reverse, but a second car pulled up behind me, blocking my way. Another guy, taller, leaner, jumped out. Before I could slam on the gas and smash into his car, forcing my way through the blockade, the younger guy took a baseball bat to my driver's-side window. The glass shattered across my lap, sparkling diamonds slicing my cheeks.

I screamed.

He popped the lock, wrenched the door open, and dragged me out onto the pavement by my hair.

I wanted to fight back, I did. But my care and concern for him made me hesitate. Made me gape up at him like I always do when he appears.

I didn't think I'd see him on this mission. I didn't think I'd see him again until I was reborn. And yet there he was, standing over me, his eyes red from whatever drug he was on, his shoulders heaving up and down, his breath shuddering through him. He grabbed me by the front of my coat and raised a fist.

"Blue," I said, throwing my hands over my face. "It's me. It's Sousa."

It was all gibberish to him.

"You think you can steal from us? Huh? Do ya?" he said in a thick New York accent. "You think we wouldn't find you?"

Oh, Janet. What have you done?

I kept silent like Porter taught me, but it only made things worse. When I didn't answer, Blue backhanded me across my face, and I flew backwards into one of the car tires, my body splayed out in the snow. I dabbed at my nose. Blood poured from my nostrils.

"What have you got to say for yourself?" he shouted as I cowered beneath him.

"Blue, please. Please remember." I knew he was in there, somewhere behind those red, raging eyes.

"Stop saying that. Stop saying *blue*." His black, shaggy hair was sweaty, plastered to his forehead. He raised a hand to me again.

"Please, come back to me. I need you right now. I need your help. Remember Chicago. Stardust. Burgers the size of our heads. Remember filling my gas tank on the side of the road in Ohio. Remember kissing me in the woods in 1876. Remember China. Remember Dante's *Inferno* and the gleaming palace."

This time he grabbed my collar with both hands and shook me, hard. "Stop it, you psycho bitch. Snap out of it." He slapped me twice, once with his palm, and again with the back of his hand, then dropped me to the ground, disgusted. He sneered and stalked off to Jimmy, like he couldn't bear another look at me.

This time Jimmy approached me, scowling. He wasn't outwardly angry like Blue. He seethed quietly, his gun held casually at his side, like it was a part of him. His silver hair was slicked back. His nose was crooked, his eyes unfeeling, almost dead. He wore a long overcoat, shiny black shoes, and a ring on his pinky finger.

He opened the back door of my car and reached under the backseat. Pulled out a package wrapped in newspaper. Inside was a neat stack of bills, so thick he had to hold it with both hands. "I always knew you were crazy, sweetheart, but I never thought you'd steal from me."

Shit. Janet had taken off with a wad of her daddy's heist money, stealing from gangsters, and thought she'd get away with it. Dumb move. Really dumb move. But I had to admire her ambition. She had to know they'd kill her if she got caught. She must not have cared.

I didn't have that luxury.

I couldn't let Janet die there on the side of the road. That wasn't how her story ended. She still had to get to the mental hospital. I know, because I have the memories. It would create a Variant, and I'd have to do a touchdown to erase it. If I did that, I'd lose the files and have to try it all over again.

Jimmy squatted next to me, moving slowly, like he didn't have anywhere else to be. Like he had all the time in the world. "I don't need this kind of betrayal under my roof, understand that? I don't need a rat in my house, stealing my cheese, understand that?" His New York accent was thick, too, his cologne even thicker. "You knew what would happen if you stole from a wise guy. You knew, but you did it anyway."

"It's bullshit, Janet," Blue said, still furious, still shaking and out of control. He slammed the baseball bat into one of the Gran Torino's headlights. The entire scene darkened a bit, and not just from the loss of light.

"Get her up, Frankie," Jimmy said to Blue as he walked away, his back to me, shaking his head.

Blue hauled me to my feet. The pain in my nose had reduced to a dull throb. My face felt numb. I wobbled, but I could stand on my own.

"Blue," I whispered. "I gave you that name, you know. The first time I met you, you had the most striking blue-green eyes. They knocked me out flat. You don't always have them in every life. Last time they were brown, almost black, like a buckeye nut. This time they're lighter. I call you Blue but you've had so many other names. Heath. John. Tao Jin. Nick Piasecki. Tre."

Blue stared at me, his face twisted, his mouth open, like he was watching someone go mad right before his eyes. He shook his head, then joined Jimmy across from me. Like they were lining up at the shooting range.

"I've had a few names too," I continued, feeling a little mad myself, for staying there, for not ascending and starting over. But I had to try one last time to save the mission. If I could call Blue back to me, maybe it would save Janet's life. "Shooter. Susan. Lo Jie. Ivy. Sousa." I paused as Jimmy cocked his gun, fire in his eyes.

"Alex," I whispered.

This was the end. And I was on my own. No Porter, no Micki, no Levi. The mission was over.

Jimmy raised his gun.

I closed my eyes.

I was just about to ascend when I heard it. Not the blast from the barrel, but a word.

"Sousa?"

My eyes flew open.

Blue wasn't shaking anymore. His shoulders were relaxed. He looked confused, disoriented. Finally, finally, his eyes widened as he took in the scene. Saw the gun pointed at me.

The iron fist of fear gripping my throat eased a bit. He remembered. I finally got through to him. And he would help me out of this mess. He wouldn't let Jimmy kill me.

He'd help me salvage the mission.

"Jimmy," Blue said, slowly lifting his hands, palm out. "Put the gun down. You don't want to do this."

Jimmy looked back and forth between us, a snarl on his face, unsure of what to make of Frankie's sudden change of heart.

Blue motioned for Jimmy to give him the gun, and after one long last glare at me, Jimmy uncocked the gun and handed it to Blue. A rush of breath left my lungs.

"That's it," Blue said, slowly taking the gun into his hands. "That's it. You don't want to whack your own kid. You don't want that kinda thing hanging over your head." Blue checked the chamber, and I assumed he was going to empty the bullets.

But he didn't.

Instead he cocked it. Aimed it right at me, his arm extended. "Let me do it for you."

And he fired.

CHAPTER 27

TURNING THE TABLES

I didn't have a chance to flinch. The bullet tore through my shoulder, just below my collarbone, and the force knocked me back onto the pavement. Jimmy got in his car and drove away, never looking back, leaving his daughter to die.

What a gent.

"Dammit, Blue," I said through gritted teeth, gripping my shoulder. "You *shot* me."

I thought I remembered what it felt like, a bullet ripping through muscle and bone.

I was wrong.

Blue strode toward me through the snow, tossing the gun to the side, his eyes sad, his mouth turned down. "I had to."

"To convince Jimmy to leave?" I sucked in a breath as I sat up, the pain white-hot and blinding. "We could've faked it, you know. *Acted* like you shot me."

He didn't say anything for a long while. He just stood there, staring at me with those sad eyes.

I sighed, clutching my hand to Janet's shoulder, her jacket covered in blood. I felt so tired all of a sudden. So very tired. "Now my mission's ruined. I'll have to redo it."

"I'm sorry, Sousa, but I can't let you go on any more rogue missions. You have to stop."

"What?" I looked up at him.

"I wanted to deliver the message to you myself this time. Make sure you understood."

His dark hair lifted in the wind, the snow swirled at his feet.

Somewhere in the distance, in the silence of the night, the universe shifted. Like a foundation of stone cracking, preparing to crumble.

I shook my head, tears of disbelief stinging my eyes. "Are you saying it was you? You told Gesh about the fountain? You ruined my Beijing mission?"

I held my breath, praying he'd deny it.

But he didn't. His face fell, revealing the truth. Porter, Levi and Micki were right all along. Blue was working for Gesh.

Blue handed me over to Gesh's Descenders on New Year's Eve, to be abducted, manhandled, groped.

Blue made me lose the cure for Audrey, kicked it right out of my hands.

I pushed myself up to stand on shaky legs, wincing from the pain. "How did you do it? Lead those Descenders to me at Jian's farm? How did you find the right soulmarks on such short notice? The exact ones who journeyed with us?"

Blue reached to check my shoulder, but I wouldn't let him touch me.

He frowned and dropped his hand. "It's a power you and I have. When Descenders connect to our soulmark in Limbo, we can pull them back in time with us wherever we go. They automatically settle into a nearby body. Hr Gesh calls it tethering."

"I know about tethering," I said, "but I didn't know we could pull people back in time with us."

Only to Limbo.

"It only works when you and I are together. Our power is stronger then; the door to the past is wide open. We can pull anyone through."

"Why haven't you done it before? Why now?"

"I was supposed to tether each time I saw you, but once I landed in one of my past-life bodies I could never remember to do it. In Beijing, my memories finally broke through. I remembered my Base Life and my mission. So when we were all alone at Jian's, I pulled my team back with me. They settled into Ning's body, Mei's, Honqi's."

"And then you fed me to the wolves." I narrowed my eyes at

him. "Did you bring them with you this time?"

He shook his head. "I wanted to do this on my own. Wanted to see you alone. You have to believe me, I never wanted to hurt you."

"Says the guy who just shot me."

"You think I wanted it to go this far? I've been trying to save you, *rescue* you, from the rogue Descenders. This whole time, every mission, that's what I've been doing. Trying to remember something, anything, that might lead me to you. Do you know how torturous it is to know things and not be able to remember? I know you told me where you were from." He tapped his temple. "I know it's in here somewhere. I just have to access it."

I hoped he didn't see the glint of fear in my eyes. I did tell him where I was from, and if he remembers Annapolis, then he'll have the key to finding me in Base Life. Alex plus Annapolis plus seventeen-year-old girl with visions she can't explain. It's the road map that will lead Gesh to my family's front door. It's how Gesh will force me to work for him, by holding my family hostage.

"Hr Gesh has been helping me," Blue said. "We've had little successes. When I remembered our meeting at the fountain he was so pleased with me."

"He isn't helping you, Blue. He's *torturing* you."

He shook his head. "It's not torture, it's purification. He's preparing me to be useful for The Cause. Each time he locks me in the chamber I remember a little more."

"He locks you in a chamber?" Blue's nightmares in China made more sense now. His memories weren't from his past at AIDA. They were current memories from his Base Life. Gesh had him chained somewhere, experimenting on his brain and threatening him with a lobotomy if he didn't remember something useful. He was forcing Blue to work against me, to lure me into trusting him and letting all my little secrets slip, just like Levi suspected. "He's using you, Blue. He's hurting you to get to me."

"He doesn't want to hurt me. He does it because it's his only option. And he'll keep doing it unless you tell us where you are. Tell us, and all of this will stop."

Gesh knew I cared for Blue. He knew, and he hoped that would persuade me to come forward, waving the white flag, sacrificing myself to save Blue from his torturous existence.

But I wouldn't trade my family's safety for Blue's. Not in a million years.

"He needs you," Blue said. "He needs both of us for The Cause. He can't do it without us. And if you won't tell me where you are, then I go back to the chamber. I'll remember eventually. I'm so close."

He was right. It was only a matter of time. And I couldn't let him take Annapolis back to Gesh. I had to stop him from remembering, and there was only one way I knew how.

If Gesh wanted me dead, he would've had his men kill me at the fountain. He would've gone back in time and made sure Ivy was never created. No, he needed both of us, me and Blue, alive and together, to tether a whole host of Descenders and pull them back in time. Why, I wasn't sure. But I wouldn't let him reach out and take whatever he wanted anymore. Just like Robbie Duncan, I was going to cut his hand off once and for all.

It was my turn to deliver a message to Gesh: YOU CAN'T HAVE ME.

Blue reached out and took my hand in his. "I just want you to be safe. I just want you to come home."

I looked down at our hands, at our cold fingers entwined like at Buckingham Fountain. "I used to trust you," I whispered.

He tucked a finger under my chin and lifted my eyes to his. "You trusted me because our souls are linked. We're partners. You can feel how much I care for you. How true it is."

Tears welled in my eyes, blurring his face, the snow falling around us.

"You feel it, don't you? That I'm in love with you. I've loved you ever since I saw you in those red, white, and blue rag curlers. Since you climbed out of that dumpster and fought those gangsters and saved my life. Since we ran through the streets of Chicago, through the city lights, just you and me."

My heart should have swelled when he told me he loved me, but it didn't. Not one bit. "Oh, Blue," I said, pulling my hand away. "You don't even know who I am."

It wasn't a relationship, what we had. It was a sickness. Both of us wanted to save the other, but the truth was, we were fighting on opposite teams, and neither of us was willing to switch sides.

Damn.

I could have loved him.

I could have.

He was the first to take notice. The first to have trouble taking his eyes off me. God, I felt so special when he looked at me. Talked to me. Teased me. Held my hand. Everything was easy when he was my Blue. I could be myself, and he'd be interested. Genuinely interested.

But my Blue was a fantasy. A version of him I built in my mind. I'd wanted it to be real because I'd needed it. Needed someone to whisk me away from all my issues.

A distraction.

And I was ashamed of myself.

Damn.

Maybe falling for someone had nothing to do with the certain way they looked, or the certain crook of their smile, or the certain color of their eyes, or the certain words they spoke, but everything to do with how their looks, their smiles, their eyes, and their words *made you feel.* Maybe it had to do with how much you enjoyed being next to them, no matter what you were doing. How much you pondered what might make them smile or sigh or swear. And whatever that feeling was, you couldn't help but want more, because it was what you needed at that exact moment.

And maybe, when that person was gone, maybe it wasn't the person you missed, but the way they made you feel. Because no one could ever make you feel that way again, so you mourn the way your chest swelled with summer sunshine and warm breeze, you mourn the contented sigh in your belly. And the only feeling that's left is your heart folding in on itself, mourning what was, what will never be again.

"We need to end this," I said, sniffing, wiping tears from my cheeks.

"Tell me where you are and all of this will be over. We'll be partners again. We'll be together."

I shook my head, because he didn't understand. "No. I'm going to put an end to it right now." I knew what I had to do to salvage the mission without a touchdown. To save the files, save the cure.

I had to create a Variant.

I didn't care about the ramifications. The mass destruction. The lives that would be lost. I only cared about the lives that would be saved. Not just my family's, but countless others. I could put a stop to Gesh's Cause, whatever it was, once and for all. I could do it in one fell swoop. And Gesh would never see it coming.

I closed my eyes as a wave of dizziness swept through me. Janet had lost too much blood, and I couldn't stand any longer. I swayed, then dropped to the ground.

"Sousa," Blue said, diving to my side. "We don't have much time. We have to ascend now, before you die."

I felt both of our souls lift as Blue pulled me to Limbo, but we didn't reach the Black. Our souls snapped back down as though they were attached to our bodies with rubber bands.

Blue's brow knitted in confusion. "What are you doing?" He tried to ascend again, but couldn't.

Then his eyes widened.

He knew. He could feel it, the soulblock I spun around us, sealing us into the past.

I felt him scramble to break through, but I held it firm. I knew what it felt like now, how strong it had to be. I'd struggled against the strongest soulblock in China, six Descenders' worth. The difference was, I could concentrate now. I only had one Descender to contend with, and I had surprise on my side.

"What the hell are you doing?" he said again, louder, panicked.

"I'm dying, Blue," I said. "It's what we do, remember?"

"You can't. If you die under a soulblock, you won't go back to Base Life. You'll go straight to Afterlife. You'll never be reincarnated again."

"And if everything goes according to plan, I'll pull you

along with me."

His expression darkened. "You can't take a life. It's against the rules. You'll create a Variant. You'll destroy history."

"I guess you should've thought of that before you shot me."

His eyes were fiery like they had been in China. "You'll ruin everything. Everything I've worked for, sacrificed for."

Didn't he know? I was awesome at ruining everything. It's what I did best.

"Then Gesh really shouldn't have put both of us on the front lines." I took in a deep, shuddering breath as the cold seeped into my bones. My whole body was shivering now. My clothes were soaked through with blood and snow.

Blue glanced at the gun resting on the ground.

"Go ahead," I said. "Shoot me again. I'll just die faster."

His nostrils flared, then he jumped to his feet and darted for his car. He was going to get as far away from me as he could to break the soulblock.

But I was ready for him.

Lo Jie was ready for him.

With the last ounce of energy I had left, I sprang up, as light as a cat, and swept my leg at his ankle, tripping him. His chest slammed into the road and he slid, snow shoved in his face.

I grabbed the gun. Aimed it at him as he pushed himself up. "I don't want to shoot you," I said, panting. I was so dizzy and my knees were shaking. "But I will if I have to. You know I will."

He knew.

"Get in the trunk." I waved the gun at the Gran Torino.

He popped it open and climbed in. I shut him inside, dark and deep, and pocketed the keys. Then I slumped onto the ground, gun still in my hand, and waited for the last breath to seep from my lungs.

I wasn't afraid.

It would all be worth it in the end.

As Death pulled at me, tugged at me to take a walk with him, I thought of my family. Eating dumplings after midnight with Mom in DC. The ride home with Dad in the Mustang, after he had my back with Mrs. Gafferty. When we fist-bumped. All the movie nights with Gran and Pops and Claire. Rolling out homemade pizza dough with Gran, passing the popcorn, throwing a pillow at Pops when he'd start snoring during the good parts. Claire and her perpetually ice-cold feet burrowing under my legs, seeking warmth. Afton curled up at the foot of my bed, his purrs so loud they carried all the way down the stairwell. Hitting Robbie in the face. Tabitha sticking up for me.

Kissing Jensen.

It was all worth it. Every single moment. And I could've died happy right then, knowing I'd lived. Maybe it wasn't the ending I had planned. Maybe I never got the chance to be a normal kid. But it didn't matter.

Being Wayspaz the Fix-It Freak was more important.

All of *this* was more important.

I wished Levi, Micki, and Porter were there with me. I wished I could see them one last time, tell them I was sorry for not trusting them, for thinking I knew better.

They were my true partners. Always had been.

I wondered what would happen after Gesh found out his two greatest assets were destroyed. Would he pick up where he left off? Continuing his Cause by searching for some new way to ferry hordes of Descenders back in time? Or would he be consumed with rage and retaliate against my team instead?

Was I leaving them to fend for themselves?

What if it didn't work? What if it all backfired?

My breaths were so shallow. I felt my soul lifting, taking Death's hand and following him onto the dance floor. A bright light washed over me, and I leaned into it, ready for the light to take me this time, not the Black.

But the light didn't take me. It made me squint and shield my eyes. I heard two car doors open and close. Saw two silhouettes approach, heard their footfalls on snow.

"Alex," one of them said.

But I couldn't hold on.

CHAPTER 28

YE OF LITTLE FAITH

Death is a tricky thing for someone like me. I never seem to finish what I started.

When I open my eyes, I'm lying in a hospital room, an IV stuck in my arm, a heart rate monitor beeping above me. Micki sits at my bedside, smiling her tiger smile.

"Good morning, Number Four."

"You're back," I say, trying to sit up, but she takes my hand in hers, easing me back down, taking care not to tug at the IV.

"I never left. I only went to follow up on a lead on your past life, that's all. I came back as soon as I was done, but you had already descended."

"A lead for the 1978 mission?"

She nods. "I was trying to find out exactly how Janet McKenzie died so we wouldn't cause a Variant."

"You were still helping me, even after I was so horrible to you?"

"It's my job." Her eyes are warm and sincere, and I feel like I don't deserve her kindness. Not yet. Not until I apologize.

"Micki, I'm sorry about—"

She waves a hand at me. "You're forgiven. It's forgotten. Case closed."

I squeeze her hand, thankful she doesn't make me grovel.

One by one, my memories flood back. Blue shooting me. The look in his eyes. The soulblock. The two silhouettes approaching me. That's the last thing I remember. "How did I get back? What happened?"

She crosses her legs and settles in her chair. "That lead on

Janet brought me to a mental facility in Ypsilanti. According to their documents, a stranger found Janet wandering in the snow near the state line, shot and bleeding. They checked her in as Jane Doe. She had no memories, no possessions. That's how she disappeared from history. They treated her at their facility for a few months, then she died a few weeks later. None of her family members ever knew what became of her. Her father believed Frankie shot her. Frankie believed it himself, that he left her for dead."

"So they did try to kill her. For stealing the heist money."

Micki nods. "Weird thing is, the money she stole was never seen again. Over a hundred grand is still unaccounted for."

"Jimmy must've taken it when he left Frankie to do his dirty work."

"Maybe," she says, biting her thumbnail. "I just wish I'd gotten there sooner. I could've swiped it."

I sit up, thinking I misheard her. "What do you mean? You were there?"

"After the China mission we knew for certain Tre was working for Gesh. Porter suspected Tre might be using tethering to pull Descenders back in time with him. He thought if Tre could do it, then you could too. Porter pulled Levi and me to Limbo, then we connected to your soulmark and watched and waited. When you thought about us, wished for us to be by your side, it was enough to pull us through to you. We descended into two nearby bodies just a few miles down the road."

I shift against my pillow, my back stiff from lying down so long. "So it was you and Levi who drove up as I was dying."

"We got you to safety. Levi patched you up, saved your life. We kept Tre with us the whole time, under your soulblock, so he couldn't do a touchdown and erase the mission. After that, we took you to Ypsilanti State Hospital and checked you in, sealing Janet's circle, her fate. All bodies were returned to where they came from. No life-altering impact was made."

"Thank you," I say, "for saving my butt."

She flashes a grin. "Anytime."

She's quiet for a while, so I say, "You can tell me, you know. Just hit me with it."

"Hit you with what?"

"We lost the files, didn't we? Since I didn't create a Variant. Once Blue ascended, I'm sure Gesh had him do a touchdown and erase everything."

"Oh, ye of little faith."

I lean forward, holding my breath, daring to let myself hope.

Micki laughs at my wide eyes. "Once you got back to Base Life, Porter put you under immediate soulblock. Tre can only ascend to Limbo for a touchdown if he can pull you with him. If he can't pull you with him…"

"Then he can't undo the mission."

"That's why you've been admitted here for the last few weeks. Porter's soulblock was so strong it completely knocked you out. Your family thinks you passed out here at the hospital while you were visiting Audrey. The doctors have been totally baffled, by the way, trying to figure out why you were unconscious. The longer you aged in Base Life, the longer Tre aged. By now he's missed his gap. He can't go back to that precise age in 1978 until his next reincarnation."

I let out a breath in disbelief. "You're brilliant. All of you."

"No, you are. You were right. Gesh wouldn't risk killing you. He needs you. You placed your bet, and you won."

"Yeah, but I didn't stop his Cause. He's still out there with Blue somewhere, trying to find me. It's only a matter of time before Blue remembers Annapolis."

"Don't worry about that right now. We'll cross that bridge when we come to it."

"And if we come to it?"

"We'll be ready."

I let my shoulders relax and lean back against my pillows.

Micki checks her watch. "I better head out. Your family will be here any minute, and I shouldn't let them see me."

"They're coming now?" The thought makes me nervous all of a sudden. Maybe because I thought I'd never see them again, and now here we are, about to be reunited.

"Wait," I say as Micki reaches the door, her heels clopping. "Did Porter get the files from Cincinnati?"

"Why don't you wait and see for yourself?" She winks at me, then disappears, and I'm left alone, listening to the sound of my heart rate monitor, the nurses outside talking about their weekend plans, their shoes squeaking across the floor.

My fingers brush my shoulder, but there's no gunshot wound. I pat my face, but there's no blood, no bruises. No painful residuals. I'm safe.

I'm saved.

I swing my legs over the side of the bed and stand at my dresser. The entire surface is covered with flowers and get-well-soon cards and balloons. I check the cards, finding some from Mom and Dad, from Gran and Pops, from Claire, from Levi, from Mrs. Latimer, even from Mrs. Gafferty, no doubt trying to smooth things over with Dad and me. There's a bouquet from Mr. Pence and my entire CAD class, including Grady and Marco. There's a small one from Tabitha. And in the front, right in the center, there's a card from Jensen with a gift certificate to Matchbox Pizza in DC. He didn't write anything, just signed his name.

"Hey, time traveler."

I turn around, and there's Audrey, standing in my doorway, free of tubes and IVs. Her skin bright and glowing, her eyes sparkling. Wearing jeans and sneakers, a striped beanie, and a black shirt that says PICK FLOWERS, NOT FIGHTS.

I remember the truths I whispered in her ear when I thought she was asleep. "You heard everything I said?"

"Of course. It was beautiful. I never knew you were such a poet."

"I'm not. Just occasionally delusional."

She shakes her head. "No, you're a poet. A poet with an old soul."

I smile at her choice of words. "Maybe you're right."

She smiles too. "But you're not an orphan of the stars, you

know. You've got all of us. You've got me."

I tilt my head to the side. "I do?"

"That's what the doctors are saying. Looks like I'm going to be around for a while."

"Good," I say, my eyes shining with tears.

She rushes to me, and I wrap my arms around her, not caring if I rip the tubes out of my arm. And then the whole family is there, squeezing into my room, laughing and crying and hugging. All of us together again.

And I swear, this living is better than dying.

So this is my team.

I make a promise to myself to live what I have left to the fullest, to see Audrey through until the end of my days with joy. No more scowls. No more anger.

No more missions.

Alex Wayfare is officially retired.

THE FINAL PIECES

I spend a few days recovering at home with Gran and Mom and Audrey swooping around me like mama birds, tending to my every need. I tell Audrey I don't need her help, she can sit down, but she says she wants to take care of me for a change, so I let her. Honestly, I just like seeing her up and moving. With energy. With easy breath.

The new treatment worked wonders right away. She went off chemo. The warrior cells only attacked her cancer cells, and she was cleared to go home after a week.

Mom still can't believe someone found copies of the lost data. She can't stop talking about her luck. The day she found out, she made homemade dumplings for everyone in the house.

She made them again the day I came home from the hospital.

It feels like everything is right again, the puzzle finally finished, every piece where it's supposed to be.

Except maybe one or two.

I swing by school to clean out my locker so I can finish the semester at home. I fill a box with stupid things I wouldn't have missed, like tattered, filled notebooks and the history textbook I never used.

On my way to the AV lab, where I left a few more things, I pass by the lunchroom and see Tabitha stirring strawberries into her Greek yogurt. There's no one at her table yet, so I slide into the seat across from her. She looks up.

"I just wanted to say thanks for the flowers, and for telling Mrs. Gafferty what you saw."

She shrugs, swallowing a spoonful of yogurt. "Well. Robbie's grabbed my ass more times than I can count. Thanks for breaking his nose."

"What the hell?" Camilla says, walking up behind me with the rest of Tabitha's crew. "That's my seat, Wayspaz."

"It's Alex's seat today," Tabitha snaps, her eyes sharp, daring Camilla to defy her.

"It's OK," I say, standing up before I cause a shift in the Mean Girl Universe. "I have to go. Thanks anyway."

"Anytime, Wayfare," Tabitha says with a nod. "I mean that."

In the AV lab, I look through drawers for anything I might've left behind. I find a sweater and a hair tie and tuck them into my box. When I look up, Levi's standing at the counter.

"Hey, you," I say, smiling. "Thanks for saving my life."

"Well," he says, "we couldn't let you die, could we?"

"I'm dying anyway."

"Yes, but at least now we can reincarnate you."

"Ah," I say, nodding. Same old Levi. Always looking on the bright side. Saving me because I'm a useful tool in the fight against Gesh.

"Have you given any more thought about taking some time for yourself the next few months?"

"Actually, I have. I've decided I'm officially retired."

"Good," he says.

"I'm going to Scotland with my family this summer, and I'm

going to enjoy myself until the bitter end." I grab the wire splitter I brought from home and toss it into the box.

"And what about Peters?"

"What about Peters?"

Levi frowns. "You know what. I've seen you two together here. You like each other. It's obvious."

I shrug and dump my backpack into the box on top of all my other junk. "It wouldn't be fair to him. You know it wouldn't. And I'm way too messed up to be anyone's girlfriend."

"How so?"

I give him a look. "Besides currently talking about dating with a guy I used to date in a previous life?"

"Besides that."

"My ex just shot me. I'm not exactly handing out trust very easily right now."

"You could learn. 'To cheat oneself out of love is the most terrible deception; it is an eternal loss for which there is no reparation, either in time or in eternity.'"

I raise an eyebrow at him. "Heidegger again?"

"Kierkegaard."

I sigh, frowning down at my box. "What's the point? I won't remember any of this in a few months. I won't remember *him*."

"You're right," Levi says, turning to leave. "What's the point of doing anything? What was the point of saving your sister?"

I look up, but he's already gone, and I want to kick him for being all philosophical again. For making me rethink things. I hadn't until now. I tried to convince myself that Jensen didn't want anything to do with me, even if he did send me a get-well card. It was easier that way. Easier to move on.

Isn't it cruel of me to want to date him? Even if that's what he wants? Lead him on, knowing I won't be around much longer?

But then again, would I deny Audrey a chance at love and happiness just because someone placed an expiration date on her life?

At the very least, I want to tell Jensen I'm sorry, so I walk through the halls, peeking in each classroom, but he's nowhere. And I wonder if maybe he didn't come to school at all.

Then, out in the parking lot, I understand why he was MIA. The basketball buses are lined up out front. He's got an away game, and the team is leaving early for the long drive. I catch a glimpse of his black-and-white duffle bag in line for the last bus, and I sprint over to him before I can talk myself out of it.

"Hey, Peters."

He turns around and lifts his eyebrows. "Wayfare? What are you doing here?" He steps out of line and guides me aside so I don't get trampled by Athletic Types.

"Came to get my stuff." I nod at the box in my arms. "I'm finishing the semester at home."

"I heard. How are you doing? Are you OK?" His eyes search my face, truly concerned about me. The cold, wintry wind gently tosses his hair.

"I'd be better if you'd come to visit me."

He frowns. "I didn't think you'd want to see me."

"I always want to see you."

He looks confused, like he's wondering why I'm being nice to him. "I feel terrible, Wayfare. I shouldn't have kissed you. I'm sorry I accused you of making that guy up. It was really ass of me. I thought maybe you were doing it because of the rumors about us. Robbie was spreading a ton. You know, before you flattened him. But I never thought for a second you couldn't get a date. I've been so jealous of this guy, and I guess when Audrey said you didn't have a boyfriend, I jumped at my chance. I'm just…I'm sorry about all of it." He looks down at his shoes.

"I'm not sorry."

He looks up, eyes wide.

"You were right," I say. "I never had a boyfriend. Not really. I cared about him, and I know he cared about me, but it wasn't ever going to work. We're just too different. Too far apart."

"You're not together anymore?"

"We never were, if I'm totally honest with myself."

He glances over his shoulder again at the rest of the team boarding the bus. "I have to go." He frowns, shifts his weight.

"Wait," I say, touching his arm. "I have something to say, and I need to say it before I chicken out."

He raises an eyebrow. "OK."

The words come tumbling out in a rush, these words I'm no good at, and stick to his jacket like snow. "Your timing sucks, Peters, and I know a thing or two about time. And I've got issues. Lifetimes worth of baggage, and I don't know if you want to deal with it all. But I do know you're one of the good ones. One of the best friends I could ask for. And I know I want to kiss you again. I want to kiss you a lot more than just 'again.' I want to do everything"—I swallow, my mouth going dry—"and try everything with you."

All the thoughts I've had about him over the years resurface— all the thoughts I'd pushed aside and buried when I was with Blue. I let them all come flooding back. I want him to kiss me, take my hand. I've wanted it for so long.

He has no idea.

He watches me, blinking, letting what I said sink in. Then slowly, all the hurt and confusion on his face melts away. A smile tugs at his lips, and he stifles a laugh.

"What?" I say, a smile tugging at my own. His grin is too damn infectious. It's not fair. My cheeks burn, and I worry I said too much, too soon.

He tries to compose himself and look serious, but his mouth keeps twitching in this insanely adorable way. "I'm trying really hard not to smile right now."

"Why?"

He gives me a mischievous look, half hidden under his hair. "Because I want to try everything with you, too." He reaches out and tugs one of the drawstrings on my parka.

We stand there, moony-eyed, each trying not to beam at the other, looking like complete idiots, because we know the moment we let ourselves smile, we won't be able to stop.

He hitches his duffle higher on his shoulder. "You want to start trying everything tonight?"

I try to act cool, like my knees didn't wobble when he said that. "Sure. After the game?"

He nods, still suppressing his grin. "Pick me up here? I'll text you when the game's over?"

"OK."

"Oh, and Wayfare?" He steps closer, reaches up and brushes the hair from my cheek with his thumb. "Think we could get a head start right now?"

I nod, holding my breath.

He leans in, but hesitates. "Are you sure? You don't have a squirt gun in your pocket, do you?"

I laugh. "No."

"A snowball?"

"No."

He smiles his lopsided smile.

I drop my box at my feet, grab his jacket, and pull him close. "Come here."

We kiss in front of his entire team. His coach. The sophomore English class sitting inside the building, gaping at us through the windows.

What the hell, right? You only live fifty-seven times.

There's no hesitation, no warring in my mind. We're free until Coach Caswell yells out the bus door, "Get a move on, Peters."

Jensen backs away, gives me one last nonsmile, then turns and heads for the bus. I watch him go, admiring the view like always. He shakes his head and, for the first time ever, I swear Jensen Peters's ears flush red as a grin spreads across his face. He rubs his jaw, trying to cover it up.

As for me, I'm dazed, and smitten, and wondering what the hell I've gotten myself into. Whatever it is, or turns out to be, I'm pretty sure I'm going to like it.

. . .

ANOTHER BREATH

Remember when I said this story was about death? I suppose it's about life too. All the tiny moments throughout each day that remind us we're alive, that we have breath, that we have worth. Taking a leap of faith. Learning something new. Stepping outside our comfort zones. Lifting our palms from the handlebars and stretching them to the sky. The little things that show us we're meant to be here, taking up this tiny bit of space on earth. Our life has meaning. *We* have meaning. And we can see proof of it every day, if we choose to look.

All these years I've turned away from it, ignoring it, letting the shadow of doubt consume me like dark clouds. I truly believed I was The Worst. That the world would be better off without me because of all the mistakes I've made.

But now I'm learning to keep my eyes wide open, to see the crocuses in the snow, the tiny slivers of light that glint through the storm. To count my blessings, gather them up in my arms and never let go. I won't let anyone take them from me, not without a fight.

Because the most beautiful things in life are unseen, unheard. They must be lived, felt, like the soul on fire.

And mine, I swear, it blazes within me.

ACKNOWLEDGMENTS

This little, obscure sequel wouldn't be possible without my agent, Holly Root, and the lovely, hardworking people at Diversion Books, especially Mary, Eliza, and Sarah. I'm so proud to have you all in my corner.

A huge thank you to Two Brothers Coffee and Brewery Becker for keeping me fueled and letting me occupy your tables for hours on end.

Thank you Rob and Penny at Blue Frog Books and David at the Rochester Hills B&N for believing in this series.

Thank you, Kelsey, for taming Hiccup. I would have never finished this book without you.

As always, thank you Myra and CJ for talking me down from the ledge and sending All The Love, All The Time.

Thank you, Nashville-Area Authors of Awesome, for kindly letting this Michigander into your group and making me feel welcome. You know who you are.

Thank you, Lauren, for being my beta, my cheerleader, when you could've been writing your next novel. Thank you for your insight and steadfast belief in Team Jensen.

To Chris and April, thank you for your inspiration and your books. I'm still your biggest fan.

Hay, thank you, thank you, for your Blessing Boxes and for letting me dedicate this book to you. You make me stronger, Soul Sister.

Special thanks to Dan M. and Mark R. for letting me interrogate you. Audrey's story wouldn't be authentic without your expertise. Thank you, Andye at Reading Teen, for recommending Matchbox Pizza.

To all the bloggers and web editors who spread the word about ALEX over the years, thank you. I owe this sequel to you.

Thank you, Malena, for making me feel like the best author in the world, and letting me use your name.

Thank you, Enduro Binders, for making me a bestseller within your four walls.

To the Beaufort Girls, thank you for your unforgettable and unmatched support. I don't know who I'd be today if I hadn't met you (probably an evil villain).

To Nicholette, thank you for always wanting to read my words. It's the best gift you can give a writer.

To my huge, supportive family, thank you for letting me be my weird little self, and for cheering me on.

To my dear, sweet Hiccup, you are crying as I write this and refusing to sleep, just like the night I wrote my acknowledgements for *The Fifty-Seven Lives of Alex Wayfare*. Some things never change, I suppose, but some things do. I wish you could stay my little one forever, tears or no tears, but then you'd never get a chance to read this book. (Did you like it? I hope you liked it.)

To Joel, my safe place, my adventurer. *Will you search the lonely earth for me? Climb through the briar and bramble? I will be your treasure.*

And finally, thank you, dear reader, for holding this book in your hands. Thank you for telling your family and friends about it. Thank you for requesting it at your library and bookstores. Thank you for making this series a reality.